A Dash of Romance

ANTHOLOGY

PAULLETT GOLDEN

This is a work of fiction. Names, characters, places, and incidents either are the product of the author's imagination or are used fictitiously, and any resemblance to actual persons, living or dead, business establishments, events or locales is entirely coincidental.

The scanning, uploading, and distributing of this book via the internet or via any other means without the permission of the copyright owner is illegal and punishable by law. Please purchase only authorized copies, and do not participate in or encourage piracy of copyrighted materials. Your support of the author's rights is appreciated.

Copyright © 2020 by Paullett Golden

All rights reserved.

Cover Design by Fiona Jayde Media
Interior Design by The Deliberate Page
Illustrations by Doan Trang
https://www.doantrangarts.com/

Also by Paullett Golden

The Enchantresses Series
The Earl and The Enchantress
The Duke and The Enchantress
The Baron and The Enchantress
The Colonel and The Enchantress

Romantic Encounters
A Dash of Romance

COMING SOON

The Enchantresses Series
The Heir and The Enchantress
The Gentleman and The Enchantress

The Sirens Series
A Counterfeit Wife
A Proposed Hoax
The Faux Marriage

This book is dedicated to the seekers of self-improvement, those who dare the journey to a deeper understanding of who they are, who look within and find the courage to brave following their hearts. Self love, growth, and care are vital aspects of our lives. I celebrate all you do to be your best self.

*A special thank you to all bloggers, reviewers,
and readers for your endless support.*

Praise for Golden's Books

"An amazing book by an author that has honed her craft to perfection, this story had me gasping with laughter and moping my eyes as the tears rolled down my face."

—*Goodreads Reader*

"Paullett Golden isn't afraid to weave complex family matters into her historical romance… The author's strong points are her ability to reveal the vulnerability of her characters while showing you how they work through their differences."

—*Readers' Favorites Reviewer*

"Character development is wonderful, and it is interesting to follow two young people as they defy the odds to be together. Paullett Golden's novel is compelling and a stellar work that is skillfully crafted."

—Sheri Hoyte of *Reader Views*

"It's thoughtfulness about issues of social class, birthrights, gender disparities, and city versus country concerns add provocative emotional layers. Strong, complex characterizations, nuanced family dynamics, insightful social commentary, and a vibrant sense of time and place both geographically and emotionally make this a poignant read."

—Cardyn Brooks of *InD'tale Magazine*

"The author adds a few extra ingredients to the romantic formula, with pleasing results. An engaging and unconventional love story."

— *Kirkus Reviews*

"The well-written prose is a delight, the author's voice compelling readers and drawing them into the story with an endearing, captivating plot and genuine, authentic settings. From the uncompromising social conventions of the era to the permissible attitudes and behaviors within each class, it's a first-class journey back in time."

— *Reader Views*

"[The Enchantresses] by Paullett Golden easily ranks as one of the best historical romances I have read in some time and I highly recommend it to fans of romance, history, and the regency era. Fabulous reading!"

— *Sheri Hoyte*

"It is an extremely well written novel with some subplots that add to the already intense main plot. The author Paullett Golden has a gift for creating memorable characters that have depth."

— Paige Lovitt of *Reader Views*

"Golden is a good writer. She knows how to structure plot, how to make flawed characters sympathetic and lovable, and has a very firm grasp on theme."

— *No Apology Book Reviews*

"What I loved about the author was her knowledge of the era! Her descriptions are fresh and rich. Her writing is strong and emotionally driven. An author to follow."

—*The Forfeit* author Shannon Gallagher

"Readers who enjoy a character driven romance will find this a story well worth reading. Paullett Golden is an author I will be following."

—*Roses R Blue Reviews*

"I would say this is a very well-written novel with engaging characters, a compelling story, a satisfactory resolution, and I am eagerly anticipating more from Ms. Golden."

—*Davis Editorials*

"With complex characters and a backstory with amazing depth, the story… is fantastic from start to finish."

—*Rebirth* author Ravin Tija Maurice

"Paullett Golden specializes in creating charmingly flawed characters and she did not disappoint in this latest enchantress novel."

—*Dream Come Review*

"…a modern sensibility about the theme of self-realization, and a fresh take on romance make the foundation of Golden's latest Georgian-era romance."

—*The Prairies Book Review*

"What a wonderful story! I have read a number of historical fiction romance stories and this is the best one so far! Paullett does a masterful job of weaving so many historical details into her story…."

— *Word Refiner Reviews*

"The novel is everything you could ever want from a story in this genre while also providing surprising and gratifying thematic depth."

— *Author Esquire*

"I thoroughly enjoyed meeting and getting to know all of the characters. Each character was fully developed, robust and very relatable."

— *Flippin' Pages Book Reviews*

"It is a story that just keeps giving and giving to the reader and I, for one, found it enchanting!"

— *The Genre Minx Book Reviews*

"The minor King Arthur plot was also a lovely touch, and the descriptions of the library fulfilled my book-loving dream."

— *Rosie Amber Reviews*

"It features characters who exhibit traits and emotions that go above and beyond passion."

— *Melina Druga Reviews*

A Letter to the Reader

Dear Reader,

This is the first book of the Romantic Encounters series, each book to be an annual anthology. Within each anthology, you'll find a short novel followed by a special bonus: a collection of flash and short fiction.

The flash fiction pieces are those featured in the monthly newsletter; thus, each piece is themed in some way to the month in which it appeared. The first piece begins with January and moves through the calendar months until we reach December. Two additional, bonus flash fictions are included within this first book, both winter themed.

There are many types of flash fiction, ranging from micro fiction of only a few words to short fiction of a couple thousand. Within this anthology, you'll find pieces ranging from approximately five hundred words to two thousand. I hope you'll enjoy them. Each is a stand-alone story regardless of brevity.

The addition of bonus fiction to accompany the novel is unique to the Romantic Encounters series. You can look forward to a similar combination of shorts plus novel every year as part of the annual anthology series.

Enjoy!
Paullett Golden

Table of Contents

A Dash of Romance *1*
Flash Fiction *229*

    Arrival 231

    Beguiled 235

    Highwayman 239

    Shipwreck 245

    Entangled 251

    Midsummer 255

    Candor 259

    Requited 265

    Persephone 271

    Haunted 277

    Masquerade 289

    Homecoming 299

    Beneficence 303

    Gorgeous 307

A Dash of Romance

Chapter 1

1795
Devonshire

The feather of the quill brushed against her chin, imbuing inspiration.

Sir Bartholomew thundered across the field on his black stallion.

No, that would not do. With a single, straight line, she crossed out "black stallion." Rewetting the quill, she wrote:

Sir Bartholomew thundered across the field on his white steed.
    Ahead, the damsel waved in distress. 'Oh, good sir,' she cried, 'my horse has lamed himself. Save me!'
    The gallant knight leapt from his horse. Had the fair damsel not been in distress, she would have swooned at the hero of our tale. Dashing, charming, tall but not too tall, hazel eyes that twinkled goodwill, brown hair that waved handsomely, a walking stick held –

With another single, straight line, she crossed out "walking stick." The hero would not have a walking stick if he had been riding his horse. Stroking her chin with the feather again, she stared at the page, dissatisfied.

"Abigail, dearest, what keeps you?" croaked a voice from the other side of the room.

Miss Abigail Walsley replaced the quill in such haste, she nearly tipped over the inkwell. Steadying herself, she turned to Lady Dunley.

"You drifted to sleep, my lady. I thought I would busy myself until you awakened. Would you like for me to finish reading to you?" Hoping the ink was dry enough, Abbie folded the paper and slipped it into her pocket before returning to Lady Dunley's side.

"No, dear, I believe I'll retire for an afternoon respite. Ring for my maid."

Before reaching for the bellpull, Abbie rearranged the shawl about her ladyship's shoulders to dissuade the autumn chill. Her ladyship had such a delicate constitution.

An arthritic hand, fingers curled and knuckles swollen, reached out from beneath the wool to grasp Abbie's arm. In a gravely voice, Lady Dunley asked, "Won't you stay with me?"

Abbie shook her head, covering the hand on her arm with her own. "I'm to visit my sister today. I'll return on Wednesday, and we can resume the chapter."

"No, no, no, you misunderstand me. Won't you please stay with me as a full-time companion? You'll want for nothing. You could have the bedroom next to mine. It's a bright shade of yellow, as befitting your charm."

"It remains a lovely offer, my lady, but my answer is the same as before. My father needs me, besides which I live close enough to continue our frequent visits."

"Pish," the woman grunted, waving her hand beneath the shawl.

Abbie accepted the dismissal as an opportunity to ring for the maid before departing.

For the first quarter mile of her walk home, her steps were stilted, her lips pursed. The renewals to serve as companion came more frequently each passing week. However flattering it was for Lady Dunley to find her company desirable, Abbie could not help but feel the sting of insult. Long gone were the hopes of marrying at the shelved age of four and twenty, but she did think her life worth more than serving as a glorified friend for hire. As fulfilling as her time with the viscountess was, this was not how she desired to spend her days. It was kindness that took her to the estate every other day, not a desire to make companionship her profession.

Ah, yes, her profession. Now there was something she had thought about a great deal.

Her gait slowed; her shoulders relaxed. For the next half mile, her mind wandered, leaving a half-smile lingering on her lips. She could see him clearly. His walking stick twirling, kissable lips whistling, that wavy hair a damsel could sink her fingers into — oh, what a wicked thought. The vicarage in sight, Abbie looked about her, hoping no one was around to see her blush. Only sheep looked back at her.

One day, her hero would win her a publishing contract. He was a real Tom Jones, by her estimation, but with more charm and morality. Sir Bartholomew would woo the world from a leather-bound spine.

That evening, after supper with her father, the vicar of Sidvale, Abbie retired to her room, intent on a good night's sleep. It was not to be had. Well into the night, the candle burned, her quill working across the page, detailing the adventures of Sir Bartholomew. She paused only long enough to pen a quick column for the newspaper under her pseudonym before returning to her errant knight as he saved another damsel, whisking this one off her feet to save her from a spring flood.

> *The knight ran a hand through his unruly locks, a wink and smile his only answer to the fair maiden. With a bow, he quitted her company, taking his leave of the entire village. He could think of no place he would rather be than by the side of his ladylove.*

Abbie sighed. A wistful smile curved her lips, her eyes unfocused. In a clear vision, she could see herself in a tower, dressed in understated elegance, a Renaissance maiden waiting for her knight. Did she dare write herself into the story as his ladylove? Or would readers prefer him a desirable bachelor? This was not to be a love story but an adventure tale. Perhaps it was best that he remained available.

Decided, she made to wet the quill to cross out the final line.

She gasped. The ink! So lost in thought, she had not noticed the ink spreading a cruel puddle over the paper. In swift movements, she propped the quill in the inkwell and grabbed a handkerchief to blot the ink.

It was no use. Rather than soaking up the excess ink, the handkerchief smeared it. The more she dabbed, the more it spread until the handkerchief was ruined, her hands were covered in ink, and the page was an illegible blob. She only just stopped herself from hiding her face in her hands. Would that not top the evening—an ink covered face? Defeated, she removed to the wash basin to clean the ink from her fingers as best she could. Sir Bartholomew would have to wait for the morrow before she could rewrite the scene.

※

Dipping her toast into the egg yolk, Abbie lamented, "They're nearly purple. I can't possibly leave the house today."

The Reverend Leland Walsley eyed his daughter's ink tinted hands and shook his head, the lift at the corners of his mouth betraying his amusement. "Is this my opportunity to ask your help with the sermon?"

She nodded, eager to serve as muse.

The youngest of four sisters, Abbie was the only one unmarried, the only one who chose to stay at the vicarage to look after Papa. It was not that he needed looking after, for he was in good health, but without her, he would surely be lonely. How fortuitous she had never received a proposal.

After a taste of his tea, Leland said, "If I were the suspicious type, I would suspect you stained your hands intentionally as a ruse to get new gloves."

"Papa!" Abbie exclaimed before a laugh. "I would never!"

"I know. I know." He winked over his cup. "Will you visit Lady Dunley tomorrow?"

She sighed, leaning against the chair back. "I have no reason not to, but I think I might put a few days between us. She's been pressing me again about being her companion."

"And you've still no notion of accepting?" He rested against the back of his chair, mirroring his daughter. "Life at the estate could be luxurious."

"I prefer my life here." Abbie laced her fingers in her lap and studied her father. "Am I being selfish to choose my own desires over helping someone?"

"I don't find your decision selfish, rest assured. Only you are privy to your calling. I support you regardless, even if that calling is not with Lady Dunley."

Abbie studied her plate. "If I were to become anyone's companion, I would choose Aunt Gertrude. You know how I love spending time with her in the summer, but even then, I would not want to be a full-time companion; neither do I think Aunt Gertrude would want someone hovering over her shoulder every day."

Dabbing his mouth with a napkin, he said, "She wrote to me, you know."

"Aunt Gertrude?"

He frowned. "No, Lady Dunley."

"Lady Dunley wrote to you? Why?" She bristled, uncertain she wanted an answer.

"Hoping I'd persuade you to serve as her companion. Although, I confess, her missive was more forceful than hopeful or persuasive. It bordered on a command. So far as you're set against it, I'll not be swayed."

Appalled, Abbie clenched her fingers. "I never thought her the interfering sort. I've a mind not to return. How dare she go against my will to have you force my hand!"

Her father chuckled. "No need to take it so harshly. It's flattering, really. She values your company."

"I find it underhanded." Folding her napkin, she returned it to the table, her appetite lost.

"I don't disagree, but let's focus on the good. A viscountess finds your company worth fighting for, and that's a fine compliment. It would do no harm to reconsider."

Wednesday arrived and departed in a flurry of quill against paper. Abbie held steadfast to her conviction—she would not relinquish her life and dreams because a wealthy aristocrat desired a companion.

Steadfast though she may be, guilt-tinged ink drops dotted the page. Lady Dunley meant well. She was kind and lonely. Her son preferred London life and rarely stayed at the estate longer than a week at a time. Abbie had only seen him a handful of times, never mind that they had both lived in the same village since birth. From her brief encounters with him, he seemed amiable, but he was always distracted and inattentive, especially to his mother. Lady Dunley most certainly must be lonely.

Blast. Another rogue ink drop.

Before she finished the chapter where Sir Bartholomew saved the burning village from the dastardly villain, Abbie wanted to write next week's newspaper column. On her way to see her sister the day before, she had witnessed a hushed argument that set her mind reeling with ideas for the latest letter from Mrs. Button to her dearest niece Lucy.

Mrs. Button was a fictitious woman of Abbie's imagination, as was Lucy, but the villagers loved reading not only the antics and schemes of dear Lucy but also the sage advice of Mrs. Button. Every letter echoed some happening in the village, offering readers a moral compass and a fresh perspective. No one knew Abbie wrote the articles. No one would trust advice on worldly topics from a maiden, the vicar's daughter no less. But they trusted Mrs. Button.

My dearest Lucy,

You were correct to write to me, as always. I understand your hesitancy with having the gentleman sup with the family. He does not sound the pleasant sort. There is, however, no need to add salt to his tea or sewing needles to his chair, though I admire your spirit. Many a time it was that my own parents invited gentlemen I did not favor to supper. It is a trial, dear, to sit through a meal with someone you feel may be pushed upon you, but I urge you to accept such trials with grace. See these times not as a moment of unpleasant matchmaking but as a testament to your manners.

Let each guest see you as a gracious hostess. The word will spread, your favor will increase, and soon the gentleman you do seek will find you, perhaps at that very table.

Yours, Mrs. Button

Customarily, Mrs. Button's letters were longer, but Lady Dunley's increasing insistence was making it difficult for Abbie to focus on her writing. She did not want to be bullied into the position, but neither did she want to feel guilty for not accepting.

If her ladyship wanted, she could make life unpleasant for the Walsleys. If truly put out, she could have the bishop relocate the Reverend Walsley to another parish. Abbie could not imagine her ladyship going to such extremes, and certainly not because Abbie refused to serve as her companion, but the worry lingered on the fringes of Abbie's mind. So insistent her ladyship had been of late, Abbie wondered to what lengths the viscountess might go to obtain what she wanted.

Abbie laughed to herself. What fanciful nonsense! She had been writing and reading far too many novels. Real life was not so dramatic. There had never been anything threatening about Lady Dunley. The woman held strong opinions and a will of iron despite her frailty and age, but she had never abused her power.

What advice would Mrs. Button give her? She wondered. With a sigh, Abbie sanded the letter's ink and folded it. Tomorrow, she would drop it in the submission box.

For now, she must focus. The village in her story was not going to save itself from the villain, not without Sir Bartholomew. The good knight needed her as much as she needed him.

Chapter 2

The spot of bother that would irrevocably change Abbie's life occurred midmorning on Friday, not even a week since her last visit with Lady Dunley.

With a finger as a bookmark, Abbie closed the cover of *Clarissa*.

She had penned a polite albeit vague missive to her ladyship that she would not be visiting until the week after Michaelmas, next week. Guilt still weighed heavily, yet steadfast she remained. This was not the first time her ladyship had tried to convince Abbie to be her live-in companion, but it was the first time the viscountess had harassed the vicar about it.

Rather than making her way to the Dunley manor, Abbie would visit her sister. Mrs. Prudence Rockford was the closest in age, relationship, and proximity to Abbie, living a few miles away in Sidbury. She had married the local physician five years earlier and was now increasing with her second child.

Her eldest two sisters were Mrs. Faith Framlers, who lived with her husband, a farmer, near Aunt Gertrude and Uncle Cecil Diggeby in East Hagbourne, and Mrs. Bonnie Sullivan, who lived south of Sidbury with her curate husband of fifteen years and their son. They had always been a close family and remained so, bonded ever more tightly after losing their mother to a fever. It was during that time when Prudence met her husband to be—their mother's physician.

Using a ribbon to replace her finger as bookmark, Abbie decided it time to set aside *Clarissa*. She could not concentrate, no matter how captivating the story. She held the book to her chest and stretched her legs. Had her father finished preparing his sermon?

Just as she rose from her chair, intent on checking on him, the parlor door opened.

Her father's face peered around the door, his eyes roaming the room until he spotted her. Leland stepped into the room wearing a peculiar expression. He was not alone. Following behind him was a man dressed so well as to be considered foppish. Blonde, blue eyed, extraordinarily tall, athletic—a handsome man indeed! Abbie flushed at the sight of him. He pulled a snuff box out of his pocket and took a pinch then paused to study the top of the box, as though it held all the secrets to the modern world. He had yet to look at her.

Her father's smile was tight, not reaching his eyes, and his brow furrowed, as though trying to sort a difficult puzzle as he looked from Abbie to the man and back.

"Dearest, I trust you're not indisposed. Lord Dunley requests an audience."

Ah! It had been so long since she had last seen Lord Dunley, she hadn't recognized him. He was much taller and broader than she recalled, certainly more fashionable. There was more lace and frill about his person than she possessed in her entire wardrobe.

It was not until her father backed out of the room and shut the door, leaving her alone with the viscount, that Abbie began to fret. Her eyes widened in alarm, the book clutched against her bosom.

"Has her ladyship taken ill?" she asked.

Guilt! Oh, dear guilt. She had been avoiding Lord Dunley's mother for purely selfish reasons, and now look what had happened! Her ladyship was ill, or worse. Could it be worse? Abbie drew the book higher until the edge pressed at her chin.

"Miss Abilene," Lord Dunley said, "my mother is quite well. It is on her behalf I have come today."

Abigail stared in confusion, her fingers tightening around the book.

For the first time since entering the room, Lord Dunley's eyes lifted from studying his snuff box and cast her a cursory inspection before his gaze rested on the book in her hands.

He frowned. "Is that a book my mother would approve?"

"I'm afraid I don't understand your question." It was not, in fact, a book Lady Dunley would approve, but that was neither here nor there, as this was her father's house not his.

His frown deepened, his eyes not lifting from the book. "Reading is an unhealthy habit for a young lady."

Bristling, Abbie bit back her response. It would not do to insult a viscount, certainly not one standing in the vicarage. Instead, she tucked the book behind her and indicated a chair.

"Would you care to join me, my lord?"

"I shan't stay long, Miss Aberdeen. I've come to secure your hand in marriage."

Abbie's jaw dropped.

"I—but you—but we've—We've never even spoken to each other, my lord," she stammered.

Not in her wildest fantasies would she have expected a proposal from a viscount, least of all this one. Had he been besotted with her all this time? Had he been gathering information about her from his mother? How flattering. How peculiar. But he had never spoken to her! Despite the absurdity, she felt a moment's blush. She could marry. She could have a family of her own. She could know love. Long ago had such dreams diminished. To have them flooding back to her in such an unexpected fashion was too much. Although not the swooning type, Abbie felt faint, her limbs cold and her face clammy.

"I see no reason why that should change," he answered, returning to study his snuff box.

It took her a minute to recall what she had said. When she did, she clamped her jaw closed, affronted and perplexed.

Pocketing the box, he huffed a bored sigh. "Well, Miss Adelaide? Shall I precure a license on Monday? A hasty and private ceremony would be best, don't you agree?"

Abbie stared. Her heart wrenched. She knew not what to say. Though it was her first proposal, it was not in any way what she had expected. These were not the words of a man besotted. The proposal felt sordid somehow, as though he wanted to hide her away, ashamed of his lowly and plain bride.

"Why do you wish to marry me, Lord Dunley?" Her voice cracked, betraying her timidity.

Regardless of his reasons for proposing, she was trapped. A spinster dared not say no to such a proposal, her one chance for wedded bliss. More to the point, one did not say no to an aristocrat.

"My mother wishes it, and so it will be done. You'll dine with us this evening. I must away to London in the morning, but it is my mother's wish you take up residence at the hall posthaste. I will send a carriage for your baggage tomorrow."

Abbie's hands began to sweat. The book still held at her back weighed heavier, tugging at her fingers.

"But my lord, I've not said yes."

He exhaled another bored huff.

Clearing her throat, she searched the room for answers, clues, an escape. If she said no, what would happen? Would the man, or more to the point his mother, retaliate against Abbie's father? Could they force her? But then, would it be so bad to say yes? They could grow to love each other. She would have children of her own. She would be respected as marriageable rather than stigmatized as undesirable. Any marriage, some said, was better than none. But what of writing? If he disapproved of her reading choices, would she be allowed to write?

Her mind reeled, so many questions, so much indecision.

"Miss Adele, I've wasted enough time. I have important matters to attend to. I'll send the carriage for you this evening at six sharp. Be ready." Lord Dunley turned to the door, his hand reaching for the handle.

"No!" Abbie screeched before she could stop herself.

He turned, his brows raised in alarm.

"I—that is to say—well, you see—I can't marry you, though the offer is flattering." She tugged her bottom lip between her teeth.

There was nowhere to go from here, no reason to decline, she a plain spinster and daughter of a vicar.

Lord Dunley's eyes narrowed. However bored he had appeared since arriving, he now looked startlingly perturbed.

"I—you see—I can't," she repeated, her words a jagged staccato.

"Pray tell, what are you on about?"

"I, um." Abbie cast about for some excuse, but it was no use. She had no acceptable reason to deny him. "I'm already betrothed," she blurted.

Abbie closed her eyes as she drew in a deep breath, her limbs shaking. There was no withdrawing the words. They had been spoken. And to a viscount! She was the worst sort of sinner—a liar.

"To whom?" asked a voice trembling with barely disguised anger.

Her eyes remained closed. She had not the courage to face him. Desperate, she found only one thing to say.

"You don't know him."

Before she could stop them, more words tumbled out of their own volition. "He's…he's knightly. Yes, a gallant knight. Brown hair, hazel eyes, charming, excessively charming, actually, a younger son, not that I care anything about that. He's—he's my knight in shining armor." If she could clasp her hand over her mouth, she would. Yet such confessions were not falsehoods, not really. Sir Bartholomew may be neither real nor her betrothed, but he was most certainly her knight. "We met in East Hagbourne, if you must know."

Why was she telling him such things? Was she so desperate to convince him that she could be loved? Was she so desperate not to be forced into a position as a live-in companion? She was mortified by her words, but once said she could not retract them.

"His name, Miss Amelie." The viscount's foot tapped against the rug in a dull, repetitive thud.

Steeling herself, she looked back to the viscount whose nostrils flared. What did he care? He clearly did not want to marry her, only was doing his mother's bidding, and for what purpose? To force Abbie to serve as companion? What a lark! He should be relieved that he did not have to follow through.

"I'll not divulge his name, my lord, for our betrothal is a secret. I should not wish to upset my family until we are ready to wed."

"Then you'll cry off. A simple solution. I'll send the carriage at six."

"No," Abbie insisted, her words bolder than she felt, for her hands trembled and her knees knocked. "My answer is no. I will not cry off my engagement to marry you. You'll need to find a different bride and a different companion for your mother."

A knock on the parlor door sent Abbie's heart leaping from her chest and the book she still held thudding to the floor.

Lord Dunley did not turn to observe Leland stepping into the room, his only acknowledgement a sniff. "Your daughter has refused me."

Abbie's eyes moved from Lord Dunley to her father, her pulse racing. Leland's brows met in confusion, his tentative but optimistic smile faltering.

"Mr. Walsley, I wish you had known she was already spoken for, as it would have saved us all a great deal of trouble and time."

"Already spoken for?" her father echoed.

"It would seem so. A secret betrothal, she says, to a knight from East Hagbourne. She refuses to divulge a name. If you'll be so good as to move from the door, I'll see myself out." With a curt bow, he left.

Abbie remained in the parlor with her father.

Leland studied her, his expression not only confused but hurt. She knew what he must be thinking—how could his daughter keep such a secret from him? It was too late now. She was trapped by her own lie. One word of truth could either free her or make it all that much worse. Would it be so difficult to live as an engaged woman for a time, and then find a way to cry off convincingly? It was not as though her false betrothed would mind. His life, being fictious, would not be adversely impacted. Yes, she could cry off—*after* the viscount had married someone else.

Chapter 3

Mr. Percival Randall, second son of the Earl of Camforth, tightened the reins of his matching pair and drew his curricle to a stop.

A swift lift of the knocker of the Merriweathers' London townhouse produced a stern-faced butler thrusting forward a silver calling card tray.

"What's this, Helms?" Percy waved to the tray. "I'm expected. And you dashed well know who I am."

"Your card, sir," said the butler without moving his lips.

Percy grumbled but tugged a card free from its case. With a *thwack* he placed it on the tray.

"I shall see if the Merriweathers are at home and receiving, sir."

The door slammed in his face.

What was this abuse? They had invited him to tea!

After an inordinate amount of time waiting, to the point that Percy began to feel dashed uncomfortable standing at the front door, regardless that the London streets were sparsely populated this time of year, the door opened.

"Mr. Merriweather wishes to see you in his study." The butler stepped aside. "Follow me."

A sense of foreboding curdled Percy's morning meal. If Mr. Merriweather wished to speak alone, that could mean only one thing: the moment of reckoning.

The man would insist on a verbal confirmation of Percy's intentions with his daughter, perhaps even on a proposal, although that may be too bold for the mild-mannered Merriweather. Was it too late to run? However serious Percy was to find a bride, thanks to his father's ultimatum, he was not ready to face the hangman's noose. A little more time would ready him. A few more weeks, maybe a year. Or two. He had until his thirtieth birthday, after all.

The walk to the study was long. By measurement, it might only be a few yards, but that made no difference to it being the longest walk Percy had made all year. Hooking a finger over the edge of his cravat, he tugged. He should have seen this coming. No father would allow his daughter to be courted indefinitely, not without some sign of commitment.

Percy had to think fast. Could he say the words? Could he propose? As sweet as Miss Merriweather was, he felt nothing in the way of romance for her, and he suspected she felt the same of him. Was a general sort of fondness enough as a foundation for marriage?

Eyeing the approaching study door, he gulped.

When the butler ushered him over the threshold, Percy found Mr. Merriweather standing behind his desk, his back to the room, chin drooped to chest. Percy waited for the noose to tighten.

"You made a fool of us all, Mr. Randall. I should have known not to expect more from someone with your reputation."

Percy's jaw slackened. What the devil?

Clearing his throat, he said, "I do beg your pardon, sir, but I must ask what I've done to disappoint you."

Had they found out about Clarice?

He knew he should have let her go the moment he started courting Miss Merriweather, but he had not had the gumption. He had, however, avoided visiting his mistress' townhouse for weeks, determined to practice celibacy to see whether he could live a monogamous life, thinking only of the woman he was courting. It was not something he was in the habit of doing, but he had to try, if for no other reason than out of respect for his future bride.

His father had raised him better than to keep a mistress. The Earl of Camforth's first marriage was said to have been a love match, a faithful one until Percy's mother died of consumption before Percy was out of nappies. Now, his father was blissfully married to his second wife and equally as devoted to her, physically, emotionally, metaphysically, metaphorically, and every other -*ly* Percy could name. The man was besotted. It set a precedent for all his sons. And yet Percy had been too much a coward to send Clarice notice, at least not until he made the official proposal.

Clearly the Merriweathers had found out. It was not uncommon for a gentleman to keep a mistress, but he could see the many reasons it would rankle Mr. Merriweather. Percy was humbled by the mere thought of the man and his family knowing about Clarice. Mortified and humbled.

Mr. Merriweather turned to face Percy, his hands curling into fists as he leaned his knuckles against the desk. "If I were a younger man, I would call you out, sirrah."

"Oh! Oh, I say!" Percy took a step back. "She's only a trifle, nothing serious. I had intended on taking care of things sooner rather than later. I promise to take care of things before Miss Merriweather hears a word of it."

"She knows," said Mr. Merriweather. "Your words pang me more than the facts. How can you be so indifferent to a young lady? Do you think of my daughter in such terms? Is this how you refer to all your intended brides—trifles? You disgust me. You are no longer welcome in my home nor near my daughter. If I catch your gaze so much as drift in her direction, I will meet you on the field. Now *get out*."

Before Percy could defend himself, the butler and a burly footman appeared to either side of him.

Right.

Interview terminated.

In some ways, it was a relief, but why the man should be so bent out of shape about a mistress Percy had not called on in weeks was beyond his understanding. All the same, it was a bullet dodged. The man had even mentioned intended brides, referring to his daughter, of course. The thought gave Percy chills.

How was he ever to go through with his promise to his father? Would it be so bad to be homeless? Between a wife and homelessness, he was beginning to think being booted out of his father's townhouse on his thirtieth birthday was not quite as bad as it had first sounded. Should the worst occur, his elder brother Freddie, Baron Monkworth, might allow Percy to stay at his estate in East Hagbourne, although his wife might feel otherwise given there were three boys to raise. Freddie would deny it, but Percy knew Lady Monkworth thought him a bad influence.

With the Merriweathers' front door firmly sealed, Percy decided it time to pay a call to Clarice. Her bills were paid, and the gifts continued to arrive regularly so she would not be cross with him for avoiding her, and right now, he would give his left foot for some tension relief. Meeting angry fathers was strenuous work.

In short time, Percival stopped the curricle at the modest townhouse he let for Clarice.

That was part of the problem, of course. His father disapproved of how Percy spent the earl's money. Money in his pocket and a roof over his head—a luxurious roof at that given it was the earl's London townhouse in which Percy lived—and this was how he thanked his father. A listless life with good money wasted on a wanton whore. His father's words, not his.

Too wild for the church. Too restless for the military. Too whimsical for law. Too irrational for medicine. What was a second son to do? It was the London life for old Percy!

The townhouse being let in his name, rather than knock, Percy slipped his key into the lock to push open the door. Or he tried. The door did not budge. He wiggled the key and pushed again. Nothing.

Staring quizzically at lock and key, he used the knocker. Within seconds, the butler opened the door.

"Ah, good to see you, Williams," Percy said as he made to push past the man.

As with the door, the man did not budge. Feet parted, arms crossed, he stared down Percy. Williams was not an ordinary butler. Given Clarice's profession as one of the most talented and sought-after opera singers in London, she needed extra protection, and so Percy had employed Williams as the butler, a stalwart employee to be sure. At the moment, however, Percy questioned having him on the payroll.

"Good heavens, Williams, let me pass." Percy laughed, a forced sound even to his ears.

"One moment, sir," Williams said with a grunt.

The second door of the day to slam in his face came close to flattening his nose. As at the Merriweathers, this was not the greeting he had expected. A sultry embrace, arms about his neck, lips to his cheek—any of these would have sufficed.

Just when he thought it impossible to wait longer still than he had at the Merriweathers' home, the door opened. Percy smiled at Clarice standing boldly in the doorway wearing nothing more than one of his old banyans, her hair spilling about her shoulders in seductive waves.

"Good afternoon, love," he said.

He heard the *thwack* of her hand slapping his cheek before he felt the sting. The sting, in fact, did not occur until after the door closed. Not the endearing greeting he expected.

What the devil was going on today?

He rubbed his smarting skin as he climbed onto the curricle. He needed a drink. And company. Flicking his wrist, he headed for White's, making a mental note to send Clarice and her staff their notice of dismissal.

Since most members of White's were in residence at their country estates this time of year, the rooms were quiet, only a handful of gentlemen taking their drink alone with their newspaper, talking in hushed tones with a friend over coffee, or losing at the tables. Through each room Percy searched until he spotted an acquaintance. Company would take his mind off the strange day. For the life of him, he could not fathom what he had done to anger both the Merriweathers *and* Clarice.

"Well met, Donaldson," Percy said, shaking the man's hand.

"Here's the luckiest man in town come to torment me." Donaldson's words slurred ever so slightly.

It was not yet two in the afternoon.

Percy took a seat next to his old Oxford mate and signaled to a footman for a drink. "And what have I done to deserve this charge, both as lucky and a tormentor?"

"You're a lifelong bachelor. What I wouldn't give to be in your shoes." The words blended as Donaldson sloshed his drink to the table.

"Ah. I see. Lady Donaldson on a rampage again?"

"When is she not? Take my word for it—don't marry." The once carefree Donaldson, now titled, married, and father of four, was not looking his best.

Percy winced to think how close he had come to a similar fate. There must be a way around his father's ultimatum. He did not want to end up like Donaldson, drinking away his afternoon at the club.

A voice from behind them interrupted.

"If it isn't the infamous Mr. Randall."

They both turned to see the bane of White's, Mr. Plumb. If there was gossip to be had, he spread it. If there was a bet in the books, he wagered. The man practically lived at the club.

Percy took his drink from the footman and raised it to Mr. Plumb. "You've caught me."

"Might as well join us." Donaldson waved at the empty chair across from them. "I was telling Randall how fortunate he is to avoid the leg shackle."

"Were you indeed? Then you've not heard the news." Mr. Plumb raised his quizzing glass to study Percy. "You may now wish him felicitations for Mr. Randall is engaged."

Percy sputtered, dribbling brandy on his chin. "I beg your pardon. I am very much *not* engaged."

"Your secret is safe with me," Mr. Plumb said with a wink.

Setting aside his glass, Percy leaned forward. "What are you—"

"It's more romantic than I would have given you credit for, a clandestine betrothal and all. The curious part is not how you managed to keep the secret for so long, but why. Is she hideous? Still in the schoolroom? A postulant doubting her vocation?"

"I say, Plumb, you do have a sense of humor," Percy replied with a hollow, nervous laugh. "Now, enough of this or Donaldson will have an apoplexy thinking I'm doomed to follow in his footsteps."

Plumb twirled his quizzing glass with its ribbon. "As I said, your secret is safe with me."

Midnight had long since passed by the time Percy stepped through the front door of the Camforth townhouse. Ignoring the letters in the tray, he tugged off his coat and dropped it on the vestibule floor. In his cups, he sidestepped his own shadow, falling against a wall.

"Watch where you're going," he slurred, pointing an accusing finger at the wall.

By the time he reached the top of the stairs, he had shrugged out of his waistcoat and lost his shirt to the wall sconce — thankfully devoid of candle. Stumbling to his bedchamber, he stripped off his breeches — stockings and shoes still snug on his person — and only just tipped onto the bed before he faceplanted on the pillow with a snore.

Too few hours later, morning light streaked across his face in rude intrusion. He had been dreaming of opera singers playing drums. Unfortunately, he could still feel the beat of the drums, or more to the point, the pounding of his brainpan. Groaning, Percy traversed through his morning ritual until he made it to the breakfast table, the world ever so hazy.

Beside the hearty breakfast, two delights awaited his pleasure: Cook's personal concoction to cure morning melancholy — buttermilk and corn flour — and a cup of black coffee. Ah, Cook loved him. With a smile that made his skull hurt, he took his seat and devoured the fare, only noticing the two letters next to his plate after his double vision merged to one reality. A peek at the letters revealed one with the earl's signet emblazoned in the wax and one with a crest he did not immediately recognize.

Ignoring his father's letter, which would inevitably be an inquiry into the bride search, Percy broke the seal on the mystery letter. His eyes first flicked to the signature.

Dunley

Pressing a finger to his temple, Percy tried to recall a Dunley of his acquaintance. A fuzzy image involving blonde hair and close-set eyes came to mind. *Dunley, Dunley, Dunley*. With a shrug, Percy read the salutatory lines.

Dear Mr. Percival Randall,

After much searching, I believe I have found the right man. My quest has taken more letters than I dare admit, which has soured my mood and depleted my paper, for which I hold you accountable.

Percy paused his reading to laugh aloud.

Ah, yes, he recalled Dunley now: a man of great self-importance, frequenter of the local molly-house, and a risky gambler. Percy failed to remember much more since they did not run in the same circles, though they had both attended Eton and Oxford together, Dunley being a year ahead of Percy.

It was not with ease that I discovered you to be Miss Walsley's betrothed. Hazel eyes, brown hair, charming, a brother in East Hagbourne, and knightly, although it has now come to my attention that you are not, in fact, a knight, yet a man with a knight's name – Sir Percival of King Arthur's Knights of the Round Table. A clever deception on the part of Miss Walsley. This betrothal must come to an end. I am under strict orders to marry the vicar's daughter for the sake of my mother's happiness, and you, sir, are the impediment. I will not have this. I demand word from you that you will ensure an end to the engagement within a fortnight. Make it a sennight and I will excuse the debt of the paper and offer a banknote of £100. I await your word. Your most venerable,

Dunley

Percy read the letter close to a dozen times trying to make sense of it. The man was dicked in the nob. Never had Percy met a Miss Walsley. He certainly would not be involved with a vicar's daughter. And he was, emphatically, *not* betrothed.

A nod to a hovering footman produced a fresh cup of coffee to clear his head. So, Dunley's mother wished him to marry, did she? She must not know — or not care — that he preferred the sterner sex. This had naught to do with Percy, however. Dunley had the wrong fellow, poor chap. Although…the banknote sounded tempting.

He sipped the coffee, thinking.

No. No matter how Percy thought of the situation, nothing would earn him the banknote without lying or misrepresenting. Even if he wrote Dunley to assure him the engagement was off, there would be the real betrothed somewhere very much still affianced to Miss Walsley.

Damn. The money was tempting. And whose fault was it that Dunley was a dunce to blame the wrong man? Not Percy's, to be sure. Alas. Dunley would have to sort out his own problems.

Taking another sip of his coffee, Percy turned to his father's letter. He knew without a shadow of doubt what his father would say.

"Find a bride now or risk being cut off," Percy said in mimicry of his father. With a harrumph, he unfolded the letter.

The first line sent the coffee cup shattering against the floor.

Felicitations on your engagement to Miss Abigail Walsley.

Chapter 4

"What do you mean the private parlor is occupied?" Percival asked the innkeeper of The Tangled Fleece.

Mr. Everitt Bradley shrugged. "Like I said. It's occupied."

"Yes, but you knew I would arrive around this time. I can't very well take my tea in the public room, now can I?" Percy laughed as if sharing a joke with the man.

Rather than laugh, the innkeeper looked him up and down. "From one until three, the Ladies Literary Society meets. From three to four we open the circulating library. Then from four until six is the Gentleman's Coffeehouse. You can have the room after six if you like."

"The Ladies Literary Society?" Percy echoed. "That's more important than an earl's son?"

Mr. Bradley nodded his head to the private parlor door. "They live here, don't they? You can take your tea in the public room like everyone else or go elsewhere."

"I say." Affronted but aware there was nowhere else to go for drink, food, or rooms in or near the speck of the village that was Sidvale, Percy sighed and took a seat.

Ladies Literary Society, indeed. As tiny as the inn was, not even space for an assembly that he could see, it seemed quite the enterprising location. Society meetings, circulating library, coffeehouse—ambitious!

Mr. Bradley came to the table with a tray and a village newspaper. Tapping the paper, he said, "Better than any you'll find in London."

Percy doubted that but flashed a grin.

The public room was empty save Percy and the innkeeper. Just as well. Percy needed to think. He needed to plan. As of yet, strategy failed him. This was not familiar territory.

It had taken two days, three more visits to White's, and a dozen more times reading the letters to convince Percival to travel five days west to Sidvale, the middle-of-nowhere village in Devonshire wherein Lord Dunley's country estate resided, and more to the point, the home of one Miss Abigail Walsley.

The need to confront the issue head on was his father's fault. Had it simply been the letter from Dunley, Percy would have ignored the situation or written a brief letter to set the man straight. As it happened, the choice had been stolen from him. He groaned at the recollection of his father's letter.

My dearest son,

Felicitations on your engagement to Miss Abigail Walsley. You have made me the proudest of fathers. It is my understanding that you wished to surprise me with the news, but I have heard it from Lord Grover who heard it from Lady Plummer who received a missive from Lord Dunley inquiring of your whereabouts, no doubt to send his felicitations, as well, since he hails from the same parish as your betrothed. I apologize if I've now spoiled your surprise, but I could not wait a moment longer to write to you of my happiness. Do bring her to the estate before long. Your proud papa,

Camforth

At this point, most of London would have heard the news. Certainly, the Merriweathers had, as had his former mistress, a few fellows at the club, and most concerningly his father. Whatever letters Dunley had sent out had caused an irrevocable stir, plunging Percy's life into potential scandal. If he did not deal with this now, it could ruin his marriage prospects. Somehow, he had to convince Miss Walsley to remedy the situation by admitting her deception to all and sundry. He could then happily return to his life of simple pleasures and search for a wife that suited him.

It had not escaped his notice that the situation presented a ready bride, but he refused to be duped by a fortune huntress and played a fool.

At first, Percy had assumed it was all a misunderstanding: Miss Walsley had a betrothed, and Dunley became confused and mistook Percy for that betrothed. But the more times he read the viscount's letter, the more he realized that could not be the case. Miss Walsley was a mistress of deception. The Randall family was old, respected, and powerful. In short—a perfect target. After realizing Baron Monkworth of East Hagbourne was in line to inherit the earldom of Camforth, she must have set her cap at him, only to discover the man was married with children. Who better to select than one of the baron's brothers? With the youngest sibling being too young and the second youngest being a girl, that left her with Mr. Percival Randall. Not having met him seemed no inconvenience.

Yes, after much thought, Percy was positive she had decided to trap him, compromise his name, and force him into marriage. As a gentleman, he would be honor-bound to marry her now that all the world thought them betrothed, for he could not call her out as a liar or break a betrothal, fictitious or otherwise. To do either of those things would ruin his reputation beyond repair, sully any future hopes of matrimony, have him kicked out of the townhouse and rendered penniless, and destroy his relationship with his family. He needed a plan for dealing with her.

Somehow, Miss Walsley had to fix this. She was a serious impediment to his matrimonial pursuits.

The image of her was all too clear for Percy. An adventuress of the worst sort. She was one of those conniving women who acted insipid to mask her skills at manipulation. Tight blonde ringlets, an enticing figure, likely the beauty of the county, but between marriage to Dunley and marriage to a Randall, regardless which was titled, she knew she could win the more sought-after prize with a bit of cunning and craft. Percy would not be surprised to find she had forged a stream of love letters between the two of them. The entire county must know of their betrothal, including the innkeeper, although he did not act as though he recognized Percy's name outside of the advanced missive booking the suite.

Percy was the last to know, the victim of this master manipulator.

A noise at the private parlor door drew his attention from his tea and the newspaper he had heretofore ignored. A group of drab women were leaving the room, too lost in conversation to notice him.

One poor girl was too tall for her own good, all long limbs and elongated neck. Another was on the short and plump side, not at all displeasing to the eye, though, with what looked at this distance to be shockingly long lashes. The third girl had deliciously bronzed skin and an enticing smile. The fourth was the plainest, chestnut hair styled in a simple knot at the nape of her neck, dress of dowdy blue with a limp ribbon about the waist, and no figure to speak of, although there was an undeniably attractive pink to her cheeks and brightness about the eyes. The four were exactly how he imagined a Ladies Literary Society would look.

Given the available goods, he was rather thankful to be in Sidvale hoping to lose a bride, not find one.

Abigail laid a page on the chair next to her and continued to read aloud from the next page:

The knight bowed to the lady with a wink and a smile. It was not every day he saved a damsel from an out-of-hand swordfight. This village, as with the many others before in his traveling adventures, would remember his brave deeds and sing songs of his valor.

She looked up after placing the final page atop the others on the chair. "Well?"

Her three friends looked between each other and then back at her.

Miss Hetty Clint spoke first, "The imagery of the battle is vivid, but…" Her words trailed off, and she glanced to the other two girls.

Abbie circled her hands in the air. "But what? Tell me. Be honest."

"He's one-dimensional," said Miss Isobel Lambeth, tugging at her too-snug sleeves until they covered the heels of her hands.

"Sir Bartholomew is one-dimensional? But… but… He's charming and handsome and… perfect!" Abbie defended, looking from one friend to the next.

Today was her day to read aloud at their Ladies Literary Society. Her turn only came every four meetings so she had saved the best chapter, one in which Sir Bartholomew risked his life against two swordsmen to save a lady who had been caught in the wrong place at the wrong time. It was, she had thought, a wonderfully romantic chapter that showed her knight to advantage. Judging from the grimaces on her friends' faces, they did not feel the same.

Miss Leila Owen confirmed. "Your writing isn't the problem. It's the knight. Yes, he's dashing, but that's all he is. There's no substance. What's his motivation? What are his fears?"

"What does he dream?" Isobel asked, nodding to Leila. "I don't feel I *know* him."

Abbie sighed. He was so vivid in her mind, but they were right. He was one-dimensional.

Hetty reached a slender hand to clasp Abbie's. "Don't fret. You'll know how to breathe life into him."

Nodding and trying not to appear too downcast, Abigail squeezed her friend's hand then focused on shuffling her pages together, rolling them, and tying a ribbon around them.

"Now," said Leila, the prettiest of the group with her East Indian tones, "the most important question of our meeting is not how you'll give Sir Bartholomew depth, rather how you're going to resolve your betrothal problem."

Abbie flushed, her grip on the rolled pages tightening. "I've not sorted it yet, but I will. I want to wait until Lord Dunley has his eye on someone else, and then I can tell Papa my betrothed and I exchanged letters, had a disagreement, and I've cried off."

"Oh, Abbie. Why haven't you told him the truth?" Leila asked. "You assured us you would consider confessing."

"I don't know which is worse: the hurt of having kept an engagement from him or of having lied about the whole thing. This is a *big* lie. I won't put Papa in a position that could jeopardize his standing in the church or community. It seems so much tidier to cry off. Then it's done. But not until I know his lordship won't renew the offer."

"Then, what did you end up telling your father?" asked Hetty.

"That we met in East Hagbourne this summer when I was visiting my aunt. I didn't say much beyond that, not wanting to exacerbate the problem. I've never lied to Papa about anything. This is awful. But what other choice do I have? Without a good excuse, the Dunleys could make life difficult for us to force my answer."

Hetty rounded her shoulders. "And life would be so bad as Lady Dunley?"

"He's so handsome and fashionable. And a viscount!" said Leila.

Touching a hand to the knot at the nape of her neck to ensure strands had not escaped, Abbie shook her head. "I'm flattered. But he couldn't even remember my name. And I don't think he would approve of me writing or reading. I'd spend all my time with his mother."

"But you could write and read whenever he wasn't around or when his mother's asleep," Isobel offered.

Leila nodded. "His mother won't live forever—don't look at me like that! It's true! As much time as he spends in London, you'd have the house to yourself to do as you pleased."

"I suppose." Abbie remained unconvinced.

It all felt wrong. Lord Dunley had only looked at her once during the proposal and seemed disinterested. She felt insignificant, even dowdy, next to him. Hiding her writing was not on her agenda, nor was sneaking into her husband's study to steal paper and ink when she was sure he would forbid her to write. She wanted more from a marriage than to live separate lives steeped in secrecy. No, she could never accept his offer. The deception was necessary. Better to remain unmarried and happy than to be married and miserable. She was not in desperate straits and did not have to marry as some women did.

The meeting at an end, the four members of the Ladies Literary Society each slipped their submissions into the newspaper box then saw themselves out of the private parlor of The Tangled Fleece.

For their next session, Leila would read her poetry. The daughter of an Indian heiress whom her father had met while working in Bengal, Leila had a love for writing romantic poems inspired by Shah Latif. Hetty preferred writing about more practical matters with her book of manners. Isobel, a lover of Ann Radcliffe, aspired to write Gothic tales.

With a smile to the innkeeper, Abbie turned into the public room. Her breath caught and her heart skipped a beat.

She stopped so abruptly, Hetty collided into her back. Thankfully, the object of her attention did not look up from his newspaper to witness the stumble. Sir Bartholomew sat in the public room of the inn, taking tea as though it were the most natural of actions. How could this be?

Blinking to clear the delusion, she stared at the living figment of her imagination. No matter how many times she blinked, he remained seated, newspaper in one hand, tea in the other.

He was not Sir Bartholomew, of course. That would be silly. Nevertheless, the resemblance was uncanny. Brown hair with a touch of gold, cut short except for the top which was just wavy enough to invite her fingers to sink into the curls. His physique. His long nose. His strong chin. They all belonged to her knight. Did he have hazel eyes too?

Hetty linked arms with her. "What are you staring at? I'll walk you home."

Isobel caught up to them and whispered, "He's out of place, isn't he? From London, I'd guess. His boots are so shiny he could see his reflection."

Hetty tutted. "Hush. He'll hear you."

Abbie made a point to look away as they passed him. Only when she had one foot out the front door did she take another look. The man had turned in his chair, an arm draped over the back, the newspaper limp in his hand. Hazel eyes stared back at her, dimples deepening as his lips stretched into a charming smile.

The nicest suite in the inn yet Percival's bed was lumpy. He tossed left. He tossed right. He alternated between staring at cracked plaster and counting the floorboards. There were no curtains around the bed, and a distinct chill that no fire could dispel seeped from a window.

While the bulk of his insomnia could be attributed to his lingering indecision on a plan for the morrow, the room contributed to a hefty portion of his wakefulness. No, not only the room. The country. Percy hated the country. Nothing to do. Nothing to see. And all the blasted quiet. His fingers laced behind his head and his ankles crossed, he listened to the unnerving silence beyond the inn. Nothing could be more disturbing than that silence. He strained for the sounds of hoofs on cobblestone, drunken laughter, the groan of the building, anything.

Silence.

He could not get back to London fast enough.

His first course of action in the morning would be to visit the vicarage. The top of the hill, the innkeeper had directed him, the stone cottage next to the church. That was where he could find the Reverend Walsley and his *lovely* daughter. The emphasis had been the innkeeper's, not Percy's, reconjuring the image of his voluptuous and ringleted betrothed, all batting eyelashes and wicked wiles.

Go in, give her a stern talking to, and then leave. The confusion would be cleared up before noon.

Twit-twoo.

Twit-twoo.

Percy jerked upright, eyes wide. What was that? Silence.

He dared not move. Was someone outside? Was someone trying to burgle him? Did a monster lurk in the dark waiting to devour him?

Hoohuhuhuhu.

The sound repeated. One part prolonged, resonating, the other part grating, as though two separate sounds merged as one. Owls? Sheep? Ghouls? Devil take it. He was going mad on his first — and hopefully only — night in Sidvale.

After long minutes of sitting rigid, he relaxed. The sound was intermittent, but clearly an animal of the night. An owl or two, he wagered. Such vulgar country sounds set his nerves on edge, but he forced himself to recline, lacing his fingers once more as a barrier against the lumpiness.

Should he explain the situation to the vicar, inform the man that his daughter was a conniving witch? Tell him outright that Percival would not be played a fool? No doubt the two were in this together.

His conscience interrupted.

Percy would be seen as a brute, a first-rate villain. To accuse her in such a baseless manner could ruin him as well as her. Regardless of the truth, he would be seen as the worst sort of rogue who had used her and tossed her aside. She would be ruined beyond repair, shunned from society, shunned everywhere word of the situation followed her. Her family, be they siblings or extended, would be dragged into ruination over the scandal. Her father would likely lose his position. Percy could not allow so many people to be hurt, no matter who was at fault. The situation would not leave him unscathed, either, his name forever tied with hers. His family would be beyond disappointed, either at his roguish behavior or his ungentlemanly treatment in calling her out. A man did not accuse a lady of not being a lady. It was not done.

This situation needed the gentlest of caresses. Dashed if he knew how to handle it, though.

As his mind worked in circles, a grin tugging at the corners of his lips—such an absurd situation! The grin masked his underlying fear. This was beyond his experience. All gentlemen knew the tales, some wise enough to heed them while others were too lovesick to listen. At how many balls, routs, or otherwise had he witnessed it? The young lady begging to see the garden only to accuse the gentleman of kissing her, thus compromising him and forcing his hand into an unwanted marriage with a fortune- or title-hunting seductress. The young lady seeking out a gentleman in the library only to be caught alone, thus trapping the man. The stories were too numerous to count, all orchestrated by crafty misses or their mothers. Usually by their mothers, although he had heard tales of some groups of friends who set out to win their trophies no matter the cost.

Not all the ladies got what they wanted, for not all their targets were honorable. Reputations on both sides were ruined, always worse for the young lady; but it was no day at the park for the gentleman, either. Invitations stopped, rumors started, good marriage prospects removed from the table.

How could he not feel the tightness of fear squeezing his heart, the tremble of his limbs? If he should have to marry the chit, he would be stuck with her. That was it. She would have the Randall name and an inseverable connection to the Earl of Camforth. He would have a loveless marriage with a smug adventuress.

Turning onto his side, he counted the floorboards.

Goodness, Sidvale was small. The distance from the inn to the vicarage was barely a half mile. As he crested what the innkeeper had called a hill — more of a bump in the road — Percy took in the cottage. The innkeeper needed to sort out his proportions.

The hill was not a hill, and this was notably not a cottage. A hall, perhaps? Not quite a manor, but sizable, nonetheless. Percy whistled. It made for a pretty picture with the church a few yards to the west and a sweeping landscape of sheep- and hedgerow-dotted pasture behind. Grey stone framed the not-cottage. A conservatory adorned by bare but bold wisteria branches extended to one side, arched windows interrupting the stone in the center block. Columned by yew trees, the two-story building welcomed him as a friend.

Despite the situation, he smiled.

Not for long did he wait at the door before the vicar himself answered. The moment of truth, and Percy stood speechless, an illogical grin on his face.

"You must be Mr. Randall," the vicar said, offering his hand.

Percy accepted, finding a firm grip from Mr. Walsley. "Ah, yes, I'm delighted you received my card in time. I would have hated to arrive unannounced or find you from home."

"My pleasure to receive you." The vicar ushered him into a pretty little entrance hall. "Is this a study or parlor visit?"

"Does my name sound familiar to you by chance?" Percy asked rather than answer the question.

Mr. Walsley tilted his head, his brows drawn in thought. "Should it?"

Fascinating. Either the father was playing a peculiar game, or he was not in on his daughter's tricks.

"Second son of the Earl of Camforth." That should jog his memory.

Shaking his head, the vicar's smile slipped. "I'm afraid I don't leave Sidvale often other than to visit my daughters in Sidbury or my sister and eldest in East Hagbourne."

"Ah, yes, East Hagbourne. Then you'll know of my older brother, Freddie, or Baron Monkworth rather." He saw the dawning in the man's eyes.

"East Hagbourne, you say?" The vicar crossed his arms over his chest, a quizzical expression replacing the furrow.

"I've spent my fair share of time in East Hagbourne to visit my brother, as well as Oxford, of course, and at my father's estate near Aylesbury." Percival hesitated for a moment before saying. "If I'm being honest, sir, I'm hoping for a word with Miss Abigail Walsley. Not that I wouldn't mind exchanging pleasantries with you, but best be upfront about these things, I say."

Any remnants of a smile disappeared. The Reverend Walsley straightened to his full height, an easy head taller than Percy. The man did not look hostile, exactly, as Percy did not think a vicar could ever look hostile, but the penetrating stare made him feel as though he were the one guilty of wrongdoing rather than the crafty Miss Walsley.

Under such scrutiny, Percy shifted his weight from one foot to the other, his own smile slipping as his eyes darted around the room for anything to look at besides Mr. Walsley. Did the vicar think him a wrongdoer? What exactly had Miss Walsley said about the betrothal? Percy gulped. Had she painted him in a bad light, as a libertine, perhaps? Oh dear.

Mr. Walsley said, "She delivers charity baskets in the morning. If you'll wait in the parlor, I'll see if she's left yet."

His tone was crisp, his words clipped, not at all the warm welcome of his original greeting. In stilted steps, the vicar showed Percival to the parlor. The door was unceremoniously closed behind him before Percy could say more. For this not to be going as planned would imply he had a plan, which he did not, but really, it was not going as planned.

Chapter 5

The frown and narrowed eyes signaled her father's displeasure. About what, Abbie could not guess. That there was a caller this early in the morning? That the caller asked for her? The only possibility could be Lord Dunley come to renew his offer by convincing her to cry off her fictitious betrothal. Another visit from the viscount would certainly discomfit her father.

She followed him to the parlor in silence, more apprehensive than curious.

When they reached the door, Leland turned and said, "You have ten minutes before I join with tea. Never say I'm not compassionate, but don't mistake my kindness for approval."

With that, he left her alone at the parlor door. Abbie watched him depart, confused and concerned. How was leaving her alone with Lord Dunley compassionate? A hand to her heart, she opened the parlor door and stepped inside.

Only, it was not Lord Dunley who awaited her.

Her breath caught. *Sir Bartholomew.*

Or rather, the man from The Tangled Fleece. So startled by his presence, she almost forgot her father had abandoned her, not even introducing the two of them. She hoped she did not blush.

Sir Bartholomew, or whoever this stranger was, removed from one of the parlor chairs and bowed. When their eyes met, he appeared as arrested as she. His eyes widened, and his smirk turned to a frown.

"Miss Abigail Walsley?"

"Yes. And you?"

His smirk returned. "You should know very well who I am."

Shaking her head and lacing her fingers at her waist, she said, "I'm afraid I don't. Have we met before?"

"Mr. Percival Randall." He sank into a slower, deeper bow, flourishing his hand.

Abbie thought for a moment. The only Randall who came to mind was one of her aunt's neighbors, Freddie Randall, though she knew of him as Lord Monkworth and had never actually met him. Aunt Gertrude spoke of him often enough. Amiable fellow, she had said.

Shaking her head again, she said, "Your name isn't familiar. I do apologize. Would you care to sit? My father will bring tea shortly."

Confused but accustomed to playing hostess to the varied guests who called on her father at the vicarage, she waved to his previously occupied chair and took a seat opposite him.

Mr. Randall accepted the chair, his smirk broadening. "I had hoped this to be an easy matter to settle, but I can tell you're going to play coy. Denial, I admit, was not the approach I anticipated."

Spine straight and hands clasped in her lap, Abbie asked, "Would you please speak plainly? I'm not in the habit of playing coy, and I have nothing to deny, at least not that I'm as of yet aware. Why have you called on me?"

He studied her, made to speak, then studied her further. In the time it took him to take her measure, she had nearly lost herself in the depths of those hazel eyes. It was unnerving to be in the same room as her hero, especially since he was not really her hero. Had other writers suffered such encounters? Fearing she was blushing, she reached a hand to the knot at her nape. All in order, no loose strands.

"I shall, as you instruct, speak plainly," he said. "You informed Lord Dunley that you were betrothed to me."

Her hand flew to her mouth. There could be no doubt she was flushed now. She could feel the flame in her cheeks.

"I did not!" Abbie defended. "I would never! I don't even *know* you."

"Hardly material in this matter. You knew *of* me enough to compromise my name."

"No! No, no, no, I said nothing of the sort. I don't know you or of you and thus gave your name to no one." A feeling of dread settled into the pit of her stomach. If the floor could swallow her, she would gladly sink. Had Lord Dunley misunderstood her, or was this man some sort of spy sent to ascertain if she were truly engaged? She had to be careful what she said for fear of the latter. "What is this about, Mr. Randall? Help me to understand."

"I received a letter from Lord Dunley naming me as your betrothed. He gave strict instructions for me to find a way to break off the engagement, complete with bribery, I might add. I confess I am uncertain if you've set about this intentionally, hoping to catch a husband of me — in which case, you will be sorely disappointed — or if there has been a mistake. Has Lord Dunley confused your true betrothed with me? If so, we can make quick work to remedy the situation."

Oh, this was too much. What had Lord Dunley done? What had *she* done? Abbie stared down at her hands, not sure how much to say.

"Do you have the letter with you?"

After a moment's pause, he said, "As a matter of fact, I do."

Pulling the letter from his pocket, a pocket she could not help but notice came with a bespoke ensemble that matched his eyes, he handed her the paper. He and his coat were far more thrilling than whatever missive she held. London tailoring through and through, not a sign of a stitch or seam. It was the most expensive suit she had ever seen. The man who went with the suit filled it admirably, a lean and unpadded physique. Not that she should be staring at his physique when there was a letter to read.

She looked over both the seal and the address on the back before reading. Could Lord Dunley have forged it in hopes of ferreting out the truth of her betrothal? She did not believe so. The letter looked well-traveled, not as though it had been handed directly from the viscount to a spy. Although she knew little of Mr. Randall, he appeared earnest.

That his lordship could have connected this man to the description she had given beggared belief. Yes, if she could have given a more exacting description of her fictitious beau, he would look like this man, but what she had told Lord Dunley had been wholly vague.

"I'm afraid I don't understand, Mr. Randall. I never gave him a name. I gave the vaguest of descriptions, something along the lines of brown hair, hazel eyes, and knightly. That could fit hundreds of men in England. I did mention I met my betrothed in East Hagbourne, which seems to be the connecting factor, but this is truly a matter of mistaken identity, one that can be easily rectified. Inform Lord Dunley that he has the wrong man."

Mr. Randall rubbed his chin in thought before taking the letter and folding it back into his pocket.

"It's become rather more complicated than that, I'm afraid."

"I don't see why. Tell him he has the wrong man, and return to wherever it is you're from, East Hagbourne or otherwise. You'll not be bothered by my affairs again. I apologize for the confusion, but this is all a silly mix-up easily rectified."

He tugged another letter out of his pocket and handed it to her.

As she read the words of Lord Camforth, the blood drained from her face. "I'm certain it's not as bad as this. Write to your father and inform him that there was a mistake."

"Miss Walsley." He paused to clear his throat. "It's worse even than this. The best way, in fact the *only* way, I can see of resolving this problem is to announce your true intended. Regardless of your reasons for keeping the engagement secret, invite him to meet Lord Dunley, a supper party perhaps. Send an announcement of some sort to the London newspapers. Have the banns read. Let it be known who your intended is and thus clear my name from this debacle. Even then, it could be messy, as it could look as though I've been cuckolded, but it's the best solution at present."

"I hardly see how a confusion with your father and the viscount is cause for such pomp. Send a letter to both informing them of their mistake, and all will be well."

Mr. Randall laughed hollowly. "You fail to understand the magnitude of this. *Everyone* in London thinks we're engaged. I couldn't walk into my gentleman's club without being congratulated by all and sundry. This has ruined my prospects with a certain young lady I was courting, broken an arrangement I had with a friend, and judging from my father's letter, spread across far more than London in a stream of gossip-filled letters. My word is nothing—a rogue's word against a young maiden who has claimed we are engaged. Only you can undo this."

Hiding her face in her hands, she could not decide whether to weep or laugh. If he were a spy, and she did not believe he was at this stage of the conversation, then so be it, for she had only one confession to make.

"I'm not engaged to anyone, least of all you, Mr. Randall."

He took his time processing the words. He folded the letter from his father, tucked it into the pocket with the other letter, and stared awhile at a spot on the wall behind her before speaking.

"At least you didn't intentionally name me," he said with a faint smile. "I won't question your reason for lying, but this must be undone. To clear my name, you'll have to admit you lied. Letters, an announcement, whatever it takes."

"I most certainly will not!" To do so would ruin her.

"Then produce another betrothed. Pay someone to do it, anyone, a local farmer. You must clear my name of all this. Thanks to your admirer, Lord Dunley, we're in a bind."

"He's *not* my—"

He held up a staying hand. "I see manners will get me nowhere. Let's skip the secrets and get to the root of this, then. Why aren't you betrothed?"

Abbie huffed. "That is none of your concern, and I will not pay someone to pretend to be engaged to me. When I find someone with whom I can be happy and who will allow me certain freedoms, I will consider a true betrothal; until then, I do not wish to bribe someone to lie. Please leave before my father returns. This is all too humiliating."

"Certain freedoms?" He gave her a sidelong look before saying, "While I realize your life is not my concern, I have been pulled into this. Why not marry the viscount and be done with it? He is, after all, titled."

"Not if he were the last man on earth. He only wants me so I can be a nursemaid to his mother. I have a life of my own, I'll have you know. I admit that I lied and told him I was betrothed since I did not think he would take no for an answer, which this situation proves. But I'll not take that back, at least not until his attention is elsewhere. With me no longer going to the estate to see Lady Dunley, I can only hope she finds a new companion onto whom she can push her son. When that occurs, I'll cry off my fake betrothal."

Leaning a shoulder against the chairback, Mr. Randall propped an elbow onto the arm of the seat and drummed his fingers on his thigh. For so long he remained silent, Abbie wondered if the conversation were at an end, though to what end, she was unsure.

"How?" he asked, those long fingers moving from his thigh to his lips where they tapped a thoughtful rhythm. "How will you cry off? My reputation must remain intact or I'll disappoint my family and ruin my marriage prospects. You clearly had a plan before I came along. What was it?"

She folded her hands one on top of the other. "Well, I have thought about this, yes, and I think I'll pretend that my betrothed and I had a disagreement, and so I broke the engagement."

"What kind of disagreement? This cannot make me look bad. I can't look like a brute or heartbreaker."

"This isn't about *you*. You're not my betrothed." When he raised his eyebrows, she added, "I suppose you have a point, though. A mutual agreement not to move forward, then. My betrothed and I can disagree on where we wish to reside or something important of that nature that does not cast him in a negative light. Satisfactory?"

"No. You said you have to remain engaged until Lord Dunderhead finds someone else. That could be, what, five years from now? This is a ridiculous idea. Had you hoped someone would come along before then so you could elope? The logic of women…" He shook his head.

Abbie harrumphed and crossed her arms at her waist. "It could be any day, weeks at most. His mother does not do well alone. At worst, she'll hire a companion and leave her son to return to London where he spends all his time anyway. I believe his proposal was only because she knew I wouldn't be hired as a companion. She panicked, I think."

"And so, that leaves me staying here anywhere from a few days to several weeks before you cry off in an amicable fashion because we can't agree on the color of the curtains?"

"Oh no; you can't be serious!" She laughed. "You can't stay here and court me! You just can't. You need to leave, go on with your life, and I'll sort this out."

"As smoothly as you sorted us into this mess? I don't think so. This is *my* name you're toying with now. Even if it wasn't your intention that I was dragged into it, I am involved, and I must come out of this as marriageable as I was before. No, make that *more* marriageable than before the, er, misunderstanding."

"Why are you so concerned with being marriageable? I can't imagine you having difficulties." The dreadful, telltale blush returned.

"Ah, the tables have turned. Now, you're inquiring into matters not your concern. Suffice it to say, I've been given an ultimatum I cannot ignore. Marry I must, though I have a little under two years in which to find a bride. As long as Lord Dunce doesn't take two years, and presuming I get out of this a hero unscathed by scandal, I'll be pleased."

She was afraid to ask but ask she did. "So, what does this mean?"

"It would seem, Miss Walsley, we are engaged."

Chapter 6

Had Percival not dined on occasion with Mr. Merriweather, he might have been intimidated by the squinty glare of the Reverend Walsley, who watched his every move as though he might elope with Miss Walsley after the third course. The invitation to join the two for supper at the vicarage had not come with a disclaimer that Percy would be scrutinized and cross-examined. He was not surprised. In fact, he found it an endearing quality, raising his estimation of Mr. Walsley. The man was a devoted father who wanted the best for his daughter, not something the marriage-minded parents he was accustomed to meeting in London could boast.

The best part of supper, regardless of the unusual circumstances by which he came to the table, was his certainty that the Walsleys were genuine. Who aside from this pair would not take advantage of having a well-connected bachelor at the end of a hook? Despite his original doubts of their sincerity, he believed Miss Abigail Walsley's story. This confusion may have come about because of her lie, but he did not take her as a woman accustomed to lying, much less manipulating.

Mr. Walsley cut his meat with a knowing glance to Percy. "Tell me. How did the two of you meet?"

Percy sputtered into his wine.

Miss Walsley set down her cutlery, her cheeks blossoming into two roses.

"By Hacca's Brook," Percy said, setting down his glass, his eyes on Miss Walsley rather than the vicar. "A rare day of sun had me desiring a walk through East Hagbourne, not to mention I needed an escape from my sister-in-law."

His temporary betrothed did not look up from her plate when she added, "Yes, by the brook. I was, um, admiring the flora."

"Just before you fell into the stream."

"Before I *what*?"

She stared at him in such horror that he bit back a laugh.

Mr. Walsley did not hold back, however, chuckling at his daughter before saying to Percy, "That is exactly what I would have expected of her."

Surprised by this insight into the young miss, Percy asked, "Is she habitually clumsy?"

"I am not clumsy!"

The vicar leaned back in his chair, smiling. "How many times this month have you spilled the ink?"

"Well—well, that's different."

Both men raised their eyebrows, but Percival suspected for different reasons. Only two courses into dinner, and he was already learning more than he ever imagined he would about this enigmatic web-weaver.

"What's this about spilled ink?" he asked. "An avid letter writer? Nervous calligrapher?"

Mr. Walsley's brow crinkled as he looked from his daughter to Percy. "Do you not know she's a writer?"

He shook his head, studying the woman across from him. "She's not mentioned it, no, but it makes sense. On occasion, she's been known to weave fanciful tales." Rather than look abashed, Miss Walsley glared at him. He flashed her a smile in response. "What is it that you write, *my dear*?"

"Nothing you'd be interested in, I'm sure." The roses returned to her cheeks as she eyed her plate.

"Anything you write is of interest to me. Come now. Confess."

Mr. Walsley watched them as he returned to his meal.

The answer came so softly, Percy almost missed it. "Novels."

"Novels, did you say?" He leaned forward, focusing on her with rapt attention. "What might be the content of these novels?"

Miss Walsley refused to make eye contact, looking everywhere at the table except him, her hands likely wringing in her lap, as they had disappeared from the table. For whatever reason, Percy found her fetching when discomfited. She looked less like a governess and more like a young country miss who had yet to discover the fashionableness of ennui. She wore this look well.

In an even lower whisper, she said, "Chivalric romance."

"With *knightly* heroes?" His smile broadened.

A nearly imperceptible nod answered him.

"By Jove. I should have known." Percy clapped and laughed. "And when will I have the pleasure of reading your prose?"

She looked up then, blanching, but she was saved by a young footman carrying in the next course. Her relief was palpable. Did one of her knights have brown hair and hazel eyes?

Once the plates had been exchanged, Mr. Walsley asked, "And what of you, Mr. Randall? What is it you do?"

"Aside from saving damsels from Hacca's Brook?" Percy asked rhetorically, directing his smirk to Miss Walsley. "I'm a gentleman."

"That may very well be, but what do you *do* in East Hagbourne? Spend your days walking the village and avoiding sisters-in-law?"

"Only one sister-in-law. I've two other siblings, both younger and of my father's second marriage. I hope they'll marry spouses who approve of me, for Freddie's wife thinks I'm—" Percy stopped abruptly.

Good heavens. What was he about to say? That the woman thought him a wastrel and a rake? He would have to do better than this.

Clearing his throat, he said, "That is to say, she thinks I spend too much time, er, reading. Yes, I spend far too much time indoors reading, and so she encourages me to walk about town when I visit. I live in London, but I do visit my brother often enough, typically spending a winter month there." A quick glance to Miss Walsley's expression set him straight. "Although this year I visited in the summer. Obviously." He hid behind his wine and took far too long of a drink.

Mr. Walsley steepled his fingers. "And is it your intention to take my daughter with you to London?"

"I hadn't thought—that is, it's not something we've discussed." He looked to her, hoping her novelist brain would think of something witty to say. When she did not come to his rescue, he said, "You see, I had hoped to sort out a few private affairs before officially announcing my intention. Come here, ask for her hand properly, that sort of thing." His laugh sounded forced. "Perhaps I'll find a place here to call home. Wouldn't that be divine, *darling*?"

With a silent crack her foot met his shin beneath the table. Hardly ladylike behavior towards the man who was saving her from Lord Dunley! Hiding his wince behind the wine glass, he reached a foot her direction to return the favor with a none-too-gentle press of his toes onto hers.

She hid her yelp by saying, "What he means to say, Papa, is he'd rather stay in London, but he knows I'd rather stay here, so it's a point of contention between us and one of the reasons we kept this a secret." Flicking her gaze to Percy, she added, "Isn't that right?"

"Of course, yes. But I wouldn't let my preferences come in the way of your happiness. If you love the country so much, I could…adapt."

Another nudge to the shin sent him back to the wine glass. This was going to be a long few days, or weeks, or however long he had committed himself to living in hell.

The meal could not end soon enough. Percival was eager to retire from the barrage of questions. Alas, such a wish was not to be granted. Although Percy and Mr. Walsley were the only men present, the vicar insisted the two should share port and cigars before joining Miss Walsley in the parlor, at which time she would charm them with a piece on the pianoforte.

He smiled, dying on the inside.

After lighting both cigars, Mr. Walsley frowned at his guest. "What are your true intentions towards my daughter?"

Percy coughed a cloud of smoke. "My intentions…" he wheezed, rubbing his chest.

Today had gone by too quickly. Not for a moment had he found time to himself to mull over how to approach this situation. Nothing had been as he expected, and he most certainly had not intended to be falsely engaged to a vicar's daughter; yet here he sat playing a charade with a vicar. He needed time to think, time to plan his approach.

"I'm waiting," prodded Mr. Walsley.

"My intentions, sir, should be obvious. Miss Walsley and I are engaged, are we not?"

"That remains to be seen."

"I beg your pardon." A soldier interrogated by enemy forces must feel as Percy did now.

"Had your intentions been pure, you would have made yourself known to my sister, Mrs. Gertrude Diggeby, while publicly courting my daughter in East Hagbourne. You would have then sought me out here in Sidvale to ask permission for her hand. Instead, you have charmed my daughter and secured her silence. Abigail does not keep secrets from me. Your power over her must be influential indeed. Now that I've met you, I can see why. It unsettles me, Mr. Randall. I don't trust you or your intentions."

Taken aback, Percy set aside the cigar.

He could not defend himself without giving away the game. In part, he blamed Miss Walsley for maintaining the lie with a father she was clearly close to, but he did recognize the sticky situation in which she found herself. Had she confessed the lie, her father would not only be upset that she had lied to the viscount, but he may have felt obligated to correct the matter by encouraging the viscount to renew his offer. A man of his position would not wish to anger the local aristocracy. Yes, Percy understood her choice, but that did not mean he approved, least of all when it put him in a position of direct blame for that which he was not guilty.

With a deep exhale, Percy met Mr. Walsley's glare and told him the only thing he knew: the truth.

"I may be a gentleman, but I'd make a sorry husband. I've lived the dissipated life expected of a man such as myself. Earlier this year, my father gave me an ultimatum to marry before my thirtieth birthday or lose my allowance and the roof over my head. I've courted, casually as it were, a young lady or two, knowing myself a catch only by name and not by profession. I have nothing to show that is not my father's. These past few weeks, I've affected changes in my life, practicing celibacy for a start." He cringed at the confession. "I want to be a better man and make a decent husband for the woman I marry, but I hardly know where to start. What if I marry only to learn I can't change my ways? What if I marry and my wife regrets it?"

"I see." Without looking away from Percival, Mr. Walsley snuffed out his cigar. "Are you using my daughter to keep the roof over your head and money in your pocket?"

"No, sir, and that's the honest truth."

Folding his arms behind his head, the vicar stretched out his legs and crossed one ankle over the other. "When had you planned for the reading of the banns?"

"Not until I know my wife would not regret marrying me."

Only then did the vicar move his gaze away from Percy. In silence they sat for a good minute or more.

"Do you ride?" the vicar finally asked.

Percy furrowed his brows at the non sequitur. "Not often."

"Care to ride with me day after tomorrow? I can show you the farms, take you around to see the Dunley estate, maybe a trip to the mill. What do you say?"

He nodded in silent agreement. Oh, he was in deep now.

"Good. I'll meet you at The Tangled Fleece at nine. Now, we've kept Abigail waiting overlong. She'll be eager to play for you."

Percival very much doubted that.

***

If Percy had to spend every evening listening to Miss Walsley play pianoforte while her father glared at him, he would go mad.

His least favorite time to be in London was during the Season. All the pretty faced chits prostrated themselves before the eligible bachelors, displaying their accomplishments like jewels for auction, singing, dancing, playing, conversing, and not all of it well. During the spring months, he avoided balls. His interests were in the routs, a soiree from time to time, and endless hours at White's. Yet here he was, about to be harassed by the subpar accomplishments of a country miss.

It was bad enough he had confessed personal matters to her father, all of which were true. In Percy's defense, there was something about the man. Despite the interrogation, there was something open about him, something that invited honesty. He must be an astonishing vicar. Had the topic not changed, Percy might have found himself admitting to every sin in his life going back to childhood, not that there was much sinning, for he was not a libertine, but he did enjoy a good party as much as any blue-blooded man in his prime.

Percival sat next to Mr. Walsley as Miss Walsley took her seat at the pianoforte, looking for all the world as though she would rather be anywhere but at the bench. He empathized.

"Need for me to turn the pages?" he asked.

Miss Walsley fingered the keys, not looking over at the men. "No. I don't need pages."

Relieved, he leaned into his chair and crossed one leg over the other. Mozart, he guessed. She would play Mozart to showcase her skill and memory. He wagered he could even predict one of five pieces she would play, for they were the favorites among the girls in London. Miss Merriweather had played all five. At every visit. Tedious business.

At the first chord, he realized he had underestimated her.

A sweet soprano voice, pure and tender, filled the room, accompanied by adept fingers against seduced keys. Percival uncrossed his legs and sat up.

Miss Walsley's eyes closed, and her body swayed gently to the tune, a subtle smile teasing her lips. She played a folk ballad, one part jovial, one part enchanting. The prim and drab vicar's daughter now shone with a spirit of gaiety and beauty. He could not help but be charmed.

Until he listened to the lyrics.

By Jove. She sang of a baffled knight taken in by a girl swimming in a brook. The girl teased him into her father's house but would not have him. A merry chase ensued, including trickery of a falsified lover to dupe the knight, and yet still the knight pursued, determined to win her love. Percy stole glances at the vicar. Rather than appear nonplussed, the man tapped his foot in time with the music.

The minx!

Chapter 7

"He's *staying*?" Hetty asked, aghast.

"But why? That makes everything worse." Isobel worried her bottom lip. "What was once a private fib is now a public reality. Didn't you tell him you would resolve this on your own with a forged letter or two to break off the engagement?"

Abigail shrugged to her friends in the Ladies Literary Society. After critiquing Leila's poetry, Abbie had recounted the previous day's events. They would soon hear all about Mr. Randall with or without her confession. The whole village would. Mr. Randall was determined to appear the consummate and faithful betrothed so that when their differences of opinion severed the connection, they could each return to their life unmarred and marriageable. Even now, she could imagine him shouting from the rooftops of his devotion to his bride. What a ridiculous, proud peacock. With the innkeeper's penchant for gossip, word could be spreading as she sat in the private parlor of The Tangled Fleece.

"He doesn't trust me to take care of it," Abbie said. "I'm so embarrassed about all of this. What I said to Lord Dunley was never supposed to leave the parlor. Papa wasn't even supposed to find out except the wretched beast blabbed it all as soon as the door opened. It would seem he blabbed it to half of the country."

Leila looked from one friend to the next before asking, "Why not keep Mr. Randall?"

All eyes turned to Leila.

"He's not mine to keep." Abbie opened her satchel, eyes averted from her friends, and rifled through her papers to appear nonchalant. "Circumstances forced him here, and he's staying only because he wants to avoid scandal. Believe me when I say he would rather be anywhere but here. Besides, I don't want to keep him. From what I know of him so far, we wouldn't suit. He's not exactly the intellectual sort, if you take my meaning. And what would he want with me? I'm hardly an ideal wife for someone like him."

Hetty looked to Isobel and Leila. "'The lady doth protest too much, methinks.'"

Nodding, Leila said, "You *do* like him."

Abbie flipped the satchel cover closed, eyes trained on her lap to hide her blush. "As I said, I don't know him. Can we please talk about something else? We have rules against gossip—need I remind everyone?"

As Leila began to respond, the parlor door opened.

Mr. Randall himself strutted into the room, an ivory walking stick at his side, his London attire the image of perfection yet again, today in garnet. The moment the girls turned to look at him, he smiled broadly enough to reveal dimples. Abbie's heart flip-flopped.

"Good afternoon, ladies." He flourished a bow, a single curl falling onto his forehead. "I heard from a little bird that this is a literary society. Is there room for one more?"

He advanced on the group, sending the girls into a simpering shamble of whispers, glances, and giggles. Abbie grimaced. How dared he invade her private life? He was only in the village because of a misunderstanding and would be gone again within days, weeks at most, never to return. Their arrangement did not include him following her about, making love to her friends and family, or showing her his dimples.

Sitting up straighter, she said, "It is a lovely afternoon, Mr. Randall; thank you for noticing. As delighted as we would be for you to join, this is a *ladies'* group, and you, sir, are not a lady." Her friends giggled when he waggled his eyebrows at them. Abbie cleared her throat. "Even if that were not the case, we are nearly finished for the day."

Unfazed, Mr. Randall took a seat next to Leila, who had had the audacity to wave him over.

"I'm not applying for membership to this exclusive club — yet — simply curious what a literary society does. Perhaps you'd be so kind as to introduce the members?" Resting his walking stick against the back of the chair, he crossed one leg over the other.

She was outnumbered. It did not take a genius to see they were all taken with him. Fickle friends. And what did they know of him aside from a handsome face? He was *not* Sir Bartholomew. He lacked all the graces and morality of her hero. Shallow, vain, pompous — she could define him from the smirk and fit of his coat. That did not stop her cheeks from warming when he turned his gaze on her.

Waving a hand to each of her friends in turn, she said, "This is Miss Hetty Clint, Miss Isobel Lambeth, and Miss Leila Owen. Everyone, this is Mr. Percival Randall, my, um, betrothed."

One by one, he took their fingers between his and kissed the air above their knuckles. The collective sigh drew Abbie's lips into a grim line.

Leila was the first to speak. "We'd love for you to join us. We're only a ladies society because no gentleman has ever offered to join."

Abbie mouthed to her friend: *traitor*.

With an innocent moue, Leila said, "We're a writing group, though we do discuss books and news on occasion. Each of us is a writer, you see."

"I sit amongst the most brilliant minds in England." Emphasizing each word with slow precision, he added, "I am humbled."

Brilliant minds indeed. All but Abbie tittered. Even Hetty! And Hetty was the most practical-minded woman of her acquaintance.

Draping an arm over the back of his chair, he looked at Abbie. "I have the greatest of hopes to hear the poetic phrasings of my intended. Will you grant me this wish?"

"I'm afraid you missed my turn at our previous meeting. Today was Miss Owen's turn."

"And you couldn't make an exception for your beloved? A short passage?"

Oh, he was too much. *Beloved*, *hmph*! What an irritating man.

Hetty nodded to the satchel. "Go on, Abbie. Read him a scene."

"Read him the part where Sir Bartholomew saves Granny Herd from the bull," Isobel offered oh-so-helpfully.

With a huff, Abbie flipped open the satchel to retrieve a page of her manuscript. "One part only." She scanned the page. "This is where Sir Bartholomew meets Lady Fowler, a temptress, but resists her charms just in time to save Lord Fowler from being poisoned."

Mr. Randall's eyebrows raised. "All of that happens in one page?"

"Well, no, this is only him meeting Lady Fowler and being tempted, but I thought you ought to know he manages to resist *and* save a life by doing so."

Mr. Randall nodded, his face the image of studious attention.

She really ought not blame him, she knew. It was her lie that had dragged him into this, and he was doing his best to make the situation work to their mutual advantage. What irritated her was the invasion into her life by a man who would be gone again as fast as he had entered, a man who could never be her knight.

Clutching the paper until the edges crumpled in her grip, she read Sir Bartholomew's summons to Lady Fowler's manor. Every third line, she looked up to Mr. Randall. Rather than derision, she saw in his expression thoughtful curiosity. He appeared to be listening. Or he was a good faker. Abbie continued to read, detailing her ladyship's beauty. Sir Bartholomew was too keen to be tempted. He saw beyond her beauty to the faithlessness of her heart. This was a new scene she had composed, an attempt to build dimension to the hero based on her friends' critique of him being flat. She wondered if the new direction worked.

When she finished, she tucked the page back into the satchel, hoping the pages were not out of order, for she could not concentrate with Mr. Randall staring at her.

"What's the moral?" he asked, rubbing a slender finger across his lower lip in thought.

"Must there be a moral?"

"No, but it feels as though you're building to one. I can't be the only one to sense that." He turned to the ladies.

Their normal forthrightness transformed to fidgets and giggles.

"I wrote the scene to add more depth to Sir Bartholomew. By the time we reach the end, we know a great deal more about his values and why he's celibate." She bit her bottom lip at her last word.

"I don't know Sir Bartholomew from a farmer in the dale, but I'm willing to bet you don't need a whole scene to build depth. You could do more with this, build in a moral. I take it he has many adventures? A traveling knight, as it were? Each adventure could have a moral, and each moral could build to an overarching theme. Yes?"

He turned to look at the ladies again, then back to Abbie. Unperturbed by the long stretch of silence, he studied her, his lips inching into a smile with each passing second. Confound her traitorous heart! If only it would not pound every time he smiled.

Leila interrupted the moment. "Would you critique my poetry, Mr. Randall?"

"Yes, and my story, as well?" Isobel leaned forward to get his attention.

Hetty was not to be left out. "I can't imagine you wanting to hear a book of manners, but I would value your input on my newest chapter. My turn to read is at the next meeting. Will you join us?"

As though he had planned the invitation from the start, Mr. Randall winked at Abbie.

Percival did not fail to notice Miss Walsley's hesitation when he offered to walk her home. His intrusion had set her on edge. That had not been his intention. With genuine interest, he had wanted to know how his betrothed spent her time, and he could not deny his curiosity of her writing after the vicar mentioned it at supper. The writing did not disappoint, least of all because his suspicions of her knight had been confirmed. Sir Bartholomew and he shared an uncanny resemblance. This truth gave him insight to her discomfort: she found Percy attractive. The knowledge puffed his chest and squared his shoulders. Even if he was not trying to lure the girl into a romance, there was a sense of pride in knowing he was desired.

His real courtship with Miss Merriweather had left him feeling less than his best, for she all too clearly had her sights on an heir, not a second son. No doubt she was relieved he had left London. Maybe he should nudge Lord Dunley in her direction if the viscount were so keen on finding a wife. The thought made him snort with humor.

"Has something amused you?" Miss Walsley asked as she stepped out of the inn, hugging her satchel to her chest.

"I'm tempted to play matchmaker with your viscount and the young lady I was courting in London."

"He's not my — oh, never mind." She stared at his open palm.

"Your satchel, Miss Walsley? Allow me to carry it."

"Ah."

Slipping the strap off her shoulder, she handed it to him. It was heavier than he had expected. Worn leather and a broken buckle marked this a treasured possession. He heaved it over his opposite shoulder, offered an arm to Miss Walsley, then set out for the vicarage in slow time, the walking stick marking the beat.

"Was it a love match, you and the lady you were courting?" she asked.

"Hardly. I was a matter of convenience for her. She loathed the thought of a second Season, seeing it as some sort of failure. Her parents wished for an alliance with my family. All tidy, really."

"You must have liked something about her if you chose to court her. Surely she was not the only unmarried woman in London."

She stared forward as they walked. With her bonnet in the way, he could not see her face.

Answering to the bonnet, he said, "Fickle reasons. She's handsome, plays the pianoforte well enough, comes from a good family, that sort of thing. We spoke unobserved no more than two or three times."

There was nothing unusual about his courtship but speaking of it aloud to Miss Walsley made him sound shallow. Did this woman dream of a love match of her own? She must if she wrote chivalric romance. Or she was a cynic.

"I've lived in London nearly a decade, and yet I don't recall ever seeing you. Did you not have a Season?"

Miss Walsley turned her bonneted face up to look at him and laughed, not a sound of mockery or harshness but a warm laugh of genuine amusement.

He took the unguarded moment to admire her. When he had first laid eyes on her, he had mistaken her understated simplicity for drabness. There was nothing drab about Miss Walsley.

She wore the pureness of country living. Her cheeks were sun-kissed with a pretty row of freckles marching across the bridge of a pert nose. Golden-brown eyes full of subdued gaiety reflected the sun. Her petite stature and slender figure made her easily overlooked in a crowd, but they housed a playful, spirited, even flirtatious woman. He had witnessed as much at supper with her behavior and song selection. Today's choice of reading verified it. However unaware of it she may be, Miss Walsley was a temptress in her own right. The unassuming temptress of Sidvale.

"Mr. Randall, I'm a vicar's daughter. How silly to think I, or any of my sisters, would have a Season. That's for families hoping to make political and social alliances. My sisters all made local matches."

Leaning closer, he said with a waggle of his brows, "*Love* matches?"

"Oh goodness. I wouldn't know. They were all fond of their suitors. I should think there is love in each marriage, yes, but I'm not privy to such private aspects of their relationships."

"And do you hope for a love match?"

To his disappointment, she turned her head back to the path, leaving him to continue the conversation with the bonnet.

"I'm not hoping or searching for a match of any nature. Should a gentleman catch my eye, he would be someone intellectual and spiritual, a kindred spirit to myself. He'll enjoy reading, church, charity, those sorts of things. I'm certain you find my ideal man droll."

"There you're wrong. You are currently betrothed to just such a man. Are you shocked? Hold on to your bonnet; there's more. I've been invited to participate in the finest literary society in all of Devonshire, and twice this very week I have spent time with a renowned vicar. I might even pen some prose this evening. How's that for intellectual and spiritual?"

His teasing had the desired effect. He could feel the hand on his arm tighten and tremble as she fought back laughter.

"You think I jest, Miss Walsley? I *am* offended. I'm not just a pretty face, you know."

She could hold back no longer. Her laughter, not unlike the deep resonation of church bells, rang out until she clamped a hand over her mouth.

Percy veered them to the path towards the church. The vicarage was mere yards away, too close for his liking, for he was enjoying her company. She did not protest at his change in direction.

With a shy glance at him, just enough for him to catch sight of her cheek, she said, "You needn't do this, this getting to know each other bit."

"Do you not want us to get to know each other? It's an important element of courtship, you realize, especially seeing as how we're betrothed."

She shook her head. "You needn't pretend to be kind or interested in me."

"If you think I'm pretending, you're mistaken."

"Don't be silly, Mr. Randall. Handsome men are all the same. You said it yourself—you only courted a young lady because she was attractive and accomplished."

"So, you confess. You think me handsome." Percy directed them around the churchyard where their pace crawled to a near stop, one calculated step at a time. "At last I have the leverage I need to pursue this friendship."

Her fingers clenched his arm. "Oh, please stop. I don't want fake friendship. If you're going to mock me, you needn't stay here a day longer. There's no point in your convincing everyone we're betrothed. It's already causing a stir and will make the split more difficult. If you insist on staying, we should be seen quarreling so that when I cry off it's believable."

He turned to face her, shielding the sun from her eyes. "If you'll recall, the plan is that we will not suit, not that we've quarreled because I'm a boor, but that we are incompatible. We disagree on the… the…" He circled his hand in the air, searching for a reason for incompatibility.

"The curtains?"

"Yes, because of the curtains. We can split as friends, an amicable break."

"But we're not friends," she protested.

"And I'm hoping to remedy that. You underestimate your charms, Miss Walsley."

Her laugh returned, and he had the joy of receiving the full force of her smile. Such a smile could turn the plainest of canvases into a work of art, but that was the thing—there was nothing plain about this woman.

"And there's another point," he continued. "If we're to be partners in crime, we should eliminate all this formality. It's unnatural hearing you call me Mr. Randall. Percival, please, or Percy, as my family calls me."

Biting her lip, she looked about her before saying, "We only met yesterday, and you won't be around long enough to warrant such familiarity."

"Please?" It would be absurd for him to bat his eyelashes, so he did the next best thing. He smiled until he knew his dimples winked at her—as good a weapon as eyelashes, if not more potent.

She sighed, not as unaffected as she would hope to appear, and said, "Abigail. My friends call my Abbie."

He jigged a reel until she was laughing again.

They worked their way through the headstones, pausing at each one as an excuse to lengthen the walk before returning to the vicarage, although Abbie could not imagine Mr. Randall's true motive for wanting to spend time with her. He was a flirt and no doubt a rake, but why pester her? She could name a few people in Sidvale who would be more apt to fall for his wiles. As discourteous as it would be to name her friend, Leila would be charmed by such a character and charm him in return. Abbie, however, was not such a person.

"Allow me to point out the uncanny resemblance between your storybook hero and myself," said Mr. Randall.

"What nonsense! You are by no means a hero."

"I beg to differ, my dearest Abbie."

He paused as though to determine with a naked glance if her name on his lips affected her.

It did.

"My presence here is heroic, no? I'm saving you from the villainous viscount."

The corners of her mouth inched into a smile. "He's not villainous."

"Oh, but he is! The villainous viscount is notorious in London for snaring unsuspecting daughters of vicars and forcing them to the altar, bound and gagged no less!"

She rolled her eyes, her smirk belying her amusement.

"And if my heroic deeds go unnoticed here, you cannot deny the heroism of saving you from Hacca's Brook. Ah, I've got you there, haven't I? I'm Sir Bartholomew made flesh! All I need is a trusty steed. And a sword. Will the walking stick do, do you think?" He gave it a twirl.

She swatted at his arm, unable to recall when she had laughed so heartily. "Mr. Randall, you are too much! The brook is barely two feet of water. Although…" She tapped a finger to her mouth in exaggerated thought. "I do confess that I'll always be grateful for your brave actions with the cart."

"The cart?" He stared, perplexed. Dawning was slow in coming, but when it did, mischief glinted in his eyes. "*That* cart! Yes, an out of control cart is not to be taken lightly. I'm only thankful I was there to whisk you out of harm's way. That was the day after the Hacca's Brook incident if memory serves.

My heart stopped altogether when I saw it careening towards you."

They laughed at their fantasy, staring into each other's eyes until Mr. Randall broke the magic of the moment. He reached a hand to her face and brushed a flyaway strand of hair beneath her bonnet. The touch of his warm fingers against her bare flesh startled her, shocking a warm awareness through her.

Frowning, she said, "My bag, please."

His hand stilled, hovering inches from her cheek.

"Could you hand me my satchel? I need to return home. I...I just remembered I promised to meet Papa to work on the sermon."

Returning her frown with his own, Mr. Randall handed her the bag. With a mumbled thank you, she stumbled across the churchyard home, hoping he did not realize the reason for her flight. It would be so much easier if they could quarrel. If he continued in this way, the end would be not only a broken engagement, but a broken heart.

Chapter 8

It had been nearly forty-eight hours since Percy last spoke to Abbie. Not that he had been pining, mind. He had been far too busy to think of the vicar's daughter. Truly.

Yesterday, for example, began with an earlier rise than he was accustomed to, for he wanted to bathe, dress, and break his fast before Mr. Walsley arrived at nine for the promised ride about Sidvale. As though testing a city boy's mettle, the vicar had arrived early. Percy surprised him by having the saddled and warmed gelding waiting outside the inn as he finished the last dregs of his cup.

Who had time to think of young ladies when spending the morning with a vicar?

In many ways, Mr. Walsley reminded him of his own father. That similarity did not exclude the occasional cross-examination. Admittedly, he enjoyed the man's companionship. Together, they toured the farms, paid calls to the viscount's tenants, rode past the gauche manor of the Dunley ancestry, and stopped by the mill.

The mill was a source of pride for Sidvale, the first of its kind in all of England, Mr. Walsley had explained. Once an old watermill, it had been converted to a wool mill with hopes of one day becoming a sizable textile business. As an earl's son, Percy had no experience with industry. The mill fascinated him. It was magnificent to behold and not without an element of country romance in the waterwheel and neighboring river. The owner, a Cornish fellow by the name of Mr. Polkinghorn, took the time to show them around, tantalizing Percy with his talk of fleece, cloth, and rugs.

Only on the ride back to the inn did the vicar mention Abbie, confessing he was hard-pressed to forgive the secrecy of the betrothal, uncertain if he had lost his daughter's trust for her to keep such a secret since this summer and unsure how far he could trust a man who had courted his daughter behind his back.

The deception rubbed Percy's nerves raw. He liked Mr. Walsley and did not wish to lie to him. This was not, however, his lie to reveal. He doubted the vicar would approve of the continued connection between Percy and Abbie if he knew the truth, even if the two were following this course of action to save each other from scandal. Nonetheless, he took no pleasure in keeping the man in the dark.

Upon returning to the inn, Percy explored the circulating library then took full advantage of the afternoon coffeehouse, befriending a couple of swells. As much as he loathed early retirement, there was nothing to do in Sidvale after dark.

Except to lie in bed not thinking of young ladies named Abbie.

Against his will, his body awoke early again this morning.

He had spent long morning hours busying himself with a walk from one end of the village to the next, twice, before finally breaking his fast in The Tangled Fleece's public room. Percival looked at the mantel clock. Barely past ten o'clock. To distract himself, he read the newspaper, eyes darting back to the clock between columns.

The local newspaper was a curious feature of Sidvale. Mr. Bradley, the innkeeper, had not exaggerated when he said it was superior to a London paper.

The contents of each edition were a surprise with only a couple of columns appearing in predictable succession, the innkeeper had explained. The column submissions were anonymous, arriving by way of a submission box poised in the private parlor, accessible only by visiting the circulating library, the literary society, or the coffeehouse; thus, the writer must be a paying customer of the inn and active participant in the community. *The Bard*, a single page publication, was printed three times per week, but only paying customers of the inn could receive a copy, gratis. The most peculiar aspect, which was not so peculiar once Percy discovered the genius of the paper, was that customers did not come for the food or drink but rather for the paper, imbibing to receive their complimentary copy, then staying to imbibe more to gossip about the contents.

Genius.

Today's edition contained political news, a couple of advertisements of local tradespeople, an announcement of available dresses by a novice seamstress, a cheeky riddle of a charade, several review columns for inns and coffeehouses in Sidmouth and Sidbury, an epistolary memoir of a family's visit to the seaside resort at Sidmouth, a poem, a brief lesson on etiquette when visiting gentry, and a letter to a girl named Lucy from her aunt Mrs. Button. The ads held little value for Percy, but he enjoyed the remaining items enormously.

It was the letter from Mrs. Button that had him most enthralled.

My dearest niece, Lucy,

It was a pleasure to receive your latest correspondence. I was especially piqued by your detailing of the handsome Mr. R. Heed my words. It would not do to reveal your interest. Men such as he could charm the birds from the trees then eat them in soup. Be ever vigilant. Guard yourself. Should there be genuine interest from both parties, remain coy, not disclosing your feelings. A woman can never be too careful when it comes to matters of the heart, and certainly not when men of his station are involved.

Although there was more to the letter, Percy stopped reading. He set the paper next to his plate and took a drink of his coffee. "Be ever vigilant." "Guard yourself." Brief turns of phrases, but he had heard them before not two days prior in the Ladies Literary Society when Miss Abigail Walsley read from her story.

By Jove.

He laughed aloud, turning the heads of the other occupants in the room. The vicar's daughter was Mrs. Button. It had not taken him long to discover the column was a special favorite in the village, a sort of advice column for young ladies, approved of by parents, but never without humor. He wagered no one knew Miss Walsley to be the author. Looking back to the paper, he chuckled again. The minx! Where was the betting book in this establishment? He had wagers to make, and this next wager was that the column was about him, however tongue-in-cheek.

Only a few more hours, and he would find out the truth, for today would be the next meeting of the Ladies Literary Society.

Nursing his *n*th cup of coffee with *The Bard*, he waited for the clock to tick itself to meeting time. Why the devil he was so eager to sit in a room full of spinsters, he could not readily say, but there was something about Miss Abigail Walsley that had him eager for her undivided attention. With his discovery of Mrs. Button, he would be certain to get that attention.

His study of the inn's mantel clock, counting down until the ladies would arrive, did not mark him a lovesick swain, merely a bored Londoner out of his element. Or so he told himself, every five minutes.

The first person Abbie saw when she stepped into The Tangled Fleece was the last person she wanted to see. There had been the slimmest of chances Mr. Randall would not show. Earlier that morning, she had convinced herself he was teasing about attending, for why would a bachelor such as himself want to talk literature with the likes of them?

And yet there he sat in the public room, tracing the rim of his cup with a fingertip—the same fingertip that had brushed her hair beneath its bonnet.

Oh bother.

The moment her cheeks reddened from the memory, he turned, their eyes meeting. Behind her, the door opened to a boisterous conversation between Hetty and Leila, but she had eyes only for Mr. Randall who stood with a dimpled smile.

Once in the private parlor with their assortment of tea, biscuits, and sandwiches, they settled in their usual places to begin Hetty's critique. Mr. Randall pulled over a chair to join them, setting it so close to Abbie's that the chair arms touched. Before she could say anything, Isobel rushed into the room.

"Have you started? I don't mean to be late. Mother wouldn't stop talking. She's in a state over my cousin's wedding."

Mr. Randall held a chair for her. "We would never begin without you, Miss Lambeth."

"You came! We weren't sure if you would." Isobel tittered, flustered by his attention.

"I'm a man of my word. I believe today we're reading from Miss Clint's book?"

Hetty pulled out her fan to help recover her nerves.

When he took his seat next to Abbie, he leaned her direction, resting his elbow on the chair arm. The scent of his shaving soap teased her, floral rather than musky, reminiscent of the rose water she used to bathe on special occasions. The subtle scent distracted her from the conversation, so much so that she shifted in her chair to lean closer to Mr. Randall.

Hetty began to read her newest chapter.

Abbie braved a glance his direction. His chin rested on his palm, his eyes trained on Hetty. He appeared interested in the reading, his expression focused, his brows puckered in thought.

Inching closer still, she inhaled the aroma and admired the man. In this moment, she was engaged to him. False engagement or not, she was engaged. Even her wildest imagination could not have conjured such a strange turn of events: Abbie the prosaic spinster engaged to the dashing son of an earl. *Why not keep him?* Her friends' words echoed in her memory.

Neither would be happy; that was why. He was a Londoner, a lover of vibrant city life, a man of fashion and frivolity. She imagined his days filled with friends and parties. He would want a woman to match him, someone glamorous, a duke's daughter with blonde hair and blue eyes, a figure to stop a carriage, a laugh of tinkling chimes. His being here was a matter of inconvenience to him. What charms did Abbie have to attract him? What excitement did Sidvale have to hold him?

Assuming she had it within her power to keep him, she could not be happy with someone so frivolous. No, she wanted a solid and steady man, someone practical, a curate like her sister Bonnie's husband, a farmer like her sister Faith's husband, a doctor like her sister Prudence's husband. Yes, someone reliable, dull, balding, with a slight pudge at the waistline. That was the man for her.

Glancing at Mr. Randall again, she gasped to find him staring at her, his eyes smiling as though he heard her thoughts and shared the vision of her perfect man. He flashed her a dimple before turning back to Hetty as she finished reading.

"Well?" Hetty asked. "What do you all think? Too much sermonizing, or did I add enough humor?"

Abbie blinked. Good heavens. She had not heard a word of the chapter.

Mr. Randall shifted in his chair to lean forward. The sound of his silk breeches rubbing as he crossed one leg over the other and the fresh waft of rose had Abbie short of breath. What was wrong with her for goodness' sake? Her skin felt flush. Perspiration beaded beneath her dress. He was *just* a man, nothing more, she told herself.

To busy a trembling hand, she refilled the teacups and took a sandwich from the tray.

Isobel and Leila were offering suggestions. Abbie chewed. A glance to the gentleman at her right had her gulping the bite. He was staring at her again, that blasted dimple deepening every time he caught her looking his way.

He would leave soon. Any day. Any week. Soon. The second that Lord Dunley showed interest elsewhere and she knew herself safe from his advancement, Mr. Randall would leave. Life would return to normal. It would be as though he had never come to Sidvale. Only a four-day acquaintance but the thought of him leaving had her gulping another bite too large to swallow.

Abbie choked.

Coughed.

Gasped.

All eyes turned her direction as she tried to recover without fuss. Reaching for her tea, she took a sip. She choked anew. Her eyes watered as she fought back the threatening coughs. She returned the cup to the saucer, her hand shaking. The cup clattered onto the plate. Tea sloshed over the rim. Oh, surely this was the most humiliating moment of her life! Then a warm hand met her back, circling and patting, strong fingers massaging over the thin fabric of her dress. Whether it was the shock of his touch or the movement itself, she could not say, but the coughs settled, leaving her calm but embarrassed.

He continued to circle his hand on her back. "Do you need anything?"

She shook her head, mortified.

When she brought herself under control and Mr. Randall returned his hand to the arm of his chair, she looked up in apology to her friends, all of whom watched her with concern.

"Carry on," Abbie said. "I didn't mean to interrupt. What were you saying about the chapter, Isobel?"

They were reluctant to continue, but once she assured them all was well, they proceeded with the meeting. Even their guest had a few recommendations. He had been paying attention. The suggestions were nothing short of brilliant, touches of humor to keep the book of manners from sounding too stiff.

This would not do. He was far too handsome, charming, and helpful. The longer he stayed and the more involved he became, the worse it would be when he left. Even now, her friends were plying him for ideas.

"Ahem," Abbie interrupted. "I would like to be the first to thank Mr. Randall for attending today's literary society. The insight you offered, sir, was illuminating. Since this will be your last day of attendance, I want you to know the visit is appreciated."

There. Uninvited in the politest of manners. This involvement in her life needed to stop. He needed to take his rose water and shaving soap far from her.

Everyone began talking at once.

"My last day?"

"Why isn't he coming back?"

"But I wanted him to critique my poetry."

"He has to come back!"

Oh dear.

Abbie strained a smile. "It's only that to be a member, one must also contribute. Seeing as how Mr. Randall isn't a writer, he can't very well be a member of our literary society, now can he?"

He leaned back in his chair to study her for a moment before reaching into his waistcoat pocket. "As it happens, I've been known to pen a word here and there. Luck is on my side for I jotted down this bit of nothing yesterday evening. Seeing as it's Miss Clint's day to read, I shan't intrude, but I am prepared for my turn when it comes around."

He unfolded the paper and smoothed it out on the table.

Abbie gawked.

She was losing ground. He could not keep coming to the meetings. He could not!

With a wary glance to the creased paper, Abbie said, "Be that as it may, you're still not a woman, and as aforementioned, this is a ladies' society."

Her friends began to protest, but it was Mr. Randall who spoke the loudest. "I begin to think, my darling, you're prejudice against my sex. Would it settle better with you if I wrote under an assumed name? I could write this as a Mrs. Stitch, perhaps. A *nom de plume* is a popular choice, I understand. You're shaking your head—why? You don't like Mrs. Stitch? How about…let's see…Mrs. Button?"

Her jaw slackened as she gaped at him. He knew. How did he know? No one knew except her friends. Had they told him? The smugness of his smile had her pursing her lips.

"Right then, *Mrs. Stitch*," Abbie said. "Let's hear what you've written."

With a wink to the other ladies, he began to read. She was in for another shock. The writing was good. Genuinely good. Wittily good. Abbie could not decide if she wanted to laugh, cry, or scream. He was nothing at all like her ideal man, and yet…

He was ideal.

The name on everyone's lips was Mr. Randall. Abbie could not walk five feet without someone complimenting him or congratulating her on such a fine match. In less than a sennight, he had made love to the entire village. Even her meals at home consisted of her father's praises of Mr. Randall's affability. To her dismay, the rake had been invited yet again to dine with them on the morrow.

The final feather was the letter from Prudence.

Dear Abbie,

You are an insufferable sister! After all the times you've visited me since this summer and all our candid conversations, I'm shocked you would keep such a secret from me — your own sister! And here I am in a delicate condition. Have you no thought for my health or sensibilities? If it were not for Mrs.

Brisby who heard from Mrs. Mercer who heard from Mrs. Staples, I would not know the truth of it. I won't lie by saying I feared you would never find marital happiness — oh, how I worried for you — but now I may set my mind at ease that my baby sister will not live her days as a lonely spinster pining for lost love — I had worried, you know. I've written to Aunt Gertrude, Bonnie, and Faith, so fear not, together we will arrange the finest of wedding breakfasts! Have you set a date? When will Papa read the banns? Why the secrecy? You must come and tell me everything! There can be no secrets between sisters, which is precisely what I wrote to Aunt Gertrude, Bonnie, and Faith, and I know they will agree. Shall we plan a betrothal dinner to celebrate? Oh, but I would not be able to attend in my condition — it is such a dreadful thing to be so indisposed, you know, but of course you don't know, but you will know now that you are to be married! I shall write Papa as soon as I finish this letter and tell him exactly what I think of your secrecy and inquire for all the honest details of the mysterious Mr. Randall — is he really an earl's son? How ever did you secure a match with an earl's son? I insist on knowing all immediately! Write to me. Awaiting your response,

Pru

Abbie buried her face in her hands.

This was a disaster. The tiniest of lies to a viscount who could not hold his tongue, and her world had unraveled. How was she to return to a normal life after this? The betrothal needed to come to an end. If Mr. Randall would not quarrel with her to help build the case for why she must cry off, no one would believe much less forgive that there was cause, for why would *she* break an engagement with a perfectly amiable man—an earl's son, as Pru so delicately pointed out.

But how was she to initiate a quarrel with the perfect betrothed?

Think, Abbie, *think*. There had to be a way.

Chapter 9

"I insist you sit with Abbie during tomorrow's service." Mr. Walsley nodded to Percy from the head of the dining table.

"I'd be honored, sir. Has she helped you with the sermon? She's mentioned working on it with you."

"Oh, yes, she helps every week. I don't know what I'd do without her." The vicar smiled at his daughter, but Percy could see the smile was laced with sadness.

Whoever she married had better be prepared to live in Sidvale. Percy imagined a compliant but melancholy Abbie should she be forced to live away from her father. Aside from her desire to be a published author, another reason she had not yet married and may be reluctant to do so was her father. Percy refused to believe any narrative that claimed she had never had suitors.

"I've had the pleasure of hearing a scene from her novel."

"Have you?" Her father raised his eyebrows, looking from his daughter to Percival. "And what did you think?"

With a teasing glance to Abbie, Percy said to Mr. Walsley, "I think she's a sly wordsmith. Did you know the hero is based on me?"

Abbie drew her shoulders back and lifted her chin. Before she could protest, her father spoke again.

"You'll not believe it when I say it, but she's never let me read her work. She tells me it's not allowed until she's ready to tie a ribbon around it and send it to the publisher. I'll live vicariously through your experiences, Mr. Randall."

"You'll be proud of her, sir. She'll put Burney and Radcliffe and all the rest to shame, especially with me at the helm of the plot."

Mr. Walsley laughed and made to speak again but Abbie beat him to it this round.

"You falsely represent my work. *You* are not in my tale. Sir Bartholomew is in my tale. He is *not* you. I admit there is the slightest of similarities, but it is, I assure you, coincidental. I've been writing this novel for far longer than I've known you."

Her volume and rate increased as she spoke, defensive quills rising in transparent threat. In response, Percy's smile broadened. He liked her all the more when she was riled, his spirited minx.

"For how long might that be?"

She glared at him. "Two years."

Percy whistled. "No wonder you fell for me at first sight after being in love with a fictional character for two years."

"I'm not in love with my own character." Abbie huffed, her quills showing barbs. "And I most certainly did not fall for you at first sight. You are the most arrogant of men to think I would ever—"

She stopped with a sharp look to her father who waited for her to continue, his elbow propped on the arm of his chair, plate forgotten.

Percy savored his wine before saying, "Do go on."

The rosiness he was growing accustomed to seeing blossomed over her cheeks. She stared down at her lap and shook her head.

"My dear Abigail," he said with the sweetest honey on his lips, "If you're not as deeply in love with me as I am with you, and are instead after my family name, you should tell me now."

He winked at Mr. Walsley who appeared amused by the whole exchange.

Rather than pout, protest, cry, or whatever other reaction he might have expected, Abbie bit her bottom lip to keep from laughing. It was no use. Her lips had already turned up at the corners, and she eyed him from beneath her lashes.

"You're incorrigible," she mumbled, the blush coloring her neck and chest.

"One of my better qualities, I believe."

Of its own accord, his foot inched across the floor until it found hers, nudging the toe of her slippers.

Without withdrawing his foot or checking her reaction, he turned to the vicar. "Tell me, sir, when did you know the church was your calling?"

"Leland, please. Call me Leland." Mr. Walsley folded his napkin and set it aside. "I believe I always knew. The church was a place of peace for me. I found myself there every day, hoping for solitude, wanting to think, looking for a sympathetic ear. I had so many ideas, so many ways I wanted to help the congregation, but I was only a boy. Seeing my potential, our parson took me under his wing. Are you thinking of entering the church, Mr. Randall? It's never too late to answer the call."

"No, I don't believe the church would suit me." Percy chuckled at the thought, leaning back in his chair as the footman took his plate. "I'm meeting Mr. Polkinghorn Monday morning, however. Being a gentleman, I've never been exposed to the gritty world of textiles. I want to learn more."

Abbie gave a laugh of her own, taking in his supper attire with a long look. "I find it difficult to believe there's something about fashion you don't know."

Her words caressed the silk of his coat, ending with a tickle of flirtation.

Temptress.

He looked back to her beneath hooded lids, a sultry gaze that had her flushing anew. "I know the side of fashion with which my tailor and my valet gift me. I know not the industry behind it. Could you picture me rubbing elbows with the likes of Mr. Polkinghorn? Owning my own textile company, perhaps?"

"No," she admitted.

Knowing he was playing with fire but unable to stop himself, he added, glancing between her and her father, "I've been thinking more seriously about living in Sidvale rather than London. What do you say to that?"

He was not, but there was something about Miss Abigail Walsley that had him speaking absurdities. Or was he continuing to prove himself the perfect betrothed? More likely, he was speaking absurdities to himself. He did, after all, have an appointment with Mr. Polkinghorn on Monday. Devil take the country. Here not yet a week, and it was already warping his brain.

A sharp kick to his shin brought his attention to his bewitching betrothed. They grinned at each other across the table, she projecting those sharpened quills his direction.

※

Long hours later, Percival returned to The Tangled Fleece, satiated and ready for his lumpy bed with an evening serenade *à la* courting owls. The villagers had other plans.

The public room was standing room only with what appeared to be every male in and around Sidvale, all into their cups and celebrating the eve of God's most holy of days. A few of the fellows he had met with the vicar waved him over, hoping to tempt him. And he was tempted. It was not the company he sought but the reminiscence of the life he left behind. The past few days had felt like a lifetime. Miles away from his mates and his club, he had not gotten properly foxed since his arrival.

Alas, he was too fagged to be tempted. Besides, who was he to deny the tawny owls their fun in keeping him awake?

Mr. Bradley caught him at the foot of the stairs. "Mail for you, sir."

He thrust two letters into Percy's hand before making his way back to the bar. Percy flipped over each and exhaled.

One from his father. One from his brother.

Not until his valet had readied him for slumber did Percival settle into bed with the letters, one ankle crossed over the other, his back propped against the headboard with a pillow. To the accompaniment of raucous laughter from below, he read.

To the loathsome beast who calls himself my brother,

Percy chuckled. However much he loved his two younger siblings, no one could replace Freddie.

You're a Friday-faced gobble-cock, and I am disowning you as my relation. Since when do you engage yourself to a woman and not tell me? Were you bored, chasing shepherdesses, and snared by the shackle? Why the secrecy? Margaret thinks you've cooked a scheme to trick Father out of his ultimatum. I've assured her you're simply in love with a vicar's daughter. For reasons unbeknownst to me, she doesn't believe my version. Can't say why. In all seriousness, are you positive about this vicar's daughter, Percy? What could such a creature have to tempt you? I hope you know what you're doing for this smells like a trap. If you've found love, I'll be the first to applaud you, but don't fall prey to a handsome face out to secure the Randall name.

F.

Resting his head against the headboard, he closed his eyes. If this were a trap, it was genius.

Not that Abigail needed to trick a man to the altar. She could capture any man she wanted with a single smile, and if not that then her wit. But this was not a trap. She did not want to be engaged any more than he did. If anything, he had trapped her, however unintentional.

Blowing air out of his cheeks, he opened the letter from his father.

Percy,

By the time this letter reaches you, I'll have arrived in East Hagbourne to call on Freddie, Margaret, and my grandsons. I plan to invite your betrothed's relations, Mr. and Mrs. Diggeby, to sup with us if the idea is amenable to Margaret; you know how she can be. Do you know yet if you'll marry in Sidvale or London? I hope to attend. From the inquiries I've made on Miss Walsley and her family, it is my opinion you could not have chosen a wiser match. She may be of humble origins, but she has a heart of gold, my sources tell me. Evie is eager to meet her, and I'll deny your stepmother nothing. When may I meet the bride? I'm proud of you, son.

Camforth

The words stung his eyes with salty tears. He had never displeased his father, but neither had he ever made him proud. The hole before him widened. He was torn between begging Abbie to cry off immediately and asking if she would be disappointed not to cry off at all. But no, that was selfish. If she did not break the engagement, she would be stuck with him, the unhappiest woman in England, and he would be trapped in Sidvale. They could live apart, she here and he in London, he supposed. No, that would be unfair. It was all unfair. They would not suit.

It was more imperative than ever that he come out of this as the heartbroken one or his family would never believe he had not sabotaged the relationship or broken her heart to force an end to an engagement he was too cowardly to see through. He had to end this as the victor or face the disappointment and possible wrath of his family.

How easy it would be if he and Abbie suited. But they did not.

Did they?

Monday morning, an hour before Percival was to meet Mr. Polkinghorn at the mill, he sat in the public room with an empty plate and a second cup of coffee, *The Bard* in hand and his mouth agape.

Lucy,

Thank you for your latest letter regarding the ignoble Mr. R. I am of the opinion, based on your descriptions of his charm, that he is not a virtuous young man who ought to be courting a young lady such as yourself. Virtuous men are not charming or fashionable. Never trust such a man. They aim to dazzle to hide their true nature.

Percy scanned the remaining contents of the letter before tossing aside the newspaper. She was blackening his name! No, it was not a direct insult to him, but as much as the villagers looked to the column for advice, they would now be skeptical of charming and well-dressed men, namely him. Even as he sat minding his own business, he could feel squinty eyes at his back, distrust settling into minds. She meant to cause a quarrel, to show reason why she might distrust her betrothed and wish to cry off, but this made him look like a villain, a libertine with base notions. Now more than ever he needed his reputation intact, needed to appear the heartbroken one.

This meant one thing and one thing only.

War.

By Wednesday, Abbie felt pleased with herself. Monday's column from Mrs. Button had planted a seed of doubt regarding Mr. Randall's charm. While making her Tuesday morning calls, several people hinted at her needing to be sure he was a virtuous young man. With just a few more columns, there should be enough of a stir to give her reason to cry off without blame, and to be fair, his name would remain untarnished. The columns were not about him, after all. But they provided a perfect excuse in the eyes of the villagers to doubt his sincerity.

It had to work. It was the closest to a quarrel she could drum up without starting public arguments with him.

This morning, her second column would have been published, planting another seed of doubt. With that satisfaction on her mind, she walked into the literary society all smiles. Mr. Randall was waiting for her.

Her tittering friends and his smug expression gave her pause. Should he not be displeased? Should they not be eyeing him with skepticism?

"It's a lovely afternoon, my darling. Don't you agree?" He greeted her with a too-broad smile.

"Why, yes, I suppose it is, if you're fond of chilly weather." She took the empty seat next to him, startled when his arm reached around the back of her chair.

"I happen to be exceptionally fond of chilly weather." He leaned closer. "Did you know that it's a gallant knight's responsibility to keep his ladylove warm?"

Looking away from him, she coughed a laugh.

He leaned closer still. "I saved you a copy of *The Bard*. I believe you'll find it more entertaining than usual."

Abbie took it from him and folded it into her satchel without a spare glance. He was acting most peculiar. Was he angry? He did not seem upset, not with the fuss her friends were making to serve him tea and biscuits and beg for him to read again, never mind that it was Abbie's turn.

Only when she had returned to the vicarage did she pull out the newspaper. Had her column not printed? Everyone at the inn had been obsequious towards Mr. Randall when they should have been leery. The Monday column had resulted in the desired effect, so why had the Wednesday column not? Her eyes roamed over the other articles until she spotted hers. Yes, there it was, just as she had written it. So, what was the problem?

Her gaze fell on the column below.

Trembling fingers gripped the page. He had outsmarted her.

The new column, penned by a Mr. Stitch, contained first a caricature of a coy young lady with long lashes hiding behind a fan, making eyes at a lovesick gentleman holding flowers and on bended knee. Below the caricature was a letter.

Dear Miss Lucy,

You'll recall we met at your aunt's dinner party. My wife, having heard of your situation with a certain Mr. R., has encouraged me to respond from a male perspective in hopes of being of some assistance. You are wise to be en garde, for there are many an unsavory sort who appear to be trustworthy. My advice is to observe his behavior. Is he seen giving attention to other women, or is he devoted to you? A tell-tale sign of true affection will have him observing you when you're unaware. There's nothing to be gained in such observations and so they reveal his true regard for you. And what about his behavior when not with you? Is he oft in his cups? Gambling? Any vices? Or is he befriending fellow villagers, taking in the air with long walks, calling on farmers and tenants? Watch for the signs. If he is living the virtuous life, he is genuine and enamored with you, a devoted suitor. I hope this advice finds you well. Your humble servant,

Mr. Stitch

The rat! He had undermined her attempts. He had turned the tide she had so carefully controlled with the Monday column. Blast! How was she to free herself of this situation without appearing a harridan or a half-wit? This sham betrothal could not end fast enough.

Chapter 10

Friday morning, Abbie arrived at the inn early, intent on being the first to see a copy of *The Bard*. Everyone else had the same idea. The public room filled to a squeeze with villagers breaking their fast over the latest edition. Conversation and laughter echoed. A quick glance showed no signs of Mr. Randall. One relief, at least.

Mr. Bradley caught sight of her and waved her to a private table tucked in an alcove. By the time she shuffled her way past the boisterous crowd, the innkeeper had a cup of tea and newspaper waiting.

"I wasn't expecting you until the literary meeting. Will you be making calls this morning?" He rocked from heel to toe, beaming at Abbie.

"Once I see what the paper has to offer, I'll make my rounds. Is Mrs. Bradley craving anything particular today?"

"Now, I'm glad you asked because she's wanting something special."

Abbie nodded, knowing just what Mrs. Bradley would like. "I'll call on her first and surprise her with Cook's rhubarb pie. She's earned a treat."

Satisfied, the innkeeper headed back to the bar. His wife was in her sixth confinement. There was little Abbie would not do to help the Bradley family, for they were the thread in the Sidvale tapestry.

Turning her attention to the newspaper, she scanned for the columns.

Lucy,

I am grateful to Mr. Stitch for his gentleman's advice in this matter, but I must disagree. Rogues do not ascribe to a rulebook on behavior. Not all villains live openly with their vices, such as gambling or drinking. Many make their way by charm and looks alone, leeches that prey on vulnerable women. They are nothing but wolves in sheep's clothing. The more charming, the more suspicious you ought to be. Stay guarded. Longevity is the way of it. Rogues do not linger for long, their attention and interest waning in short time. Insist on time, allowing you to know his true character before declaring your love. Always your favorite aunt,

Mrs. Button

Below the column, as with Wednesday's edition, was a caricature of a young woman with her back turned to a gentleman who lay prostrate on the ground, his eyes drawn of hearts and an arrow protruding from his shoulder. Cupid, hovering in a corner, held a bow. *What a cheeky monkey*, Abbie scoffed.

Miss Lucy,

What confusing times are these when we cannot know a villain from a hero, a rogue from a gentleman? Something for you to consider is that a sheep is most often just a sheep. If your young suitor, the noble Mr. R., has declared his affection for you, there is but one way to ensure his sincerity. Has he made this affection publicly known? Secret vows of affection should not be trusted for long. A gentleman, as with a lady, may at times have reason for keeping love clandestine, but such an understanding should not outlast a season. Keep the lover at arm's length for a season. As the leaves turn, does he declare his sentiments publicly or maintain concealment? If his intentions are true, he will announce his affections proudly, for what honest man would want to hide you or his love for you? Trust the honest men, for they tell no lies.

Mr. Stitch

Abbie harrumphed until naught but tealeaves remained in her cup. Wretched scoundrel.

A commotion near the stairs caught her attention. Leaning around the alcove, she spotted a figure carrying a chair overhead and making his way to the center of the public room. Curious, she stepped around her table to get a better look. The chair thudded to the floor, creaked and groaned, and then above the heads of the patrons stood Mr. Randall, poised on top of the chair in all his fashionable finery.

She inched her way back to safety. No one had noticed her hidden in the corner.

"Honored guests of The Tangled Fleece," Mr. Randall said, his words enunciated, his voice loud and clear. "I have read the sage advice of Mr. Stitch from Sidvale's prestigious newspaper, and I have taken his words to heart. Mr. Stitch is a wise man, far wiser than myself."

The crowd mumbled, a hushed buzz circling the room. Abbie sank lower into her chair.

"Although Mr. Stitch's words were for Miss Lucy, I must heed his advice if I am to prove my affections for a certain young lady who has stolen my heart. I stand before you today, a man struck by Cupid's arrow. From the moment I first laid eyes on Miss Abigail Walsley, I knew myself affected. There is no cleverer or more enchanting woman of my acquaintance. Would my betrothed please join me?"

Heads swiveled. Abbie sank until only her eyes peered over the table.

"Abbie, my darling love?"

She ducked under the table. Boot heels against wood clopped their way to her, louder as they approached until she could see the black sheen. A hand reached beneath the table, palm up. When the floor did not open and swallow her, she heaved a sigh and took his hand. Hoisted to her feet, her first sight was the dimpled smile and hazel eyes of her counterfeit intended. Her heart flip-flopped.

Turning her to face the onlookers, he laced their fingers. "My love for the vicar's daughter runs so deeply that nothing could tear us asunder." He gazed down at her, his expression full of doe-eyed, false love.

"My only hope is that we will share the same taste in curtains, for if anything could fell our affection, it would be pink, lacy curtains."

The crowd erupted in laughter, a few of the patrons sighing with contentment.

Smiling, Abbie clenched the hand holding hers. If it was the last thing she did, she would bury the *Honorable* Percival Randall in the flower garden.

He might have overdone it. Abbie had not spoken a word to him since earlier that morning. Even his jeers and leers during the literary society meeting had her casting frosty glances. Subtlety had never been Percy's style. With a war to win, he needed bold action. All signs pointed to his having won this round. He did not feel victorious, however.

The ladies of the literary society sat in their reading circle, tea table in the middle, all eyes on Miss Owen while she read her poetry. Percy's attention on the poetry waned, his focus riveted on Abbie. He angled to see her better. She had an unassuming profile, the window-filtered afternoon light illuminating wisps of chestnut hair struggling to escape the knot at the nape of her neck. Such an understated beauty. Her lips were plumper when she was mad. Rather than purse her lips, she pouted them. An errant thought stole into his mind—what might it be like to release her hair from the knot, sink his fingers into the strands, and kiss those ready lips?

Devil take it. He had been in the country too long, and celibate far longer. Dragging a hand down his face, he refocused his attention on Miss Owen. There. Now she was a beauty. Bronze skinned and as flirty as an opera singer. She had been making cow eyes at him the entire meeting. But as she continued to read, Percy's gaze involuntarily returned to Abbie's profile.

More than once she caught him staring and huffed. He ought to be the one huffing. Yet another fine afternoon wasted. If he were in London, he could be at the club or the park, maybe walking Tattersall's. He should leave. What was he doing here? He could make an excuse to return and let her cry off in a letter, just as she had originally planned. But he felt compelled to stay, to see this through, to ensure all went as planned. If he left it to her to resolve…

The fact that he could not yet bear to part with her company held sway in his decision, even if he was not ready to admit what such a feeling meant.

His eyes still trained on Abbie, the ladies around him began chattering. Miss Owen must have finished reading. Heaven help him if she asked his opinion. They would not wish him to share his thoughts, such as the thorough examination he had conducted on the shape of Miss Walsley's right ear, concluding from said examination that the lobe begged to be nibbled. Had she been kissed before? A pimple-faced youth she pulled behind the church one Sunday? An older, dignified widower who took advantage of her charity? The thought of anyone kissing her turned his stomach sour.

How he escaped providing Miss Owen a critique, he could not say, but he was happy when the meeting ended. He rushed to Abbie's side and offered his arm.

"Shall I walk you home?"

She glared at his arm, taking it only out of politeness.

Without her satchel to carry, and with his walking stick left in his suite, they walked unencumbered. Neither spoke until they crested the hill. Percy turned them towards the church rather than the vicarage.

She slipped her arm from his as they entered the churchyard. "You've ruined everything. Now I'll appear a villain for breaking it off. What sort of ninny ends an engagement with the most devoted man in history?"

"I acted rashly, I'll admit, but only because you were turning *me* into the villain. You would have had the entire village believing me a rake who had used you."

"They certainly don't think that now, I can assure you." She scoffed, walking away from him and down the row of headstones. "If you had simply let it be, I could have taken care of this. I see now this is some sort of game to you, some jest you're having at my expense. You can tell all your friends how you humiliated that dreadful country mouse. It'll be good for a laugh."

Falling in step with her, Percy said, "That's not my intention. I want this resolved as much as you. Hang on, how do you know I wasn't genuine this morning? I could have fallen for you somewhere between supper and Mrs. Button."

He laughed at his own joke.

She did not.

Abbie turned to him, her face pale. "That's the trouble with you. I wouldn't know your truth from your lies."

"We're in this together, Abbie. We're on the same team. I don't mean to upset you."

"You're so wrapped up in charming everyone, you can't be honest with yourself. You've never had to do anything with your life, just live off your father's fortune and your personality. Do you even know what you want? Is your only plan to find an heiress so you can live off her fortune and continue to charm your way through life, spending your days and nights at a club with men who don't care a fig about you?"

She turned away, crossing her arms over her chest. "I think you should leave Sidvale. Make some excuse. I'll break it off in a letter. Everything will die down in a week, and before long, no one will remember this happened."

Percival was stunned, unable to move or speak. His thoughts jumbled, confused by her questions and insights, wanting to grasp the branch of freedom she offered while also wanting to rail at it. Shaking his head until his thoughts settled, he did the only thing he knew to do in times of drama. He made another joke.

"Our second quarrel is much worse than our first. Do you remember our first?" He tightened his coat about him to fend off the chilly air. "It was this summer. I wanted to carry you over the fallen log, chivalrous and all, but you wouldn't have it. We quarreled because you were too independent to accept my heroism."

She turned to face him, her chin quivering. "Is my life a joke to you?"

"I meant no harm. I only wanted to make you smile. You have a lovely smile." He reached a hand to cup her cheek. "You're beautiful, Abigail. I mean what I say. You're beautiful."

A crease formed between her brows.

Percy took two steps forward, clasped his hands on either side of her face, and kissed her. With a gasp, she made to step away. He relaxed his lips against hers, moving with her. Her breathing sharpened, but she puckered her mouth into a delectable pout, returning his kiss. Her lips were soft, pliant, and moist—heaven tasted of ginger biscuits. He angled to embrace her more fully. Running a thumb down her cheek, he nibbled and suckled, inhaling the intoxicating scent of jasmine. She returned as good as he gave. Hot blood pumped through his veins, invigorating him, fueling him. His tongue teased the seam of her lips.

Her hands covered his, and she stepped away, quitting the kiss. With an expression of confusion, marred by the flush of her skin and the red of her lips, she looked up at him.

"What if we didn't call it off?" Percy asked.

Her brows knit, she stared back at him as though he had sprouted two heads. "You want to remain here? With me? Why?"

"Would you consider it? I know it sounds mad, but would you consider staying engaged? Have the banns called…marry?"

Now that he said it aloud, he warmed to the idea. The solution had been staring them in the face all this time, but they had been too stubborn to see it.

A hint of a smile teased the corners of her lips.

Oh, to kiss her lips again…

He smiled with a soft laugh. "I mean, it makes sense, doesn't it? I need a bride, though she doesn't have to be an heiress, and you need a hero. We could solve each other's problems by marrying, couldn't we? We're not ideal for each other, and in fact, we're not even suited, but—"

Abbie stuttered a laugh. Wiping her lips with the back of her hand, she turned and walked away.

Chapter 11

Crying into a pillow was not Abbie's style. She took out her frustration on an unsuspecting band of robbers who Sir Bartholomew happened to come across, her quill working furiously across the page, the inkwell receiving an equal abuse to the highwaymen with her jabs for more ink.

All along she had known Mr. Randall was a rake. It had not taken two full weeks for him to live up to her expectations. A first-rate rake.

What hurt was not that he had tried to use his wiles on her, taking advantage of her as he had done in the churchyard, confusing her mind and senses, sending her heart reeling. No, what hurt was how desperately she had wanted it to be real. From the moment he stood on the chair in the inn, she had wanted it to be real. Of course, she had known he was posturing, but that had not stopped her traitorous and irrational heart from wanting his words to be true. For him to be in love with her, find her beautiful and witty, an ideal bride.

He was right. She wanted a hero. And for some stupid reason, she had wanted it to be him.

These were all thoughts she had not allowed herself to have. Now that she had tasted sin, she let the thoughts flood her mind as a way to torture herself into accepting what a naïve fool she had been. From this point forward, she would guard herself with brambles. For starters, she would heed the advice of Mrs. Button. Over and over, she had written to guard oneself against rakes, and what had Abbie done? Listened instead to the inane jabber of Mr. Stitch. How had she allowed this to happen? It was his dratted dimples that had distracted her.

If he refused to return to London—she ignored the twinge of panic at the thought of his leaving—she would make new rules clear to him. This situation was in her control. She could, after all, break off the engagement, while he, as a gentleman, could not, no matter what situation he found himself in. Thus were the legalities and rules of society. This engagement, false or not, was a legally binding verbal contract. She was in control. She needed him to stay to avoid further pursuit from Lord Dunley, and she did not want his reputation harmed, and so the best course of action was a truce, but on her terms. If he refused her terms—well…

Scowling at her story, she returned her quill to its stand. Only when she looked about the desk did she realize she had written two entire chapters without stopping. What an unexpected turn of events—the rake was a muse.

It was not until Monday that Percival sought out Abigail. The days between the disaster in the churchyard and his visit to the vicarage were a blur of self-berating. He could not say what had come over him. From kissing her to proposing they follow through with the engagement, he had been a man possessed. Only after private reflection did he realize the error of his ways.

He never should have lusted after her—where had that come from? He never should have pushed himself on her—she was a vicar's daughter! He never should have insulted her—oh, yes, this was the real sticking point.

He was not such a dolt as not to realize why she had fled. It had nothing to do with his kiss or his proposal but his foot-in-mouth words to follow. The attempt to keep things light and friendly had been botched the moment he kissed her, practically a declaration of love to someone like Abigail. And then he had swiftly kicked her by all but saying it had nothing to do with love. Well, it did not…did it? That was not the point. The point was he should not have said what he said or how he had said it.

Best do this before he dug his own grave.

Knocker to brass, he struck the front door of the Walsley home. The wait was long, requiring a second strike. Just when he wondered if they were from home, the door opened.

Mr. Walsley smiled in greeting. "Mr. Randall. A pleasant surprise. Do come in." He stepped aside, opening the door wide. "Our footman is tending to a family matter, so I'm afraid we're shorthanded today. May I take your coat?"

Shaking his head, Percival shrugged out of his coat and pulled off his gloves and hat, setting them on a table in the vestibule. The weather had taken a nasty turn on Sunday, raining most of the night and bringing with it a frosty chill far too early for the season. With luck, the sun would return to warm the temperatures.

"Abbie's in the parlor if you'd like to see her. She's been in a writing frenzy for days, so I hope you don't mind ink-stained hands. Thankfully, no spilled inkwells." He chuckled. "I presume you can find your way. I'm in the middle of a project. I hope this doesn't cast us in a bad light, me being a derelict chaperone and all."

Mr. Walsley patted Percy's arm then disappeared behind a door down the hall.

Seeing himself to the parlor, Percy peeked into the open door. Abbie sat at the escritoire, quill in her hand, feather stroking her chin. He grinned at the smudge of ink on her cheek.

"Ahem." Percy cleared his throat before stepping into the room.

Abigail turned, her hand nudging the inkpot as she looked up at him. She shrieked as the container tipped over, splashing ink on her pages. Handkerchief brandished, Percy dashed to the rescue, blotting the ink as she tried to do the same with her own handkerchief. Thankfully, it was mere splashes, not the entire bottle.

He stopped himself short of making a joke about being her hero. Instead, he surrendered his kerchief to her expectant palm and stepped away from the desk, having the courtesy to look chagrined for startling her.

"Mr. Randall. What are you doing here?"

"I've come to apologize for my behavior on Friday. You must think me the worst blackguard."

She pulled her shoulders back and clasped her hands at her waist, a proper posture for a headmistress, though ruined by the ink-tinged hands and smudge on her cheek. Now that he had a better look at her, he realized the smudge was not singular, as a thin streak also graced her brow. There was something bewitching about those smudges. If he had not schooled himself already, he would have half a mind to kiss her in the parlor.

"Would you care to take a seat?" Abbie waved a hand to the chairs by the hearth.

They sat in silence for a minute or more, she holding her prim pose, he tapping his emotions onto his thigh.

"Well?" She raised a single brow — the brow christened with ink.

He hid his smile behind his hand. This was no laughing matter, but who could not be amused in such circumstances? A serious discussion with an outraged woman and, well, the *ink*!

"You said you came to apologize. I'm waiting."

Right. Percival cleared his throat once more, pulling the edges of his lips down with his fingers. "Yes. About that. Please, accept my apology. I never meant to, er, accost you. Pressing advances where they're unwanted is disrespectful. I shall keep my, *ahem*, hands and lips to myself in future."

However intent she was to remain poised, the flush of her skin hinted to her true thoughts. He knew she remembered as well as he how sensual had been that kiss.

"I'm relieved you've called on me, to be honest," she said, her voice a notch higher. "We need each other for this to end to our mutual advantage. I must make one point clear, however. I am not like your London women. I will not be abused by your…" She hesitated on the last word, as though searching for an appropriate term to call what she had mistaken as rakish lust.

Not that it was anything but rakish lust.

"Charm," she concluded.

Percy crossed one leg over the other, uncomfortable by the direction of his own thoughts. Of *course* it was rakish lust.

A hand to her brow, she rubbed her forehead as though warding off a headache. The ink smeared into her hairline.

"We must maintain boundaries, strict boundaries," she said. "I insist upon it. We are business partners and nothing more. We will never be anything but business partners. If you're to stay here rather than return to London, you must agree to keep your… *charm*…far from me." With a strained expression she asked, "You are staying, aren't you?"

"If you're not planning to run me out of town with a pitchfork and blazing torch, then yes, I'm staying."

"Splendid. Shall we shake on our agreement to maintain boundaries and conduct this situation as business partners?" She thrust out a purple-blotched hand.

Taking her hand in his, a simple action that caught his breath, he asked, "Not as friends?"

"Don't toy with me, Mr. Randall." She gave his hand a squeeze.

"Very well. Business partners." He liked it when she was feisty. Hoping to prompt a pout of disapproval, he added, "And our first business transaction needs to be you calling me Percy. Don't think I've not noticed you still using my surname."

Stealing her hand from his, she sighed. "If that'll be all, Mr. Randall, I'm terribly busy and must return to my work."

Of all the jests he could make, he resisted. He held his tongue, gave a business-like bow, and excused himself.

For two days, Percy avoided his business partner, not for any logical reason, rather to clear his mind of her kiss and temptations. Of all the kissing he had done in his life, he never would have guessed a kiss from a vicar's daughter would keep him awake at night—much to the disappointment of the determined, hooting owls who declared that their right.

All the distancing he had accomplished, and he nevertheless felt compelled to see her. Had the Reverend Walsley not invited him for tea, Percy would have invited himself.

An overeager footman showed him to the parlor where Mr. Walsley and the fetching Abigail waited. There were no signs of ink this time. Pity. Flashing a smile to both, Percy accepted the offered chair, exchanged pleasantries, and waited for the tea to be brought in by the same industrious young footman.

"Have you thought more about where you might live after the marriage, Percival?"

The first question from Mr. Walsley had Percy spluttering into his teacup. Blast Abigail for laughing behind her hand.

Dabbing his chin and nose with a napkin, he said, "I confess I've not given it much thought since our previous conversation about it."

"What he means to say is it's a point of contention for us, Papa," Abbie offered, ever the helpful business partner.

"Oh, I wouldn't say it's a point of contention so much as acclimation," Percy countered.

Abbie was not to be outdone. "But we've spoken about this. At some length, if you'll recall. And your heart is set on London, while mine is not."

"People change. Plans change. My heart is set on you, not a place." There. That ought to be a point in his favor.

Mr. Walsley intervened. "You've lived in London for some time. I've not been in years, decades, truth be told. Noisy, smelly, crowded, from what I remember. What is it you like about the place?"

Percival stared into his teacup, lapsing into thought. Where else was there for him except London? His brother had a family of his own. His father had a second family. Everyone had a place, a purpose. Percy had…what?

He savored a sip. It was exceptional tea, a bold flavor but with a sweet aftertaste.

"London is a place to lose one's self. You can be anything, see anything, do anything. The noise is the essence of life, a symphony of people thriving. The smell is one of industry, culture, refinement. The crowd is full of promise, everyone from chimney sweepers to nobles, all walking the same street, all with a dream of their own. In a single day, one can visit with friends, watch a horserace, attend an opera, and attend a soiree."

"It sounds exotic," Abbie said, her eyes revealing her curiosity. "I might like to see it."

Percy cast her a curious expression. She sounded sincere.

Mr. Walsley mirrored the curiosity when he glanced at his daughter before asking Percy, "How have you found the country, then? Dull, I suppose."

"Not at all. Well, at first, yes. But I'm growing accustomed to the pace. The country is a place to find one's self. It's a sort of looking glass if you will. If there's nothing inside of substance, the silence can be far louder than any noise in London."

The vicar set his saucer on the table and leaned back into his chair, lacing his fingers over his chest. "What have you discovered in this looking glass?"

Percy chuckled. "You manage to pull out my confessions every time. How do you do that?" he mused. "No matter. I've found I like my company. I don't mean that in any conceited way, merely that I don't need the distractions I thought I did."

In his periphery, he spied Abbie watching him, her fingertips absently touching her lips. Percy kept his focus on Mr. Walsley, enjoying the feel of her attention when she thought he would not notice her gaze. Only when she spoke did he turn to her.

"How did you like the mill?" she asked, her hands having returned to her cup and saucer.

"Would you be shocked if I said I'm returning on Friday?"

A lift of her slender brows and a quick dart of her eyes to her father answered the question.

"Mr. Polkinghorn likes some of the ideas I shared with him," Percy said. "Difficult to believe, but there might be more to me than fluff and fashion." With a wink, he returned his attention to his tea.

Abbie laughed. "Of course there is. Did you know, Papa, that he's been attending the literary society? He's quite the adept writer."

"You exaggerate, darling. I've no more interest in writing than you have in owning a wool mill. I'm only attending the meetings to bask in the brilliance of my betrothed." His eyes met hers, and his smile faded as the reality of his words registered.

She continued to stare at him even as his attention fell to the fare of sweets and savories before him. Food would distract him from that inconvenient realization. It would also distract from the awareness of her gaze which had him feeling warm under the cravat.

"As it happens," Mr. Walsley began, "Abbie will be visiting her sister in Sidbury tomorrow. Have you been to Sidbury? Far more hustle and bustle than our quaint village. Her friend Miss Clint was to accompany her, but we've received notice this morning that she's unable to join. Would you consider escorting Abbie? It would ease my mind that she's safe with a protector and give you the opportunity to consider Sidbury as a potential residence should you wish for someplace more engaging than Sidvale but not as far as London."

With so much to unpack, Percy delayed his response with a conveniently timed bite of a biscuit. Abigail, he noticed, was staring wide-eyed at her father, obviously not privy to either the invitation of accompaniment or the suggestion of living in Sidbury. He took his time with the biscuit then refreshed with a spot of tea.

"It would be my privilege to escort Abbie and an honor to meet her sister." He relished in her consternated expression. Had she expected him to say no? Not a chance! "As to Sidbury, I suspect Sidvale is where she would be happiest. If, in the end, I were to choose London or even next door to her sister, she may cry off the engagement and send me packing."

It was her turn to hide behind a teacup.

"I don't wish to be an influence," Mr. Walsley said, "but as it happens, the McVey place is for sale. It neighbors the Dunley estate, though a quarter mile or more stretches between them."

"Leigh Hall? But no one has lived there for ages," Abbie said, returning her cup to its saucer. "I can't think it would be in good condition after all this time."

"With some love and care, it would be grand. I doubt it's anything like what you're used to, Percival, but it's a sizable estate all the same. When Mr. McVey lived there, I spent many an afternoon in his study. He was a good man and took pride in his home. It's been a shame to see it sit empty for so long."

Unable to resist, Percy offered, "If we start our journey early tomorrow, we can plan a visit."

Abbie grimaced. "I can't see why you'd want to visit Leigh Hall if you have no intentions of purchasing it. You love London, and that's that."

"Ah, but you forget—love compels me. Your happiness is all I desire." Percival raised his cup to a pleased vicar and a frowning betrothed. "For Leigh Hall, we're bound!"

Chapter 12

Abbie snuggled deeper into her traveling cloak, battling the chill that persisted despite a warm morning sun. She watched Mr. Randall approach in a curricle. Dread mingled with curiosity. After experiencing his *charm*, she was less than enthusiastic about having him as an escort to Sidbury, but she could not deny that pesky desire to see him and get to know him further.

He was dashing atop the sporty vehicle, two mismatched horses leading him to her. Even when traveling in a shabby, hired curricle, he was dressed in splendor, his greatcoat caped and revealing glimpses of a crimson coat and waistcoat with floral embroidery beneath.

"If it isn't the loveliest of lovelies, Miss Abigail Walsley!" He drew the curricle to a stop and climbed down, his smile never wavering.

"Good morning, Mr. Randall. You're punctual." Try as she might to look prim, her lips curved as he reached for her hand.

"And miss a moment of time with you? Never." He waved to the curricle. "It's a far cry from my own, but it'll have to do. The innkeeper knew a fellow who was willing to part with it for a day. I'm beginning to think there's nothing and no one the innkeeper doesn't know."

Slipping her hand in his, she allowed him to help her into the seat. Her first curricle ride! The slight dizziness and racing pulse of anticipation swept over her. She endeavored to make herself comfortable, smoothing out her dress. How impossibly high off the ground she was! Mr. Randall leapt into the seat next to her. Her faintness increased. The seat was so narrow, her leg bumped his as he situated himself. And they were to ride thusly to and from Sidbury? Heaven help her.

"Have you packed provisions in your reticule? Dressed in an extra layer or two? Prepared yourself for a lengthy journey with me?" He angled his body to face her, the ribbons in his hand.

"We're only going to Sidbury, Mr. Randall, not London." Even so, the trip would feel hours long with their legs touching.

"And you're positive you don't want to bring a maid? Your father may feel confident your betrothed serves as an adequate chaperone, but given the truth, I can't think you'd be comfortable on such a trip without an eagle-eyed biddy ready to thwack me over the head with her parasol should I so much as look at you. I'm sure I can find one if you'd prefer."

Abbie laughed. "I trust you to be a gentleman. And who's to say I don't have rocks in this reticule to defend my honor?"

"I would be surprised if you didn't." He eyed the bag. "If you need an extra layer over your cloak, say the word. You can have my coat. I've no idea how long we'll be on the road and don't want you catching a chill."

"How chivalrous you're being today. I'm warm enough. It's not even five miles, you know."

"Is it really?" His shoulders slumped, and he cast her an exaggeratedly glum look. "And here I thought I had you at my side for at least an hour's drive."

With a smirk, she said, "I'm ready for my adventure, sir. Tally-ho!"

He flicked the ribbons. Abbie jolted backwards and grabbed the arm of the seat to hold steady, the air filling with peals of her laughter.

―――

They rode for but half a mile before Mr. Randall turned the horses from the road to Sidbury onto an overgrown lane. Abbie looked about to gain her bearings. Another quarter mile would be the drive to the Dunley estate. It was a walk she knew well. She had never in all her walks turned here, but she knew where it led: Leigh Hall.

"Where are we going?" she asked, already knowing the answer.

"Leigh Hall, of course. Did I not promise your father we would see it?"

"Oh, come now. You jest. Telling him is one thing, but doing it is quite another. There's no point, is there?"

Mr. Randall slowed the vehicle to better take in the surroundings. The lane was narrow and winding, enclosed by woodland and overgrown foliage. Leigh Hall was said to be beautiful; she had never seen it to judge for herself.

"I see no harm in touring the estate before we head to Sidbury," he said. "I've been in correspondence with the steward, and while it was short notice, he seemed eager at the prospect of a potential new owner. His only complaint was he wouldn't have a chance to air it out."

"You've misled him, then. He thinks you're going to purchase it."

The driveway meandered through autumn-touched trees, a creek snaking to meet it then running alongside. With better clearing, this could be an impressive entry. As it was, she wondered if they were lost in the woods, never to find their way to the house.

"I've not misled anyone. Who's to say I won't purchase it, with or without you as my bride?" He winked at her when she turned to scowl at him. "If you will, think of today as writing research. Imagine Sir Bartholomew is visiting his aged great uncle, and Leigh Hall is the man's estate."

Abbie harrumphed, but she did not bother to hide the grin. Unwittingly, he had added depth to her one-dimensional knight. No, a great uncle did not add character development, but foolishly, she had never questioned whether her knight had family. The possibility of a great uncle, or whoever the person might be, gave her new subplots to explore and added more to Sir Bartholomew's backstory and motivation than she had planned. How silly that one offhand remark had her imagination running wild!

Until the estate came into view. All thoughts of her stories fled.

A three-bay, stone block covered in overgrown, leafless vines awaited their arrival. A sizable wing branched perpendicular to the main house. The windows were gabled, the entrance arched, and the view spectacular with woodland to one side and open fields to the other, sweeping out and down into the valley.

It was serenity.

From the right angle, she wagered she could see the church.

Her escort pulled the curricle to a stop in the circled drive. As he secured the horses and came around to help her down, she ran her hands under her bonnet to ensure her hair had not worked itself into disarray during the ride. Feet met gravel to the tune of the front door opening.

"Mr. Randall!" waved a man who Abbie assumed was the steward.

A plump fellow with old fashioned, powdered curls came bustling from the entrance. She knew him from church, but they had never exchanged conversation outside of the polite discourse after Sunday service. He had always seemed a genuine sort of fellow.

After a brief introduction of all parties, the steward clasped Mr. Randall's hand in his.

"Mr. Randall and Miss Walsley, such a pleasure to meet you both."

"Mr. Wynde. Thank you for meeting us on short notice. As my missive said, Miss Walsley and I heard the good news about the hall's availability. We couldn't resist coming for a look."

"Yes, yes, come in. I'll show you around."

They followed the steward inside, Mr. Randall continuing the conversation, Abbie taking in the house. It was considerably larger than the vicarage, but not as grand as the Dunley estate, rather a modest country manor, if one could call a manor modest. Her first step into the vestibule had her wrinkling her nose. It smelled damp and stale. Nothing a good air out could not remedy. The condition, at least, appeared pristine.

"Once a monastery," Mr. Wynde was saying as Abbie walked about the entrance hall. "Then converted into a manor. Not much evidence of the old monastery, though. A stone arch here and there perhaps. Twenty acres of woodlands. The gardens overlook the valley, though the beds aren't a pretty sight, left to weed."

The steward carried on. Abbie saw herself into the first room, a ground floor parlor of some sort, perhaps an anteroom for guests. Linen and blankets covered the furniture. Layers of dust coated the mantel and sheets. She peeked under one to spy an ornate chaise longue.

Still talking, the steward and Mr. Randall joined her.

"House's been tied up in legalities for years, McVey's kin battling to get their grubby hands on it. All's settled finally. I've not had time to air out or hire staff; been overseeing the farms like. There are tenants and farms to look after, all which come with the house, and seeing as how I've been looking after them for so long, I'd like to say I come with the house, as well. Been heartbreaking to see it go to dust. McVey was a good man, loved this house. I hope it'll go to a good family, a couple like you two perhaps."

Abbie met her betrothed's smirk with one of her own.

"Mr. Wynde," he said, walking over to stand beside Abbie. "Would you mind if we explored the house on our own? We could meet up with you in half an hour at the foot of the stairs."

"Splendid idea. Of course, you'll want to discuss it all without me present. Half an hour." With a few too many bows, he left the room.

"Well?" Mr. Randall cupped her elbow. "What would you like to see first? This is, after all, Sir Bartholomew's great uncle's house."

Swatting at his arm, Abbie said, "You're incorrigible. Let's find the drawing room, shall we?"

Room after room, they explored, admiring the view, peeking under sheets, commenting on the condition and décor. When they found the drawing room one story up, they were in no hurry to leave, or at least Abbie was not, and neither was Mr. Randall, it seemed, for he swept one of the linens off a couch and took a seat, stretching his arms across the back.

She felt his gaze follow her as she moved from window to window, taking in the view from the back. Beyond a line of yew trees, the land sloped into the valley. As she predicted, she could just make out the church, partially obscured by a copse of trees.

Beneath one of the windows was what Abbie assumed to be a buffet. What she discovered was even better. With a tug, she freed the sheet, uncovering a long, narrow desk carved from mahogany, all the little drawers and cubbies still filled with paper and writing implements. An empty inkwell waited to be refilled. Lost in the moment, she sat at the desk and stared out the window. What a glorious place! It filled her with inspiration, not for Sir Bartholomew and some fictitious great uncle who may or may not make it into her novel, but for *her*. She could see herself sitting here every afternoon, writing.

"Do you like it?" Mr. Randall asked.

Dazed, dreaming of this view and this desk as part of her future, she whispered, "It's perfect."

"I've been thinking about what you said. You're right, you know."

It took long minutes to shake herself from her fantasy and realize she was in a room of a dusty house with a rake of a fake betrothed. It took longer minutes still to understand he was speaking to her. The fantasy lingered on the fringes of her mind, demanding attention.

She turned to face him, startled anew to be here with him. "Right about what?"

"My life. I have no direction, no purpose. An estate like this could be the answer."

Caught between a scoff and a laugh, she settled for a frown. "But I thought you hated the country, didn't want the responsibility, and wouldn't dare give up your London fun."

"Is that what you think of me?" Mr. Randall stared into the distance, lost in thought. "It must be true, then."

"Are you serious, or are you jesting again, Mr. Randall?"

It was his turn to frown. "My name's Percival. Will you forever insist on this formality, even while I call you by your given name? Please, Abbie. Call me Percy."

Biting her lip, her pulse accelerating, she nodded. "Very well. Percy. Now, are you being serious about this estate? I don't believe you are."

His absent expression passed, replaced with a dashing smile that nevertheless seemed wooden. "You know me too well, darling. I couldn't be serious if my life depended on it."

"I believe you're actually joking now, which tells me you were being serious before. If you're considering purchasing an estate, be it this one or another, you must be positive it's what you want to do. You would have staff and tenants who depend on you. It's a life change you'd need to be ready to make. There would be no changing your mind after a month to return to London. Well, I suppose you could, but what a mess that would be."

"What about you? Where do you see yourself this time next year? Or two years from now? Five years? What will Abbie be doing with her life?" He stood and walked to the window next to her, looking out onto the valley.

Abbie opened her mouth to speak a ready answer until she realized she had none. Published. Writing her next novel. Calling on her fellow parishioners. Attending her literary society. Yes, that seemed right. Her life would proceed exactly as it was currently, and that was how she wanted it. What if her friends married? Would they continue to attend the literary society after marriage and children? She could not say with certainty.

This was a silly conversation. She did not know or care what next year looked like as long as she was content with life now.

When she did not answer, Mr. Randall—or Percival, rather—turned to her. "Ah, darling, I believe our guests have arrived for loo. Will you prepare the table? You know how Mr. Pendergast loves to sit on the fattest cushion with his bum facing the hearth."

It took Abbie only seconds to catch on. Fluttering her eyelashes, she gave him a demure look then headed to the table near the fire, yanking off another sheet.

"Let us hope his frock does not singe like last time," she said.

"Oh, yes, dreadful business. I owed the man a new suit, never mind it was he who continued to move his chair closer to the fire. Shall I ring for tea?"

As Percy's hand tugged at the bellpull in the corner, Mr. Wynde stepped into the room. The steward looked from one to the other of them, perplexity tainting his brow.

"Not yet half an hour, I know," Mr. Wynde said. "But I wanted to see how you carried on. I'm afraid there's no staff for tea."

When Abbie met Percy's gaze, the pair dissolved into laughter.

―⁂―

Less than an hour later, they pulled up in front of Prudence's house in Sidbury, a terraced, thatched cottage that reflected the owner's disposition with its colorful array of flowers, all still blooming despite the late October chill. When they knocked, it was four-year-old Fanny who answered the door. Wide eyes, a cherub mouth, and satin tresses adorned the oval face. Wordless, she reached her arms to Abbie to be carried, her stare riveted on the stranger.

The house erupted in noise the second they walked over the threshold. Chattering, chittering, and chuckling combined with the wails and whines of children. It was not only Mrs. Prudence Rockford, her husband Mr. Rockford, and the baby to greet them, as Abbie had expected. No, gathering in the hall from the parlor was their sister Mrs. Bonnie Sullivan, her husband, their thirteen-year-old son William, and several neighbors either poking a head around the parlor door or conversing within.

Casting an apologetic glance to Percival, Abbie's cheeks flamed. All this fuss over a misunderstanding, not that anyone in the house knew that fact.

The next long minutes were filled with uncountable introductions by an overexcited Pru, one hand on her round belly, the other patting the arm of a grinning Percival who did not at all seem to mind the overfamiliarity of Abbie's family and acquaintances. Seated in the parlor next to the inglenook fireplace, exposed beams overhead and flagged floors below, Abbie nodded and smiled when necessary, trying not to become overwhelmed. Fanny soon lost interest in her aunt with a newcomer in her midst. The little girl poked and tugged at his coat.

"And what have the two of you been doing this fine day?" Pru asked, her eyes moving from Abbie to Percival and back. "I was telling Mrs. Brisby this morning—wasn't I, Mrs. Brisby—that he'd be a fine gentleman with a fine carriage and escort my sister in the style to which she would soon become accustomed. And here you both are, arrived in a sporty, racing vehicle that meets my expectations in every thinkable way, and I know—didn't I say, Mrs.

Mercer—that Abbie has had the time of her life this morning, riding in such stylings with the man who has caught her eye. There's love in the air—am I not correct, Mr. Rockford—there is *love* in the *air*."

Percival, the devil, replied, "You are most perceptive, Mrs. Rockford. They say it's not at all the thing to spend too much time with one's bride. But you'll understand me when I say I can't stay away from Miss Walsley for long before I feel a dreadful tug at the heart."

"You are a man besotted!" Mrs. Brisby exclaimed, setting down her needlework to clasp her hands over her heart.

"Guilty, I'm afraid. Guilty. The only thing that will keep us apart is our difference of opinion on the décor. My beloved has the worst taste in curtains." He winked at Abbie. "Just today, she was eyeing a picturesque window at Leigh Hall and wanting to cover it with emerald green draperies. Now, I ask you, who covers such views with emerald green?"

All in the room laughed, except Abbie who was too busy covering her rouged cheeks with her palms.

Pru placed a hand on Percival's arm once again. "What were you doing at Leigh Hall? I've not been there in years, not since old Mr. McVey passed. He always had the best cakes—didn't he, Bonnie?"

With an uncharacteristic expression of unadulterated bashfulness, Percival shuffled his toe on the stoned floor and said, "Now, now, Mrs. Rockford, don't have me revealing such confessions in front of all and sundry. It was idle curiosity more than anything, but I do aim to make Abbie the happiest of brides, if you catch my meaning."

The room erupted in conversation, everyone talking over each other, all speculating on whether Percival would purchase Leigh Hall, and if Abbie had liked it, while asserting how wonderful to stay so close to home and family when they worried he would whisk her off to London. Abbie sat in silence, her palms glued to her cheeks, her stomach in knots. Percival, the wretched bounder, grinned at her like a hound to a fox.

Mr. Sullivan, a curate and her eldest sister's husband, was the only one who appeared to recognize her discomfort, likely mistaking it for bridal nerves. He made an excuse for the gentlemen to retire into the study, and shortly thereafter, the neighbors removed to their own homes, taking their children with them. Fanny went to the nursery for a nap. From chaos to quiet, Abbie soon found herself in the parlor alone with her sisters.

Bonnie and Pru both clasped Abbie's hands.

"He's as taken with you as any man I've ever seen," Bonnie said, squeezing her hand with the reserved but heartfelt support she was known to offer.

"Don't be silly," Abbie protested before she recalled she was supposed to be a blushing bride deeply in love.

"No modesty. You're with us now and can speak honestly." Bonnie nodded to Pru for affirmation.

Releasing Abbie's hand to grab her mending, something she always hid at the bottom of her embroidery basket when guests were around, Pru said, "He's been stealing glances at you since you first arrived. Besotted, just as Mrs. Brisby said—she's always observant about such things, didn't I say so, Bonnie? And oh, so attentive is Mr. Randall!"

"We couldn't be happier for you. It's about time you did something for yourself, Abigail."

Pru touched Bonnie's arm before returning her attention to the repairs of a shirt sleeve. "You said so the other day. You said Abbie is the most selfless person you know, never doing anything for herself and only living for everyone else's happiness. And I said how well spotted that was for I can't remember a time when Abbie did anything for herself—didn't I say that?"

Smoothing the already tidy hair behind her ears, Abbie said, "You needn't discuss me as though I'm not here. I'm touched by your perception, but that's not at all true. I see to my happiness every day. I would also like to point out that marriage does not guarantee happiness."

Her sisters exchanged meaningful glances.

"And your visits to Lady Dunley?" Bonnie asked, threading her needle for the embroidery Pru had given her to busy her hands.

Abbie's jaw slackened. "She's a lonely woman whose son neglects her. I wanted to bring a bit of happiness into her life, just as I do with a great many other parishioners. I hardly see my visits as material."

"But that's the point," Bonnie said. "You spend all your time helping others. When's the last time you did anything for yourself?"

"I—but I—Well, the literary society. My writing. Those are for me. Who's to say visiting my neighbors for charity isn't for myself, as well? It brings me happiness to see them happy, to know they had sunshine in an otherwise lonely day."

"All we're saying," Pru offered, "is how happy we are to see you taking your own happiness seriously.

You can't carry on with literary societies and charities forever and think that's all you need from life. This engagement means so much to us! Papa wouldn't dare say it to you, but he's ecstatic. He's written every other day since Mr. Randall arrived to Sidvale, and though he was skeptical at first, he's quite taken with the man; we all are! He, too, sees it's a love match. He also quite agrees it is time you do something for yourself."

"Papa said all that?" Alarm speared through Abbie's chest.

She had hoped he would remain dubious so that when the engagement ended, he could share in the relief that nothing came of it. Together, they could resume life as normal. Did he not want her to remain with him at the vicarage?

"He wrote just yesterday how much he hopes Mr. Randall will choose to live close because he desires more time with his future son-in-law. He quite likes the man's company. Not that I would say this to Mr. Rockford, but I'm under the impression Papa likes Mr. Randall far better than my husband. For, you see, Mr. Randall's presence reminds him of your happiness, while Mr. Rockford's presence reminds him—and this is merely my opinion—of Mama's passing since Taylor was Mama's attending physician. Now, he's never said so, and they're good friends, but I suspect that might be the case—don't you agree, Bonnie?"

Of all the contributions Abbie could make to the conversation, she chose to allow Prudence and Bonnie to carry on without her, which they did without prompting, moving to the topic of the wedding breakfast they hoped to plan and hinting at hosting a betrothal supper at the vicarage.

What could Abbie say? She nodded and smiled, embroiled in her own thoughts.

While she could confide in her friends, she could not bring herself to confide in her sisters, and certainly not when the truth would crush their spirits. So happy for her were they, she was nearly caught up in it. If she ignored the melancholy of carrying on a deception with the people who loved her most, she could feel their elation, absorb the joy, and believe it all to be real.

Percy's words from earlier mingled with her sister's words. What did she want her life to look like in five years? What was the ideal image of life? She had resigned herself to spinsterhood some time ago, not needing a man to define her, not wanting the limitations marriage could bring to her writing or other aspects of her life. There were not many advantages to marriage for someone like her. Her sisters, yes, but not her. Her father's wages, while not enough to support four daughters indefinitely, were enough to support Abbie and himself. Should Abbie publish, she could contribute.

Some women, she knew, had no choice but to marry, for their families could not or would not support them. Others found self-worth from someone else's opinion, believing they were only fulfilled by someone else's presence, regardless if the marriage was loveless. From Abbie's point of view, it was better to be a spinster than trapped in an unhappy marriage. She had far too much self-respect to throw away her life for the sake of society's perceptions of her worth as a woman. There was nothing in her world she wished to escape, no funds she needed, no alliance desired, no part of herself that could only be resolved by allying to someone.

As such, she had never imagined herself as an advantageous bride. She had never imagined herself as a wife or mother. Did she want a knight in shining armor? Did she deserve a knight in shining armor? Would such a knight find her...*desirable*?

Her thoughts settled on the churchyard. The kiss. Percival's words. How easy it would be to convince him that by continuing the engagement he would meet the requirements of his father's ultimatum. She *could* keep him. But what a gamble! He had made it clear after kissing her that his only attraction to her was the threat of being cut off by his father if he did not marry. He had no interest in her, no...*desire*. He was not a man besotted.

The gamble was too great.

He would be back to his old ways before the honeymoon ended. However convenient the situation, however much her family adored him, she could only marry someone who knew what he wanted from life and saw her as part of it. Some flighty Londoner who would forget her in a fortnight was not the man for her.

Chapter 13

Percy was not prone to introspection. If someone inquired of his friends at White's, the answer would be that Mr. Percival Randall had never had an introspective thought in his life. Either his friends did not know him well or the country was casting a spell.

Since returning from Sidbury, there was little Percy had done except introspect. He mused over supper. He mulled over life from bed. He minded possibilities over morning coffee. As he waited for the literary society ladies to arrive at The Tangled Fleece, he pondered further. There was no end to his contemplation. The crux of it all was where he saw his life in the next year, two years, or even five years, as he had put to Abigail. No, on second thought, that was not the crux. The crux was what the devil he would do about his growing attraction to Abigail considering where he saw his life heading.

There was no denying it. He was attracted to her, and he had been for some time. The way the sun shone through her eyes, the way she tucked her hair behind her ear when the locks were already tidy, the way her smile warmed him to his toes, the way her voice sent his heart pounding—*blarg*! Percy growled. He was besotted by the vicar's daughter.

Oh, it was worse. He was besotted by the family, the villagers, the country, the mill, the deuced dusty hall. How he was to cure himself of this illness, he was uncertain, but he would need to find an apothecary soon: *Dear sir, do you have an herb that will restore my senses and return me to London?*

"Are you ready to read?" asked the dulcet tones of the recipient of his affection.

He turned, taking in her petite frame, governess' hair, and plain dress with its shade of dreadful fog grey — had it once been blue but seen too many winters? All he saw was the most beautiful woman of his acquaintance. The slope of her neck, the twist of her knot, the freckles across her nose, the blush on her cheeks… Good heavens. He was lost to her.

Gulping his feelings, he said, "Is it my turn already? I thought it was Miss Clint's. I've nothing to share, I'm afraid." Who could write nonsense prose when Miss Abigail Walsley haunted one's dreams? He was more apt to pen romantic poetry.

"She won't be joining us today. I hope all is well." Abbie tugged at her bottom lip with her teeth, her brow puckered. "This is the third time she's canceled plans this week. I'll call on her tomorrow." Her smile returning, she added, "I'm positive Isobel and Leila will have something to share. If not, I do. I wrote *three* chapters last night! You'll be shocked that I've added a moral to this adventure, as you suggested."

A witty remark stalled on his tongue. He had lost his train of thought somewhere between the natural rose of her lips and the two crinkles around her eyes when she smiled.

With Percy's attention trained on Abbie's profile, the literary meeting passed lightning fast. His escort from the inn to the vicarage flew by faster, his focus on her laughter about her excitable sisters. Somewhere between now and tonight's supper, when he would be dining with the Walsleys, he had to pull himself together.

※

Declaring his best point combination, Percy looked across the table at Abbie.

With a cheeky smirk, she studied her cards before saying, "Not good."

Narrowing his eyes with a returning smirk, he declared the best sequence.

Her smirk dipped. The twitch was imperceptible except to someone with a trained eye, and Percy had spent far too many nights at the tables not to see it. His smirk deepened in response.

There was nothing more romantic than a game of piquet after supper. Mr. Walsley had sequestered himself by the hearth, a book in hand, spectacles perched on his nose, leaving the pair to entertain themselves over cards and tea.

Percival laid the ace of clubs on the table, waggling his eyebrows.

Abbie frowned. After some thought, she laid down an eight of spades.

Percival won the trick.

He accepted the win with grace and dignity — a whistle, a whoop, a seated jig.

Whoever said a gentleman must allow a lady to win at cards had never played against Miss Abigail Walsley. Percival had a score to settle. He was already down two full games. This game, he was determined to win. Now that he knew her hand's weakness, he felt self-assured. He laid another club card and watched her sweat it out as she followed with a ten of diamonds. Flicking his ace of diamonds, he accepted this trick's win. Abbie began shifting in her seat, her smirk fallen.

"What is Sir Bartholomew up to today?" Percy asked, distracting her.

She blinked rapidly, her attention shifting from her cards to him. "Let's see… I left him in the middle of a field, about to help Granny M retrieve her stolen sheep from the clutches of the Swine Brothers."

Absently, she set down a card.

Chuckling at the ease of his strategy, he collected another win. "Have you thought on my comments from the meeting about the moral revision?"

Although her hand tilted, attention on her cards waning, it was the pinkening of her cheeks that excited him more. "I hadn't thought you would like it. I was nervous to read it aloud to you, if I'm being honest. Your suggestions on strengthening it have been helpful. More than helpful. In fact…no, that would be silly. Never mind." She placed another card without consideration.

He collected the win.

"Go on. Tell me. Nothing you say is silly."

The blush blossomed, and she dipped her head to look at her hand. "I was wondering if you might consider reading everything I have so far, beginning to end. To see if there's continuity, a steady arc, character development, that sort of thing. I've reworked several scenes to help add more depth to the hero, but I...I'd value your opinion."

Now was Percy's turn to be distracted. His opinion was of value to her? She wanted him to read the *whole novel*? Good heavens. He felt honored beyond words.

Tossing a card in the center of the table, he proposed, "What if you read it to me? I daren't take it with me, and how unnerving for you to watch me read. I'd much rather hear it in your voice, just as we do at the literary meetings. We could start tonight. Now. Dash this game."

Abbie's smirk returned as she won the hand.
Minx!

⁂

His feet propped against the edge of a chair, ankles crossed, Percy lounged on the parlor rug, a pillow beneath his head and his fingers laced over his midsection. The clock on the mantel read a quarter after eleven. The air filled with the soft snores of Mr. Walsley, his spectacles askew on his face, his book folded over his chest.

"'The widow looked up at Sir Bartholomew. She puckered her lips and leaned in to reward the knight for his deeds.'" Abbie paused reading to tap the paper. "Right here. I'm not sure how this should go. He's going to reject her, obviously, but would she be so forward? Would he know what she was about?"

Percy looked over to Abbie who sat with her back to the escritoire, her stockinged feet tucked beneath her. His favorite ink smudges were back. One graced her bottom lip, the other across her cheek where she had swept her finger behind her ear.

"He would definitely know what she was about," Percy said. "And yes, some women are that forward. I think, however, she would try to lure him inside first. Offer him something to drink. Get him inside the cottage. It's up to you if you want him to be gullible enough or tempted enough to go inside before rejecting her. Unless he's thick, any man would know what the invitation entails. From the chapters we've covered so far, I wouldn't say he's thick. Benefit of the doubt. Trusting. Only seeing the good in people. That sort of thing. But not thick."

"So… strike through the puckered lips? Instead, she invites him in for a drink? He'll sound rude not to accept the drink. I can't see how readers will understand her intentions from a simple drink invitation."

"Hmm. You're right." Percy thought for a moment, flicking his waistcoat buttons with his thumbs. "Have her give him a 'knowing' look. Or how about a gaze from beneath half-lidded eyes. That'll get the point across."

"A what?" Abbie laughed, incredulous.

"You know. The *sleepy* look."

"No idea what you're talking about, Percy. I hardly see how her appearing exhausted or tired is going to show the reader or Sir Bartholomew how she intends to reward him."

Tutting, Percival raised onto his forearms. "Look at me. No, not a quick glance. Put down the paper. Now, watch me."

When he had her full attention, he awarded her his most seductive gaze: half-lidded eyes, coy smile, dimples.

"Oh." She averted her eyes to stare down at her paper.

A delectable rash of red started at the bosom's edge of her supper dress and worked its way up her neck and onto her cheeks. Victory! Flopping back onto the floor and lacing his fingers behind his head, he stared at the coffered ceiling, tongue in cheek.

"Describe that look," he instructed. "With that look, he'll know, and so will your readers. Nothing but trouble awaits behind the door. She probably won't even offer him a drink once the door closes."

He stole another glance to find Abbie's blush had deepened to a dark crimson.

Without looking up, she said in a soft stutter, "But…but she invited him for a…a drink." Her hands fidgeted with the corners of the paper. "Wouldn't she offer the…the drink first? Work her way to…" She swallowed audibly. "You know."

"To *seduction*?" Percy rolled onto his side and propped himself onto his forearm. "The look is enough. The look says everything. If he walks into the house, they both know there's a different sort of thirst to be quenched."

"Oh, my goodness." Abbie exhaled from her cheeks with a huff and turned back to the escritoire.

Rewetting the quill, she drew a long line across the paper. Back and forth the quill worked from inkwell to paper in a furious blur of movement. This evening was more fun than he could ever have found at White's, her blush more satisfying than any kiss from a mistress.

The vicar sputtered a snore, his book sliding down his chest until it caught in a waistcoat button.

The situation was tricky. Not being in a room with Abbie in the presence of her father. No, the whole of the situation, Percy's admiration for her, the engagement, all of it. There were more ifs than answers. If he moved too fast, Abbie would flee. If she suspected he was trying to trick her into continuing the engagement, she would flee. If he confessed his ardor, she would mistake his intention and flee. If he purchased the estate as a demonstration of his affection, she would feel pressured and flee. All ifs led to her fleeing.

From his estimation, there was little he could do that would prove his sincerity. Then, to whom did he need to prove it? Her or himself? To marry Abbie, to love her, was a lifetime commitment that came with more than half-lidded looks and kisses in churchyards. It meant responsibility to her, the community, tenants and farmers, even himself.

He knew the answer.

All his examinations of ifs, but he already knew the answer, though he remained uncertain if he was willing or ready to face it. It was the greatest gamble of his life. To woo her, he could not seduce her. To woo her, he had to prove himself man enough to support her and accept the responsibilities of life. If he gambled, and she did not fall in love with him….

Well, at least he would have found a place in the world, a place he had never known he needed until now.

In time, anything could happen, even love.

Chapter 14

Three days later, the first Monday in November, Percy sat in a drawing room chair at Leigh Hall. Several windows stood open, airing out the stale musk. Upon closer inspection, Percy and Mr. Wynde had discovered a pinhole leak in the roof. Thankfully, no damage had been done aside from a damp smell and a repairable water stain. Mr. Wynde would arrange for the repairs.

For much of the morning, Percy had been at the hall. Lengthy conversations with the steward had helped him to better understand the running of the estate, something he confessed to the man that he knew nothing about. While Percy would prefer to trust the family solicitor with the numbers, he believed what Mr. Wynde told him and felt confident all would resume smoothly if the steward remained employed at the hall. A long talk with his father was in order before he could purchase the property. Oxford education or not, he knew nothing about managing an estate, much less purchasing one. More importantly, his father served as gatekeeper to the finances.

Before he could write to his father, he needed to decide a course of action. He was not yet convinced he wanted to purchase Leigh Hall. It was still a gamble in terms of Abbie, and it was still a commitment of responsibility. The more he explored the manor and its grounds, however, the more at home he felt—a novel concept for him, feeling at home—and the more in love he fell with the life it offered.

The views were not half bad either.

The drawing room was fast becoming his favorite room. Hardly a rational reason to like the house. And yet… Time and again his eyes fell to the desk with its empty ink pot. The steward had not replaced the sheet Abbie had removed when they visited. The vision of her sitting there, gazing out of the window, her hand poised to write, charmed the desk. That desk was hers. It waited for her. And Percy longed to see her at home there. He could feel her presence in the room, joking with him about the fictional Mr. Pendergast. With eyes open, he imagined them together, sharing a life in the house.

Sometime later, he met Mr. Wynde in the study.

"Would you consider removing the sheets?" he asked the steward. "All of them. I'd like to come tomorrow and see the place more fully."

"Yes, yes, my pleasure. I've already arranged for a housekeeper. Be good to have the place dusted if it's to sell. Not that the owner has to keep her on staff once purchased, but she has impeccable characters."

"Friend of the family?" Percy winked.

Chagrined, the steward countered, "Well, I say, we're all close around here. Not many people don't know each other or everyone for that matter. Can't go a quarter mile without running into someone you know. We're all friends and family in that way."

"She sounds charming. Would you care to show me the farms tomorrow, as well?"

Soon after leaving the hall, Percy joined Mr. Polkinghorn in the study at the Core Copse Mill. The man genuinely liked Percy's ideas, and Percy likewise genuinely liked the mill and owner. As repugnant as industry was to his society, he could not give a fig what anyone beyond Sidvale thought of it. If he wanted to ally himself with a textile mill, why should he not? He was growing fond of the idea of feeling useful.

After leaving Mr. Polkinghorn to his work, Percy spent the remainder of the afternoon in the coffeehouse of The Tangled Fleece, the private parlor having become a familiar haunt. He rejoiced at the time spent with new friends, capital fellows he found far better company than the lot at White's. No offense to his old friends but talking politics and philosophy and even poetry over a mug of coffee was superior to the drunken gossip he was accustomed to in London.

That night, his favorite pair of tawny owls hooted a duet of symphonic proportions, the sound reverberating in the silence of the country. Percy was none the wiser. He slept the night through, content with his lumpy bedding and the future he envisioned with perfect clarity.

***

The following afternoon held a rescheduled literary meeting to meet Miss Clint's needs only to be sans Miss Clint after all. Again. She had not been home when Abbie called on her, and both Misses Lambeth and Owen were as concerned as the vicar's daughter. Percival was not concerned. It made the meeting cozier, offering more opportunity for Abbie to read and for him to admire her profile, which was becoming a habit he hoped no one else noticed.

What struck him about this literary meeting was not the absence of Miss Clint with her book of manners but Abbie's startling change of appearance. When she walked into the inn, his breath caught.

She was still Abigail. Still understated. Still unadorned by jewels and rouge other than her natural blushes when she caught him staring. Yet today, she was different. Her hair, typically pulled back into a severe knot, was swept up and pinned, chin-length tendrils curled about her face. What made her hair so charming was not the style so much as the slight lopsidedness to the pinning and the curls that did not hold, unraveling and straightening as she read to the group. If this was what he could expect from her hair styling without a lady's maid, may she never want one, for he found the imperfection sensual and *perfect*.

Her hair was not the only aspect different. Rather than her usual, shapeless sack of a dress, she wore a high-waisted round gown of periwinkle blue, topped with a modest fichu tucked into her bosom. The dress hugged her frame deliciously, revealing promises it had no intention of keeping. The figure it displayed took him by surprise. He had always assumed her figureless, flat in the chest, narrow in the hips, but this dress showed otherwise. There was nothing voluptuous about her. She remained petite and slender. But there was undeniably a curve to the hips and an invitation of the bosom, an invitation he had no business hoping to receive, despite wanting to flatter himself that she might have dressed for him.

Percy counted the minutes until the end of the meeting so he could have her alone, selfish rogue that he was. He vied for the privilege to walk her home, those handful of insignificant minutes when he would have her undivided attention.

With a reverent bow to Misses Lambeth and Owen, Percy watched them walk together down the road in the opposite direction, each looking back thrice at Percy and Abbie before he led her away from the inn. Her hand on his arm, they proceeded to the vicarage at a stately pace, his walking stick tapping the rhythm of their walk.

"Will you stay for tea?" she asked not fifteen feet from the inn.

"Ah, the lady invites me in for a drink, does she? I'm sensing a trap."

"Percival!" she shrieked, unable to hide her grin or her blush. "That is inappropriate, and if you're going to say such things, we can't be friends." Her laughter gave her away.

"It's a good thing we're betrothed, then." He waggled his brows. "Now, is my memory faulty, or did we not just take tea at the inn?"

"Oh, you're spoiling my invitation. I'm hoping to trick you into picking up where we left off in the book."

"The lady is a trickster! Even knowing a ploy is afoot, I can't resist your wiles." He teased though speaking the truth.

A sharp wind cut through the center of the village, sending Percy burrowing into his greatcoat. Abbie tugged the corners of her cloak tighter around her. She stepped closer to him. He started to remove his coat to offer it to her when her hair unraveled, coming unpinned in a disheveled disarray. She reached up, but the wind would not be outdone. It whipped her hair about her face, tangling the pins. She screeched, trying to pin it all back up. No use. By the time the wind died down, only one thin lock of hair remained pinned in the delicate styling; all the rest frizzed about her face.

He worried she might not see the humor of the moment and dissolve into tears as most women of his acquaintance would do, but no, not Abbie. Even with hair covering her face and sticking out at awkward angles with hairpins hanging on for life, she laughed.

Tucking his walking stick under his arm, he parted the hair curtaining her face and tucked the strands behind her ears. She was a mess.

"Shall we make a run for it before anyone sees you in such a state of undress?" He chuckled as she continued to shove strands beneath hopeless pins.

"Yes. Let's."

She grabbed his hand and tugged him to follow. They raced the remaining short distance to the vicarage door, only rousing the suspicions of a distant sheep and one old tabby in the last cottage, spying between the wisps of curtains. By the time they stepped inside, they were winded from laughing while running, cheeks pink from the wind.

"If you'll excuse me. I'll meet you in the parlor." Yet again, she did not wait for his response but raced upstairs, her dress hem raised as she ascended. Slender, stockinged ankles peeked in tease.

The Walsley footman helped Percival with his coat, hat, walking stick, and gloves, then showed him to the parlor. Mr. Walsley, the footman informed him, was in the study, recently returned from his rounds, and would join them presently.

Abbie arrived before her father, her hair pulled into the familiar knot. To his delight, the periwinkle dress had not changed.

Taking a seat after she waved an invitation, Percy said, "You're lovely, even with that lone pin poking behind your ear."

Her hand flew to her hair, wide eyes meeting his as she discovered the forgotten pin. With a nervous laugh, she said, "I'm hopeless."

"Lovely, as I said. You were a beauty with the new style, but I prefer you as you are now. This suits you. A simple look for an extraordinary woman."

Rather than reply, she tugged at her bottom lip with her teeth, fighting against a determined smile.

"I was promised a story, remember?" He raised his brows in mock seriousness. "Don't tell me you brought me here under false pretenses."

The parlor door opened to the vicar carrying in a tea tray. "After seeing me walk the hall with the tray, Martin, our footman, may worry I expect him to take my job in exchange," he chided, setting the tray on the low table between the chairs. "Cook forced me to accept three slices of cake. If no one is hungry, I'll eat all three. Can't have her feelings hurt."

"There's no fooling me, sir," Percy said. "I've sampled enough of her baking to know heaven awaits me on that plate."

Abbie busied herself as hostess by preparing the tea and passing the cakes.

Mr. Walsley said after a sumptuous bite of his cake, "Couldn't resist my daughter's temptation, I see."

The fork paused inches from Percival's mouth as he gaped at the vicar. Heart in his throat, he stuttered a laugh. "I beg your pardon?"

"Abigail was in a twitter this morning about tempting you with the story. And here you are. She's a clever girl. Did she ply you with promises of tea and cake?"

Relief swept through Percy. Silly of him to worry her father suspected him of being attracted to his own betrothed. "Indeed she did. Tea, but no mention of cake. I anticipated arriving to a broken promise about the tea once she had tricked me into the parlor, but here I am being rewarded for my loyalty." He savored a bite, closing his eyes and sighing in exaggerated contentment, though not too exaggerated. The cake truly was sinful.

Abbie made a quick dash to the escritoire to collect her papers. Percival wondered what her father thought of the story so far. The man had not heard much of it, given his propensity for dozing off, but he had been present for most of Percy's calls over the past couple of days, and thus had heard a fair few chapters. If he were wise, and Percy knew him to be just that, he would recognize his daughter's talent.

"Shall we?" she asked, looking to the two gentlemen with a rustle of paper. "*Ahem*. Chapter eighteen. 'The sun shone overhead as Sir Bartholomew rode through town.'"

Percival sat back in the chair, saucer held at his waist, his ankles crossed. He listened, interrupting only if prompted or if a scene fell askew of the arc. Mr. Walsley spoke only twice, both times to offer advice on the conviction of the chapter's moral and its contribution to the overarching moral of the story. By the time she finished reading, over an hour had passed, but Percival wanted more. He was not ready to leave.

Alas.

Abbie saw him to the door and stepped out to bid him adieu. Greatcoat taut about his shoulders, walking stick in hand, he touched a finger to his hat and gave a little bow.

As he turned to leave, her hand touched his arm. "Have you given more thought to your future?"

His brow knitted.

"When we visited Leigh Hall," she continued, "you had remarked on your future. You were toying with the idea of buying the estate. Have you thought more about what you want?"

Her. He wanted her.

All the *what ifs* circulated. He could not scare her away. He could not say what he felt. Not yet.

"I have, yes. I believe I'd make a debonair landowner." With a shake of his head, he mocked, "Can you imagine anything more ridiculous? Percival Randall the estate owner, calling on his tenants and seeing to his farms, observing the world from his first-floor drawing room, welcoming neighbors for tea and biscuits. Ridiculous, isn't it?"

Abbie shook her head. It did not escape his notice that her hand remained on his coat sleeve.

"Not at all ridiculous. The life would suit you. I apologize if I seemed to laugh at your idea before. I thought you jested. I thought—well, I thought you would be eager to return to London and all the diversions it offered."

"If you think London could ever compete with you, then you're dashed mistaken."

Capturing the hand on his sleeve, he lifted it to kiss the air above her knuckles before heading back to the inn, his mind made up to write to his father.

The wind howled, blustering and blowing with the threat of a storm. Early Wednesday morning, Percival stood at the front door of the vicarage, his shoulders hiked to his ears. He had offered to see Abbie from house to house this morning. Not the best day for charity rounds, but had he not volunteered, he would have fretted about her blowing away in the wind or being caught by rain.

His favorite footman answered the door.

"Mr. Walsley will see you in his study, sir."

"Ah, will he? Good of him. And where's my charitable intended? I thought she'd be ready when I arrived." He stood still as the man removed his greatcoat and took his gloves and hat.

"Mr. Walsley will see you first, sir. If you'll follow me."

Something about the moment wiped the smile from Percy's lips. It reminded him too much of his final visit to the Merriweathers. Heaven forbid someone else claim to be betrothed to him. He could handle only one of these situations per lifetime.

But then, what if something had happened with Abbie? What if she had cried off without telling him? Or told her father the truth? None of these thoughts would have worried him before, but now that he was on a mission to woo her, he feared the opportunity ripped away, without even a chance to prove to her he was a man of responsibility, a man of commitment, a man besotted.

The walk down the hall to the study must feel like the long walk to the gallows, Percival thought as he swallowed twice and rewetted his lips. The hall narrowed. The sounds of shoes against floor echoed.

"Percival. Come in, please."

Across from the study door stood the Reverend Leland Walsley, a desk serving as barrier between suitor and father, the scene all too familiar. Behind Percy, the door shuddered close.

Opening a drawer, the vicar pulled out a cigar. "Would you care to join me for a smoke? We have time before she's ready for her rounds. Abbie paid an early call to Mrs. Bradley this morning. False alarm, as it were. The baby wasn't ready to make an appearance. Mrs. Bradley wants Abbie nearby when it happens. She overstayed, as she does, and hasn't had time to change or eat. Cigar?"

Percy nodded, letting the information wash over him. So, nothing was amiss? Abbie merely needed time to dress and have a cup of tea. Relief relaxed tense shoulders. Why he had thought this moment was the end, he could not say. A funny feeling. An intuition. A premonition. A fear he would lose love now that he had found her.

The vicar walked around to the other side of the desk, readied both cigars, and waved Percival to join him at the mirroring chairs in front of the hearth. He crossed one leg over the other and handed Percy the cigar.

His smile returned, Percy sorted himself into a comfortable position and puffed.

"It's good we have this time to talk alone," the vicar said. "You've been here a month, dancing attention on my daughter. I've humored you both because the betrothal is now public, and I know how young love can be. But I put to you this question: when am I to read the banns?"

Exhaling a cloud of smoke, Percy clenched his jaw.

"You'll have three months to marry," the vicar continued, "after the reading of the banns, so I see no point in delaying them. You *do* plan to marry Abigail within the next few months, don't you? Or is this a long-term betrothal?"

Tricky. He had no answer to offer.

The cigar forgotten between his middle and forefinger, Percy fidgeted with his waistcoat buttons, twirling one way then the other, awarding them a hard flick of his thumbnail. The silence stretched. Mr. Walsley remained patient, wearing a placid, friendly smile, the only interrogative aspect about him being his eyes.

Those eyes seemed to read every thought and memory in Percy's head. And why in this moment did he suddenly recall every sin he had committed? He recalled with clarity the time he kissed his sister's governess in the garden, the time he broke his brother's nose, his employment of his first mistress, the gambles he lost that wasted his father's monthly allowance, the lustful thoughts he had entertained of Miss Abigail Walsley on more than a dozen occasions. More sins sifted through his brain, revealing themselves to the vicar in a bright bubble above Percy's head. Or so it felt.

Giving his cravat a tug, he took two long puffs of the cigar and confessed.

"Mr. Walsley, sir. Leland. There's something about this betrothal you should know."

One more puff to calm his nerves. He hated the smell and flavor of cigar smoke, but he could not deny the calming effect of sharing such a vice with a man of God.

"I'm in love with your daughter."

There. He had said it. He had admitted it aloud. He leaned back in the seat to better observe the vicar's reaction.

"Yes," Mr. Walsley drawled. "I had assumed as much, seeing as how you're engaged to her."

"That's not the whole of it. You see, I'm in love with your daughter, but I don't believe she's in love with me. At best, she may be fond of me. If I'm that fortunate."

The vicar furrowed his brows but remained silent.

"She's content as she is. There's no reason for her to marry me. Why choose a life with me when she's perfectly happy as she is? I've an inkling she's under the impression that I'm some sort of London rake, which I'm not, just to be clear, but how do I dissuade her of such notions without her thinking me insincere? How do I convince her life with me offers more than her current happiness? I don't want to scare her or send her running. And while I'm being honest here, I fear she's going to cry off. Wouldn't you, if you were engaged to someone you didn't love? You'd cry off, wouldn't you? For now, she's trapped in this betrothal with me, but what will she do when she realizes she doesn't have to be? What's going to make her give me a chance?"

His ramblings filled the study, accompanied only by the crackling of the fire and the faint whistle of wind through stone.

Head bowed in attentive concentration, his companion made no rush to respond. "Has my daughter given you reason to believe she's unhappy with the betrothal?"

Percival thought for a moment, rubbing his temple. "Only at first. She was…" He circled his hand in search of a way to phrase this. "…reluctant to enter the betrothal in the beginning. It was impulsive. Since then, she's not seemed unhappy. Lately, she's enjoyed my company, I believe. She smiles more. Talks more. Laughs more."

"Then I rather think you have the answer, son."

"But is it enough? Smiling and laughing doesn't equate to love. Love doesn't even equate to trust. How's she to believe I'm sincere and won't bolt to London?"

Mr. Walsley took a deep breath and rubbed his chin. "I heard you've visited Leigh Hall a few times this week." At the perplexed look Percy gave him, he shrugged and said, "It's a small village. People talk."

Letting the cigar burn out, Percival set it on the corner of the ashtray and folded his hands at his waist. "I've done more than visit. I've written to my father. I proposed that in lieu of the next two years' worth of allowance, he front me the funds for the estate. I want it, Mr. Walsley. I've never wanted anything this badly. I want it, and I want to be an influencer at the wool mill, although to find the investment funds, I'll need to work the estate for a few years. And—and I want to marry your daughter."

The vicar nodded, snuffing out his own cigar. "You're a good man, Percival. I'm proud of you."

Tears stung Percy's eyes at the words. They were the words he had always wanted to hear from his own father, but when he had finally seen them in writing, they had been in reference to something he could not take credit for doing.

"I believe you've found your path, and I've no doubt Abigail will realize it. Give her the benefit of the doubt." Mr. Walsley stood, gave a squeeze to Percival's shoulder, and opened the study door. "Shall we see if she's ready?"

Abbie skipped downstairs, unable to contain her enthusiasm. Both her father and Percival were waiting in the vestibule. What else could she do but beam at both of them with a smile that defied the dark clouds outside? There was no reason in particular for her good mood. Life, she supposed. The progress of her novel. The joy of a new friend. The promise of spending the morning rounds with her hero.

As soon as they stepped outside, the wind blew right through her, chilling her to the bone. She could smell the coming rain. Tucking her hand under Percival's arm, she sidled closer, smelling more than just moisture in the air.

"*Eew*. You smell like a cigar," she said, wrinkling her nose.

"That's the greeting I get for being your noble escort today? You need lessons on how to treat a knight in shining armor. I expect compliments, simpering, forelock tugging, knee scraping."

"Aren't knights supposed to be humble?"

He scoffed. "Not when told they smell bad. I even added a little something special today for my lady fair. Here, sniff."

Percival leaned in and pointed to his neck. Bashful but too curious to resist, Abbie angled her face to the exposed skin between his cravat and his ear. She gave it a little sniff.

Although the cigar smoke hung on his clothes, she could not deny the seductive aroma of rose water. When he did not immediately move away, she lingered, inhaling the combination of scents, the subtle hint of man, roses, and cigars, a heady mix that had her closing her eyes and leaning against him until her nose brushed his ear.

He straightened, his fingertips to her lower back to steady her. "Well?" he asked, his voice deepening. "Does that absolve me of the sins of the tobacco leaf?"

"I'll think about it." She giggled. "But only if you remind me of your good deeds. To make amends, tell me about the dragon you slew."

She tugged him in the direction of their first stop. Mrs. Cleo Tuxton, a widow with four young children, lived with her sister-in-law, Mrs. Ayda Tuxton, who cared for her stepdaughter and elderly brother. They were partial to Cook's Cornish stargazy pie, so Abbie always packed it in the basket especially for them.

"The dragon was grossly misunderstood, I tell you. I arrived on the scene, sword brandished, and called out, 'Ho! Dragon! I challenge you at the behest of the villagers whose relatives you unceremoniously roasted.' To which the dragon stepped out of his cave, gave a mighty roar, and declared he was framed!" Percival pointed to the child's face peeking out at them from the cottage window.

"Framed?" Abbie laughed, waving at the face in the window, which ducked down at being spotted, the curtains swaying in response. "I don't believe a word of this. Knights slay dragons. Dragons are not *framed*."

"Who's telling this story, you or me? In my version, the dragon was framed, or at least that's the story he gave me. And you know what? I believed him! Still do, as a matter of fact."

She knocked on the cottage door. "Then who roasted the villagers if not the dragon?"

"The blemmyae, of course." He winked at her as the cottage door opened to the trills and howls of five unruly children.

They had little time to talk on her rounds since each visit was one door down or three doors down or one cottage away. But every time they stepped out of a house, Percival picked up where he left off without missing a beat. By the time they reached their last stop, they had cobbled together a fantastical story that interweaved not only her role as his squire—a lady in disguise as a boy so she could save her family from the wicked clutches of Prince Dungheap—but also her role as the clandestine betrothed of Sir Bartholomew, who had just been gifted by the Crown a home at Glee Abbey.

The two were in hysterics over their tales, drawing the curious eyes of the villagers scurrying to and from their homes, hopeful to escape the coming rainfall.

The sky was ominous, and the wind had picked up its pace, tossing her cloak about her legs.

As far as she was concerned, Lord Dunley needed never to marry. He could instead pursue her with more gusto so she could continue this betrothal charade longer. She was not ready for this fantasy to end. She did not want Percy to return to London. Eventually, he would leave. He was a man of City and Society. Should he stay much longer, he would bore of her, and if not of her, then of the country.

Now, however, was divinity.

They approached the vicarage door, but she was unprepared for the morning to end.

Selfishly, desirous of more time with him, she kept her hand tucked in the crook of his arm and asked, "Would you consider reading another chapter before leaving? We've only two remaining before we're caught up to where I am in writing. I believe, and I'll value your opinion on this, that I've only a few more chapters to write until finished."

He tucked a finger beneath her chin and looked at her with a twinkle in his hazel eyes. "It would be my honor, darling."

Before she lost her nerve, she stood on her tiptoes and kissed his cheek.

The door opened as she rocked back onto her heels, startling her into a little jump backwards.

The footman greeted her with, "Ah, Miss Walsley. I thought I heard your voice. You've a guest in the parlor."

As much as she dreaded Percy leaving, with a caller waiting, it was for the best. Out of her peripheral, she watched him walk away, not wanting to appear too lovesick with her longing gaze.

Removed of her cloak, gloves, and bonnet—something she would not leave home without again after last time, when she had declined to wear it in fear it would muss silly ringlets—she headed for the parlor. Martin had apprised her of the identity of the caller. The knowledge afforded no explanation for the reason of the visit. Normally, it would not be unusual, but seeing as how Abbie had not seen or heard from Hetty in over a week, the unexpected visit piqued her curiosity. If aught had gone wrong, a sick relation, for instance, word would have spread through the village, and yet Abbie had heard nothing of the sort.

Her first thought upon seeing a puffy-eyed Hetty was that rumor had failed. A relation had died. Abbie was positive of it. Hetty never cried.

She launched herself at her friend, hugging her as Hetty burst into fresh tears. "Oh, Hetty. All is well. You're with me now. Have a seat, and I'll fetch fresh kerchiefs and ring for tea."

Hetty dabbed at her eyes and sat down, waving off Abbie's attention. "I won't stay long enough for tea. After I've had my say, you won't want to take tea with me."

"What nonsense! We've been friends forever. Nothing you say could upset me."

The sobbing renewed. "I've done a terrible thing. This is the happiest day of my life but also the worst. I almost didn't have the courage to face you, but I'd rather you heard it from me."

Abbie clasped Hetty's hand and refused to let go, despite a brief tug of war.

"I—I—I'm engaged!" Hetty screeched, flailing her handkerchief.

When she volunteered no further information, Abbie gave the hand a squeeze.

Another sob. "To Lord Dunley."

Releasing her friend's hand, Abbie covered her mouth in shock. Hetty was engaged to *Lord Dunley*? Impossible! They had never even met.

"You're angry. I knew you would be. This is the end of our friendship, isn't it?"

"Of course, I'm angry!" Abbie exclaimed, her hands coming to rest over her heart. "I'm furious. How could you do such a thing?"

Hetty blanched. "I'm a terrible friend. I'm selfish and took advantage. It was all a ruse to steal him for myself. I knew you would be angry, and you've every right to be."

Abbie shook her head and reached for her friend's hand again. "I don't know what you're talking about. I'm furious because you've allied yourself with someone who could never make you happy. How could this be what you want?"

Her friend's sobs turned to hiccups. "Wait. You're not angry that I've gone behind your back?"

"Not at all. I'm only worried you've made a mistake."

Hetty's shoulders slumped with relief. "I don't believe I have." She balled the kerchief in her fist. "As soon as I knew Lady Dunley wanted a full-time companion, I took up your post of calling on her daily. At first, she didn't take to me. All she could talk of was you. But she warmed to me sooner than I expected. She loves my book, Abbie. She wants me to write more, says writing books of manners is a perfect pastime for a young lady. I did as you had, knowing what she was after, and refused to be a full-time companion, but I continued to visit, staying all day on several occasions. Today, at last, Lord Dunley proposed. I'm the happiest of women. I am. I only worried you would be angry."

"But you'll be more companion than wife. Don't you see that? He'll spend all his time in London. You won't be happy."

"That *is* the happy part. He won't be there. And I love spending time with Lady Dunley. She likes for me to read to her from my book and has sage advice on how to improve it and what to add. She's even promised to see it published. Lord Dunley is a kind man, I believe, even if he has no interest in marriage." With a laugh, she added, "Not everyone wants a Sir Bartholomew to sweep them off their feet."

Abbie mustered a little smile, wrapping her arms around her friend's shoulders. "I do want a hero. I never expected a heroine would come to my rescue, though."

Not long did Hetty stay, worried of the coming storm. After Abbie saw her friend to the door, she closed it, resting her head on the wood.

No, no, no. She was not ready. This was too soon.

With Lord Dunley engaged, she was free to call off the engagement. Percival would expect her to. It was the moment they had both been waiting for, and yet now that it had arrived, she was uncertain she could bring herself to follow through. But she could not trap him. She could not force him to love her. Whatever flatteries he had uttered recently were just that, flatteries. A rake making the best of a bad situation by doing what a rake does best: flirting with the maidens. If he knew she had fallen in love, she would be beyond humiliated.

She needed to end this with all the dignity she could muster.

This was the end, of course. All she could do was let him go.

Chapter 15

By the time she knocked on her father's study door that afternoon, the storm raged outside. Gusts of wind vibrated the window frames. Sheets of rain pelted the glass.

Half hidden, she peered around the door. "Are you busy? May I have a word?"

Leland waved her in, removing his spectacles and setting them to one side of his notes.

"I have a confession," she said, shutting the door behind her.

Her father stood and indicated the chairs by the fire. "Is this official, or have you spilled ink or tea onto the rug?"

"It's official, Papa."

"Ah." He sat across from her, lacing his hands over his chest.

Abbie blew air out of her cheeks. This may very well be the most difficult conversation of her life, and she had not prepared for it.

"I'm in love with Percival."

There. She had said it. She had admitted it aloud.

Her father remained silent, watching her with compassion and encouragement.

"The trouble is, he could never love me in return. Ours is an impossible situation." Her eyes averted, unable to meet his gaze, she waited for a response.

It was a long time in coming, the rain peppering the glass in waves.

Leland spoke in subdued tones, the even and steady tones of a vicar. "It's the greatest gift any of us can bestow, love. The giving of love is simultaneously the most selfless and the most selfish of acts, for while it fulfills us to offer, we do so freely, without reservation, without expectation, for the sole purpose of *loving*. Love asks for nothing in return."

She nodded, her mind warring against the words. What was the point of loving him if he did not return the love? That wasn't fulfillment. That was heartbreak. She heard her father's words but did not understand them.

Her affection had deepened the more Percy invested himself in the village, in her interests, the more he made steps to better himself, such as his interest in the mill. But such affection was unrequited. His was all a farce, an over-the-top farce. He was accustomed to charming others and so had used that charm to convince everyone of the betrothal and build his reputation as a consummate gentleman not to appear a blackguard when they broke off the engagement. He might have expressed a passing interest in the hall and the mill and life in Sidvale, even in her, but it was just that, passing. The best she could do was let him go.

"Have you told him?" her father asked.

"Goodness, no." She scoffed. "He would laugh."

Leland propped an elbow on the arm of the chair and rested his forefinger against his temple.

"What gives you the impression he doesn't feel the same way?"

She worried her bottom lip, eyes still averted. "Lord Dunley has proposed to Miss Clint. She has accepted."

Her eyes flicked to her father to gauge his reaction. He remained attentive, unmoved by her announcement.

"The betrothal wasn't real," she blurted.

Heat surged behind her eyes. To admit to such deception to her father was too much.

Her vision blurred. Her throat constricted. But she continued, "I lied to Lord Dunley to escape his proposal. I worried if I declined, his mother would find a way to pressure me and force my hand. So, I lied."

Abbie took a deep breath and explained the whole of the tale as best she could. Her father made no interruptions, asked no questions, and made no expressions. When she finished her confession, she looked up, meeting his eyes at last.

"I'm the worst of daughters. I understand if you cannot forgive me."

Leland cleared his throat, shifting in his chair. "I forgave you before you confessed, Abigail. It's what I do. You're a strong woman carrying a heavy heart. I hope telling me helps lighten the weight."

"Aren't you going to reprimand me?"

"You came here to confess, not to receive punishment. Do I wish you had told me? Yes. Anything else I'm feeling is immaterial. This is about you, Abigail, not me."

The guilt she had carried was a far greater punishment than any reprimand he could give, but she did not need to say that to know he felt the same. Brushing the dampness from her cheek, she gave him a half-hearted smile.

"This next question," he said, "is a difficult one. There's no need to tell me the answer. Think it over and trust your best judgement. What will you say to Percival when you next see him?"

The storm kept Percival and most of the villagers indoors the next day. He did not get to see Abbie or the hall. There was no walk through the village nor companions in the private parlor for the coffeehouse hours. The weather was fierce and inconvenient. For most of the day, he alternated his time between studying estate management from the materials Mr. Wynde sent over and studying textiles from what he could find in the inn's circulating library. It was not much. But not much was more than Percival had previously read.

How differently would his Oxford days have been had he discovered such studies then? The classes he had taken made no mention of textiles, management, or land ownership, but they had taught him several languages and the best countries in which to use those languages while shopping for new furniture or a mistress. No, that was unfair. He had the very best education, and it had covered a great many subjects. The trouble was, nothing about the offered professions—law, for instance—had interested him. He had been bored and restless.

His studies had not included the running of an estate. Such training was for the heir. His brother, the heir of the Camforth earldom, had private tutors to teach such intricacies. As the spare, Percival should have, or rather *could* have, been privy to those lessons, but being the hellion he was in his younger days, there had been far more trees to climb and lakes to swim than a single day allowed—who had time to be cooped inside with his brother's tutors?

His father had been too lenient, too accommodating, and then too distraught over his wife's death, then too in love with starting a new family with a new wife.

No, Percival could not blame his father. It was his own fault for being a lazy son. But how differently the past decade might have been had his education been taken more seriously, his days more disciplined. And perhaps his actions would have remained the same. It had taken a strange twist and a vicar's daughter to help him find his way.

Fueled by newfound passion, he poured over the material at his disposal. The rain could almost be said to be a Godsend, forcing him to focus and prepare for his new life.

The following day, Friday, brought yet more storms. The rain and mud did not stop the mail coach. Percival sat in the public room, enjoying a coffee with Mr. Bradley, who was sharing possible baby names since his new son or daughter would arrive any day when the mail arrived with a letter for Percy.

The seal was unmistakable. The Earl of Camforth. Percy nodded to his companion and returned to his suite.

His father had written sooner than expected. It had been only a handful of days since he posted his proposal, a proposal that would nullify the ultimatum and free Percival of his dependence. It would set in motion the beginning of the rest of his life as a landowner and investor. If his father agreed, all allowance would come to an end. If his father agreed, Percy was free to marry whoever and whenever he wished.

Squeezing his eyes closed, he gripped the letter, his breath held, his hopes and dreams dependent on the contents.

With a shaky exhale, he thumbed under the wax and unfolded the paper.

My dearest son,

By the time this reaches you, I'll be on my way to Sidvale. We'll talk when I arrive.

Camforth

He blinked.

His father was coming to Sidvale. Ronald Randall, the Earl of Camforth was coming to Sidvale. Percy panicked. Did this mean his father disapproved of his proposal and was coming to talk sense into him? Did he distrust Percival or think he had gone mad? Did he like the proposal but want to see the estate for himself? Or was his coming nothing to do with the estate and all to do with the betrothal, a way to meet the supposed bride?

Then it dawned on him what this entailed.

His father did not travel lightly.

The man would bring a caravan of carriages, along with his wife and two children, and if Percival could place a wager, he would put money on his father's bringing his eldest son and family along with, in all likelihood, Abbie's relations from East Hagbourne, for the man would want pomp, fanfare, and a wedding. He would expect the banns to be read his first Sunday in Sidvale.

His father did not travel lightly.

He could be wrong. But he knew he was not. It was imperative to get word to Abbie. Should he tell her about the proposal he put to his father? It would be best to mention something, but he did not want her to be disappointed if his father declined.

With a flourish of a quill, he jotted her a message that they needed to speak on a matter of urgent importance. He would come to her tomorrow morning at the vicarage, rain or shine.

Percy stared down at his missive, uncertain. It was best to sort their betrothal once and for all before the earl arrived, but it was too soon. What did he have to offer her without the estate in his possession? Promises could be broken.

Nevertheless, they could not go on as they were with the earl coming. Something had to be settled. If he explained his plan, his reason for writing to the earl, maybe, just maybe, she would believe him sincere. Over the past several weeks, he had gone to such lengths to publicly prove his faux affection that convincing her of actual sincerity would be a daunting task. If she would not believe he had fallen in love, just maybe she would believe he had found a new life here in Sidvale, which was the most he could ask for under the circumstances.

In time, anything could happen, even love.

Saturday morning, the rain had lightened considerably. While Percival had not received a response from Abbie about his visiting that morning, he had not expected to. His missive was an announcement of his morning call rather than a solicitation of invitation. He trudged up the muddy road to the vicarage, a dodgy umbrella overhead. His valet had apologized to find it in less than its best condition when unpacked. A steady drip down the back of his neck kept him company on his walk from the inn.

They had far more to discuss than the earl's visit. Percival had awakened to yet another letter, this one delivered by staff from the Dunley house.

Lord Dunley had written to inform Percival of several points of interest.

The first point of interest was that he would be expecting as guests the Earl and Countess of Camforth with their two children, and Baron and Baroness Monkworth with their three children. A subtle but not impolitely worded invitation was extended for Percy to join them, which Percy could not decline fast enough. Lord Dunley also anticipated the vicar would have lodgings for his out of town relations from East Hagbourne, but the viscount would ready additional rooms for them in the event the vicarage was too *quaint*. Percival had chuckled at this since there was nothing small about the vicarage, and undoubtedly, the vicar's family would much prefer to stay there than the Dunley estate.

The second point of interest was that Camforth had left it in Dunley's capable hands to arrange a betrothal dinner.

The third and final point of interest was that the betrothal dinner would be a double celebration in honor of Mr. Percival Randall's engagement to Miss Abigail Walsley alongside his own to Miss Henrietta Clint.

Percival's eyebrows had risen high on his forehead at the final bit of news. As to which was more shocking, he could not say—the bridal choice being Miss Clint or the engagement of Lord Dunley. One thing was for certain; this marked their freedom from the betrothal. The time had come at last where Abbie was free *not* to be engaged. The freedom had him grinning from ear to ear. Now they could *choose* to be engaged. No pretenses, no games, no questioning when or if she would cry off. Now the engagement would be real.

If she would have him.

Heart in his throat, he knocked on the front door. There was no waiting this time, much to his relief since the drip down his back was cold and unpleasant.

Rather than one of the Walsleys, the footman greeted him. "I'm afraid they're from home, sir."

Percival stared at the man as though he were daft.

"It's Mrs. Bradley, sir. The baby's coming. They both left less than an hour ago."

"Right. Tell them I came 'round, eh?"

With little choice, he sloshed his way back to the inn in hopes of dry clothes. So much for his grand plans. Instead, he spent the day hunched over the desk in his suite, resuming his studies.

Tomorrow was Sunday. Rain or shine, he would see Abbie. Tomorrow was the day everything would change.

The curious thing about services that morning was the contradictory expressions worn by Miss Abigail Walsley.

When she thought he was not looking, she frowned. No, *frown* was not the correct word. It was a frown all right, but such a word did not depict the myriad of emotions he detected. Melancholy, worry, concern, anxiety.

When she caught him looking, her expression transformed. *Smile* was not the correct word for that expression either. It was forced, and yet it conveyed, or attempted to convey, a message of mutual understanding and mutual happiness, the two in this together, whatever *this* might reference.

He could not say with confidence what such expressions meant. They did not bode well. She knew about Dunley's engagement because the first of the banns were read. Whether or not she knew of the impending arrival of her aunt, uncle, sister, and brother-in-law was unknown. Whatever she knew, it had affected her, and he did not like the direction of those expressions as an indication of how it had affected her. Her considering him as a real suitor was precarious to begin with, but those expressions signified a death knell.

Did she feel nothing for him? Was his affection unrequited? Surely not. She had kissed his cheek only days ago, for heaven's sake! She valued his opinions on her novel. She had dressed with care on more than one occasion. She had enjoyed their kiss in the churchyard, even if he had made an arse of himself afterwards. The affection could not be one-sided.

And yet affection did not mean love or a desire to marry.

He had known he needed more time to woo her, for she was not a woman to fall for flatteries she perceived as false. Now everything was happening before he had his chance. Just a little more time. Just enough to prove his sincerity, to show himself not a man of dreams and lies and false promises but a man of substance, dimension, action. Just a little more time.

Had it not been for her expressions, he would have escorted her back to the vicarage with the grin of a love-struck fool, ready to propose. Or at least ready to propose a future proposal, once the hall had been purchased, once all had been settled. Now, he escorted her in silence, anticipating the end. Where had it all gone wrong?

Today proved a light drizzle only, but enough to warrant an umbrella, even one with a bend and dribble. Percival held the umbrella over them both, Abigail's hand tucked in the crook of his arm.

"How's Mrs. Bradley?" he asked as they approached the vicarage.

"Doing well. A little boy. They named him Everitt after his papa. Their sixth child, the fourth boy. He was so very tiny, but the midwife assured he was healthy. Certainly a healthy pair of lungs," she said with a quiet laugh.

He stood dumbly at the door as she opened it and stepped over the threshold.

"Will you come inside? Papa will be at the church for another half hour at least. We can talk in the parlor."

As with her expressions, her voice now contradicted. It was low, soft, sad, but she wore a sunny smile, even if it did not meet her eyes.

Devil take it. He had been counting down to this conversation. They were *free*, and he was about to be freer still if he could convince his father to advance him the money for the estate. *Think, man. Think. What can I say to convince her I'm the man for her?* His mind blanked. The fact that she was beyond beautiful today did not help him think straight. All he wanted to do was pull her into his arms and kiss her senseless.

He followed her to the parlor. Although she took a seat near the hearth, he was too antsy. He propped an arm against the mantel instead, a hand tucked into his waistcoat pocket.

They spoke simultaneously:

"I wrote to my—"

"Now that he's—"

They stopped, shared an awkward laugh, and then Percy waved for her to go first.

She took a deep breath, not meeting his eyes. "Now that he's engaged, we can finally be free of this farce. It could have taken longer, so we have Hetty to thank for moving this along. But at last, freedom!" Her laugh was a touch too loud, her smile a touch too wide. "Neither of us wanted this betrothal, so now we may resume life as it was before the disruption. You'll return to London, naturally, and I'll return to… well…my life. You must be feeling as relieved as I am. I thought it would never end!"

Percival narrowed his eyes, trying to judge the honesty of her words. Was she saying this because she meant it? Or was she saying this because she thought he would feel that way? There was only one way to find out.

"We most certainly are free," Percy said, trying to catch her gaze which kept flitting to the floor. "We're free to make the choices we want to make. You don't want to end the betrothal, do you?"

She looked up at him, a sharp look, startled look. "What do you—but of course, I do. That's what we agreed. I'll cry off publicly so there's no confusion. I'll say you chose to live in London, and I refused. It's believable."

"No, it's not," he argued. "I wrote to my father about Leigh Hall. About purchasing it. I'm dependent on his answer, but I did write to him. I proposed an end to the ultimatum and my dependence. If he fronts me the next two years' worth of allowance, I can purchase it."

Every expression he had noted at the church crossed her face before she said, "Write him again and tell him there's no need. It was a ridiculous notion anyway, and I don't know why you did it. You'd be miserable as a landowner. Before the first month ended, you'd be back in London. Write to him and tell him you've changed your mind, or that you were never serious about it, which we both know you weren't, or that I've cried off so there's no point anymore."

He shook his head.

If he could only know whether she was trying to convince herself or him, this would be easier. Had he misread the signs? Devil take it; he believed he had. She had been friendly because they were stuck together, but this whole time, she had no more interest in him than she had in Lord Dunley. Unless she really was trying to convince herself.

He was no more accustomed to begging than he was to being rejected, and yet he could not stop himself from saying what he said next.

"If I told you I'm in love with you, would that make any difference?"

The moment the words left his lips, he wished he could retract them.

The look of horror on her face told him everything he needed to know. He might as well have told her he ate dogs for breakfast.

"I don't believe you," she said at length. "Whether you *think* you are or are so accustomed to telling women you are, I can't say, but it's not possible. I believe you're a man who tumbles in and out of love faster than I change bonnets. We've been thrown together in unusual circumstances, and that's the whole of it. If you take time to think about it all, you'll see I'm right. You don't want Sidvale. You don't want me. The country would bore you, and so would I. It's best to end things now as we planned than be stuck together, miserable and unhappy because you developed a passing fondness for a damsel you thought needed saving."

Percival laughed, a harsh sound that made her flinch. "You've defined me from the start, Miss Walsley. You've known me better than I've known myself. Without your wisdom, I would throw my life away on estates and love. How will I ever get on without you to tell me who I am and what I should do?"

"I can't speak to the future, but for now, you should take your chance to escape. Be free. Go back to London and live the life you love. You're not Sir Bartholomew. You're Mr. Percival Randall, Londoner, rogue extraordinaire. Take this chance while you have it, and don't look back. You'll see I'm right. You already know I'm right. I see your relief."

"What you see, Miss Walsley, is a far cry from relief."

He ran a hand through his hair, the back of it damp. Getting out of this room was the best course of action. He needed to think. He needed away from her.

In the back of his mind, a voice whispered that she was on the offense, so afraid of rejection or insincerity that she had to attack to save her own vulnerability, to save her own heart from breaking. This was exactly what he thought might happen if he did not woo her, convince her of his sincerity first. But that was only the whispered voice in the back. His rational mind told him he had fallen for the one woman he could never have, perhaps because he knew he could not have her. What a wicked woman was love.

"Right," he said, crossing his arms over his chest. "Of course, you're right. Don't know what I was thinking. Thank you for setting me free, for breaking the shackle." He eyed the door. "I ask only one favor. Will you wait to say anything until we can make the announcement together? We'll show a united front, as business partners, and admit to being incompatible."

Her chin wobbled. Or maybe he was seeing things.

"Yes, naturally. When do you think would be best to make the announcement?"

"The betrothal dinner. It'll be the most public, and both our families will be there to witness the end of it."

Her eyes widened. "What betrothal dinner?"

"Ah. I assumed you knew. My father is coming. He'll be here next week, any day really. He's bringing with him my entire family, as well as yours. I think he hoped to press the banns and be present for the ceremony, see this through in case I spoil the match with my rakish ways; you know how men like me can be." Closing his eyes, he said, "I apologize for that last comment. I don't wish to say things I don't mean. If you'll excuse me, I must take my leave of you. But please, let us wait until the dinner. We can announce the end together."

He gave her a bow as she nodded in agreement, then fled the house with what dignity he had remaining.

Chapter 16

The vicarage was in chaos. The village was in chaos. Abbie was in chaos.

Mere days later, without notice, her Aunt Gertrude and Uncle Cecil, accompanied by Abbie's sister Faith and her husband Tom, arrived at the Walsley's home. Had Percival not warned her, and she then not warned her father, the welcoming reception would have been even more chaotic. Aunt Gertrude had sworn everyone to secrecy. A surprise, she said. A surprise of epic proportions. She wanted the first sighting of her to be waving from the carriage window, part of the earl's caravan. Imagine, she had said, *she* riding with an *earl* and his *countess*! And had she mentioned—at least five times in the first hour—that she had dined with his eldest son and daughter-in-law, Baron and Baroness Monkworth, on more than one occasion since learning of Abbie's betrothal?

Abbie and Leland were the last to know of the visit and the betrothal dinner. Even Prudence and Bonnie had received letters to come and bring the children, for it would be a reunion to remember.

The vicarage was not small, plenty of room for a vicar, wife, and four young daughters. Not quite enough room for a widower, four grown daughters with three husbands, said vicar's sister and brother-in-law, and two youngsters, not to mention the baby one of the daughters was carrying, which nearly had a seat at the table with how much attention Prudence required for her needs in this delicate condition. They all fit. Just.

The noise did not fit. It spilled into the garden and down the road, boisterous chatter and laughter. It was almost enough to guilt Abbie into retracting her decision to cry off. To tell all these people who were so happy to see her happy, or what they thought was her happiness, that the betrothal was at an end was overwhelming. But which was worse, she asked herself on more than one occasion: disappointing them now or living with a mistake for the rest of her life?

She could not allow herself to give in to her own heart's yearnings. Her decision had been for the best. She had set him free. There were no trappings, no strings, no shackles. He no longer needed to placate those around them with fictions and fantasies or to overcome his boredom with their country trifles.

There had been a moment when she had wondered if he were sincere. He mentioned the estate. He spoke of falling in love. Her heart broke to be toyed with, for he could not mean such things; he had not even sounded sincere! He had tossed the declarations in the conversation with a bitter edge to his tone. Why wait to tell her those things in the moment they both realized freedom? If he had been sincere, he would have already proven it somehow, not waited until the moment of rejection to gain the advantage. He had not even denied her charges.

Percival could never fall for an inexperienced wallflower.

Or so she had told herself every hour of every day since the moment he walked out of the parlor. Abbie could not bear to think he might have been sincere. She could not bear it. Not after rejecting him.

"I'm impressed," Ronald said, looking out to the church spire in the distance. The two stood at the highest point on the property, admiring the valley.

"Is that a yes, then?" Percival asked, his eyes on his father rather than the view.

"It's not a definitive yes until my solicitor studies the paperwork, but the answer is merely my opinion, son. You may do what you like with or without my opinion. Should I agree to your proposal, and from what I see here, I have no reason not to, the money is yours to do with as you like, be it purchase this estate or squander it at the tables."

Percival laughed. "I'm not much of a gambler, and you know it."

"No, but you understand my point." Ronald turned in a circle, whistling. "I never would have thought you would hear the call of the land. A city boy through and through is what I thought. It's modest, but that's all you need. And it's a beauty. Now, what's this about the Core Copse Mill? Planning to sully our good name with industry?"

"That I am." He chuckled, knowing his father jested, one of the few aristocrats who would jest about industry. "From what I understand of the accounts — not much, mind — the estate isn't profitable enough to yield what I would need for an investment, at least not for many years to come, but I hope to change that. With advice from Freddie. With advice from you. After a long talk with Mr. Wynde. I think we can find a way. With enough profit, I can invest in the mill."

His father turned to walk back to the estate, his hands clasped behind his back. "If you want it, you'll have it, son. Never underestimate the abilities of my solicitor and his team. He'll have the price of the estate reduced, especially with the roof dilapidation you discovered and its long-term vacancy without even a staff to care for it. With a reduction in price, you'll have more than enough remaining to invest and take your bride on a honeymoon. I assume she'll want to tour the continent?"

Before he replied, Percival allowed the news of the investment potential to sink in. Joyous indeed! As good as he was with numbers, there was still much to learn about management.

"About Miss Walsley…" Percy swallowed, uncertain where to begin or what to say.

"Either you're about to tell me that now you're free of my ultimatum, you don't wish to marry and have convinced her to cry off, or you're going to say you've already married her and forgot to send me notice." Ronald's shoulders shook with his good humor.

"Neither, you'll be relieved to know. I was merely going to say that I'd rather us wait until the betrothal dinner to meet her, if that's acceptable. More pomp in the moment rather than trying to arrange for a meeting beforehand."

His father eyed him with skepticism. "So, you're saying I shouldn't have sent my card to the vicarage this morning?"

"Why doesn't this surprise me?"

The two re-entered the hall rather than walk around to the courtyard. There remained a few more aspects of the home he wished to show his father, never mind that the man was already pleased with the estate. Percival felt too much pride not to show off his accomplishment.

The betrothal dinner was only days away. Saturday, to be precise. However brutal of a rejection he received, he was not disheartened. He knew the moment he made the decision to stay in Sidvale that it was all a gamble. Should she not accept his official proposal, he would back away and move forward as a landowner, happy to have found his place in the world and a village he loved, even if that meant seeing her every day of his life as an acquaintance rather than a wife. But it would not be for a lack of trying. He had set everything in motion before her rejection, and he would see it through. This time, his wooing of the vicar's daughter would be sincere for there were no shackles, no strings, no trappings. With no other motive than love, she had to be convinced.

The tying of twine about the manuscript was a monumental moment in Abbie's life. Yes, it marked the completion of her first novel, but more importantly, it marked her courage to send it to a publisher. The address had been written for Mr. Bradley, who said he had a post-boy chosen for the task. It would go out tomorrow.

Should this publisher decline, she had a list of others, but this one was her first choice, for he had a reputation for being open to women writers. Several letters of introduction lay in crumpled wads about the table, wasted paper, wasted ink. Her first signature had read *Mrs. Button*. She had rewritten the entire letter so the signature would read cleanly, and then altered it to *Mr. Button*, thinking she would gain more favor by posing as a male writer. At last, she took a deep breath, rewrote the letter again, and signed it as *Abigail Walsley*.

While work would not begin on her next novel yet, she already knew her plot and characters. Now that Sir Bartholomew's story had come to a close, she could not stop her mind from whirring with countless others. There was something to be said for the many fantasies she and Percival had weaved, tales that provided a plethora of ideas. Her next story would be of a young girl who disguised herself as a squire to save her family. She was itching to tell that tale. There would not be a Prince Dungheap in this version, but it was too good of a story not to write.

It seemed too soon to be thinking of what she wanted from the next year, two years, or five, as Percival had put to her once upon a time, but with the betrothal dinner fast approaching and her plans to cry off imminent, she needed a plan, something to encourage her.

She envisioned herself as a published author, known and loved by readers. Once every year, or at the most every two years, she hoped to publish a new novel.

The trouble with her vision was she could not stop seeing Percival as part of it. All visions of the future were intrinsically tied to him. Each plot referenced something they had playacted on one of the many walks from the inn to the vicarage or on her charity rounds. And each vision of her writing had her sitting at the desk in Leigh Hall, Percival at her side. Somehow she had to replace those visions with her desk in the vicarage parlor or the table in her room, the chairs about her empty or with her father reading quietly by the hearth. Any day now, Percival would return to London, delayed only by the presence of his family and this dreadful, impending dinner. Try as she might, Abbie could not get him out of her head.

The knock on her door would have sent the pages of her manuscript flying had they not been tied by twine. Clumsy girl. Thankfully, no spilled inkpots today. Opening the door unleashed a trumpeting of squeals, titters, and guffaws from her family in the parlor below.

"A letter for you," her father said, handing her the folded paper. "Join us soon? Your aunt is insisting on pairing off for games, and I'm notably without a partner."

Once he reached the landing on the stairs, Abbie closed the door and returned to her table. She turned the paper over in her hands. The only marks were her name scrawled across one side in bold, looping letters, the other side sealed with a wafer. It had not been posted but hand delivered. Unfolding it, she smoothed it out, her eyes first moving to the signature: *Mr. Stitch*. With an intake of breath, she leaned against the chairback and stared into space, gathering strength.

Lucy,

As I understand the situation, the trouble you've been having with a certain Mr. R. stems from your uncertainty if his actions and affections are genuine. This is the plight of many young women, so do not feel alone in the struggle. There are rogues who mean ill, as your aunt Mrs. Button will attest. I applaud you for guarding yourself against their charms. The trouble is, my dear Lucy, that should you mistake a sincere young man for a rogue, you will break more than one heart through the rejection.

Being of a wise vantage point, I thought it prudent to offer a different perspective. You can spot a man in love easily enough. Does he spend as much time with you as possible without motive? Does he focus his attention on you during those times? Does he support your endeavors, goals, and dreams? Does he act in a fashion that plans for a future wherein the two of you might be together? Does he admire you even when your hair is mussed? Does he embrace your family as though they were part of his own? These are only a few of the signs to gauge, but if you answer in the affirmative to these, it could be a sign your young man is sincere. Trapped men, bored men, men who toy with the affections of young women, either do not do any of these or cannot maintain the façade for long.

I offer my thoughts freely and with no obligation. It is only for you to say if Mr. R. is a rogue or genuine in his affections. A pity it would be, don't you think, to charge him too soon, especially if his affection runs deep? Think on my words, and perhaps, just perhaps, give Mr. R. a chance to prove himself. Your humble servant,

Mr. Stitch

Abigail slumped into the chair. Did he have a motive? Was his father pressuring him? She could not think what he could gain from an alliance with her. This was his moment of freedom. She had offered him every chance to escape the snare. He could return to London with his reputation secure and marry an heiress, a beauty, anyone he wanted, and yet he sent this.

Folding the paper along its creases, she smoothed it into its original, tidy square. What did it mean? She had no beauty, no dowry, no connections. She was simply Abigail.

Did she dare hope his words of love had been sincere? Patting the letter, she tugged at her bottom lip, chin quivering, and smiled. *Oh, she dared!*

With a loop and flourish, Percival signed the paperwork. The hall and demesne of Leigh were his, for better or worse. The weight of responsibility settled onto his shoulders, a contrary that lifted the burden of dependency and listlessness.

He looked to his father and solicitor. Both wore stern expressions. The twinkle in his father's eyes, alone, showed the pride in his son's decision. The executors of the estate were not as eager to sell as

Mr. Wynde had implied. They tossed around words like long-term lease and termed leasehold, as well as impetuous, followed by squabbling over a reduction since the vacancy was to do with an understandable contention between the settlement and the will rather than their choice to let the hall sit unoccupied. His father's solicitor, and now by right of purchase his own solicitor, put an end to such squabbles.

A shake of hands around the table sealed the deal. Mr. Percival Randall was a landowner.

Once in the earl's carriage, his father said, "Next thing I know, you'll be running for parliament."

Percival howled in laughter. "I'll leave the politics to you, but I appreciate the vote of confidence."

"Your first action as a man of means?"

The carriage rocked into motion, moving away from the executors' law office in Sidbury, on the road for Sidvale, his father's solicitor following behind in his own conveyance.

"My first action," Percival said, a hand on the leather strap as they bumped along the roadway, "is to write the butler in London to arrange for the transport of my possessions. What I wouldn't give to have my curricle. And my horses. Good heavens—I'll be able to move out of the inn and sleep in a decent bed at last. I swear my backside has bruises from a month of lumpy stuffing."

"Staff would be my first order of business, but what do I know? I'm just an earl." The smugness of his expression had Percival renewing his humor.

"Too right. And what do I know? I'm merely a wastrel of a second son, my priorities on carriages and fashion." This tickled them both into laughter.

It was good to have his father here. A more loving papa a boy could not ask for, even if Percy did oft avoid family gatherings.

The humor faded, his father eyeing him. "Now that my ultimatum is void, will you still be marrying Miss Walsley? Pardon my skepticism, but I had not anticipated you'd choose a vicar's daughter. I had wondered if it was a ruse."

His smile slipped. Percival looked to the barren fields from the carriage window when he said, "I can't speak for Miss Walsley, Papa, but I'm in love with her. If she'll have me, I'll marry her any time on any day."

Although he continued to face the window, he could feel his father's penetrating stare. Not until they turned down the single carriage lane leading to Sidvale center did his father say, "I do believe you are in love, my boy."

Abbie accepted the cup of tea from Lady Camforth, moments before her father did the same. They occupied a private parlor in the Dunley manor. To her relief, Lord Dunley's whereabouts were unknown, and Lady Dunley was with her future daughter-in-law and a modiste to arrange for a bridal gown befitting of a Dunley. Even more relieving was Percival's absence. He and his father were on an errand, although no one would say what that errand might be or when they might return. She had not yet met his father. Her more pressing concern was avoiding Percival, especially with his family looking on, for she had not seen or spoken to him since the rejection. She wanted to see him, especially after the curious letter, but she did not want the awkwardness of meeting with onlookers or with so much confusion now in her mind.

Her rejection had been final. And yet she could not stop thinking of the implications of the letter.

"We're delighted you've called on us, Mr. Walsley, and that we have this opportunity to meet Miss Walsley. My husband is keen to meet you both and will be forever envious that we had the opportunity to do so before him," Lady Camforth was saying.

Joining them was Percival's older brother, Lord Monkworth, his wife Lady Monkworth, to whom Abbie did not warm although everyone else was amiable, and also Percival's half-siblings Mr. Samuel Randall and Lady Sally. The two younger siblings were treasures with nothing but kindness to share. The elder brother looked strikingly like Percival with the same hazel eyes, golden brown hair, and dimples, but without the youthful exuberance. The slight peppering of his hair made him appear older than his years. None save Lady Monkworth acted high in the instep.

"Have you always lived in Sidvale, Mr. Walsley?" asked Lady Camforth.

"My family is from Northbourne. The church needed me in Sidvale. I've long since made my home here, my wife—God rest her soul—being the rector's daughter, born and raised in Sidvale. Our daughters have grown up here, although only my youngest remains in residence. It's peaceful here. Good people."

"You're a writer?" Lady Sally asked Abbie, drawing her attention away from the current conversation.

A tad prissy but without airs and bearing a quiet beauty she would grow into in a few years the girl could not be more than fifteen. Abbie liked her straight away.

Lady Sally prodded, "Your sister mentioned it during the drive here."

Glancing around the room, Abbie tried to gauge the reaction of the family, all of whom had turned their attention to her. The only negative response came from Lady Monkworth who gave an audible sniff at the question.

"Yes, I am. I've only just finished my first novel."

"How diverting." Lady Sally giggled. "Is it a tale of horror and murder?"

"Sally!" Lord Monkworth hissed.

"Papa doesn't disapprove of my reading Radcliffe, so neither should you," Lady Sally said with a scolding glare at her brother.

For the first time, Lady Monkworth spoke. "I can see why my brother-in-law favors you." She looked Abbie up and down with a sneer. "He's always been the fanciful sort. Prefers fantasy to reality."

With a warning look to his wife, Lord Monkworth said to Abbie, "What my wife means to say is my brother is a dreamer and a visionary. I believe he could accomplish anything if only he set his mind to it."

"And this is why it's fortunate he's the second son," said Lady Monkworth. "He would set his mind to naught if it weren't forced. There are visionaries, and then there are *dreamers*. You must make the distinction." Another sharp look at Abbie, she added, "You do know which sort he is, yes? It would be unfortunate for you to find out after the wedding."

The room shuddered into silence, all eyes moving from Abbie to Lady Monkworth and back.

Abbie gave her best vicar's daughter's smile. "It has taken some time to get to know him, my lady, but yes, I believe I do know which sort he is. He is nothing if not honest. Wouldn't you agree?"

Her ladyship gave a tight smile and a titter. "On that point, we can agree. No artifice about him. He's a proud Lothario."

If Abbie bristled, she did not let it show. The words were not hurtful so much as the realization that they reflected Abbie's own thoughts of him. Here she sat with a loving and kind family, and her views had been more in keeping with Lady Monkworth's than theirs—a humbling and frightening thought. The riposte on the tip of her tongue was to doggedly defend Percival, however hypocritical given her recent words of rejection. She thought carefully of her response, not wanting to appear impolite.

After a moment's reflection, she said, "Mark my words not of naivety, my lady, when I say I believe him more of his namesake than either of us would have suspected on first acquaintance."

She felt her father's arched brow before she saw it in her peripheral. Lady Monkworth mirrored the expression but said no more, looking into her teacup, either chastised or self-righteous.

Lady Sally, in her infinite sweetness, said with a teasing look to her brothers and a conspiratorial tone, "Don't tell Freddie or Sammy, but Percy's my favorite brother. I hope you'll convince him to call on us more often."

They stayed no longer than half an hour, but in that half an hour, the Walsleys were made to feel as family. The Randalls asked more about Leland's work with the church, another question from Lady Sally about Abbie's writing, and one not quite impertinent question from Mr. Samuel Randall as to what Abbie's impression of Percival was on their first meeting, which resulted in her father relaying the fictionalized tale of the fall into Hacca's Brook and Percy's gallant rescue. The blushes sealed Abbie in their good graces.

The kindled hope flared within her breast. She hoped it was not too late to rectify her mistake.

Chapter 17

The Dunley estate was grand and stately to be sure, but an odd combination of Tudor and modern architecture and décor. With some ceilings of wooden beams and others of gilded scenes, sashed windows in one room and casement windows in others, and even stone fireplaces here and ornate marble there, the house revealed the history of ownership and changing tastes of the time.

Hands clasped behind his back, Percival stood in Lord Dunley's drawing room, thinking not of splendor or history but of his preference for his new home. He owned a home! The thought appeared at random moments, striking a silent tremor of elation. Should he eye his father across the room, the thought appeared. Should he catch a glimpse of Lord Dunley's boredom, the thought appeared. Should his gaze rest on the back of Abigail's coiffure, the thought appeared.

Especially when his eyes alighted on her. The home was meant for the two of them, after all. If she would reconsider.

Several groups occupied the drawing room, conversing before dinner. Lord Dunley, Lady Dunley, Miss Clint and her family on one side of the room entertained Percy's stepmother Evie, Freddie, and Freddie's harridan of a wife Margaret. On the other side, Mr. Leland Walsley chatted with Sammy and Sally, who were enthralled by the man, while the Walsley sisters chatted with their husbands and Mr. and Mrs. Diggeby about the Dunleys, or so Percy guessed from their glances across the room.

In the middle of the madness sat Abbie with Percival's father. It did not take a genius to see his father was engrossed in the conversation and infatuated by the novelist disguised as Percy's betrothed.

Percival did his devil best to blend in with the wallpaper. His motivation was two-fold: admire Abigail, since it may be his last opportunity to do so and fret in silence regarding how the evening would progress. Her reaction to seeing him when she entered the manor, her first time to see him since the previous Sunday, had been indecipherable. She wore her charity expression: a polite smile that reached her eyes but gave away nothing of her heart.

All his plans to talk to her again before the dinner had failed. Each time he called on the vicarage, she had been calling on the Bradleys or the Owens or the whoevers, or she had taken her sisters for a walk to who-knew-where. The one time she and her father had returned Ronald's invitation to call on the family at the Dunley manor, he and his father had been in a law office in Sidbury. Fate mocked him. Fate shook her fist at him and laughed. *This will be one woman you cannot woo*, said that wicked temptress.

Not knowing if Abigail liked flowers or if such a gift would be too bold given she planned to publicly spurn him today, he had taken the risk. After all, what did he have to lose other than his pride? With the help of the innkeeper—no surprise there since the man knew everything, or so it seemed to Percy — he was able to send from a hothouse to the vicarage an embarrassing number of flowers. An unsigned note accompanied:

Dreams become reality with sincerity and love.

If the flowers were not ostentatious enough, then the new set of writing implements and paper would be, a gift he hoped would demonstrate his serious interest in her endeavors. And if she remained determined to end this, at least she would have a useful gift even after the flowers died.

There was so much to say to her, so much he should have said before. Now, it was too late. The time of the dinner approached. The casement clock ticked to his doom. No excuse could draw her away for a private talk, not without appearing conspicuous and violating at least ten rules of decorum.

Should Percy face his death, be it by sword, pistol, or illness, his last thought would be not of regret or longing, but of the state of Miss Walsley's coiffure.

Her hair was styled again, ringlets framing her face, the back swept atop her head and wound with a turban, exposing a kissable neck. He memorized each strand, the fallen ones providing him a lifeline. His heart skipped beats each time she tilted her head. Her dress teased him with that delicate figure he had spied only once before. She wore another round gown, this one with a silk open robe of basil green.

Lost in thought, he missed the butler announcing dinner. When guests stood, voices rose, and a queue formed, Percival snapped to attention. Good heavens!

It was time for dinner! The rush of blood in his veins roared in his ears until he could hear nothing but the end of days. Panicked, he rushed forward to Abbie. All around him assumed he would offer his arm. This was, after all, a betrothal dinner partly in their honor. He did not, however, offer his arm.

He darted forward as she took a step with his father. His shoe met the train of her robe.

It was not cataclysmic. Dresses were not harmed, and no one fell. But it was enough.

Abigail made the slightest stumble, the Earl of Camforth offering his arm to steady her while one of her relations joked about her clumsiness. There should have been a smoother way to hold her back, a subtler way, a more gentlemanly way, but panicked men do panicked things, and Percival panicked.

Abigail blushed and apologized to the earl but had the wherewithal to stab a sharp look at Percival.

He rushed to her side. "Wait, darling. It was my fault, not any clumsiness of yours. Allow me to ascertain if your dress has survived unscathed." A quick look to his father and the other guests, he said, "Go on, please, we'll be but a moment."

No one protested. No one lingered or gave them a second glance.

He knelt at her feet, fiddling with the hem of the green, until they were alone in the room. The door to the dining room remained open for all to see their exchange. Not ideal, but it would have to do. It was all he had.

When he stood, she looked up at him with eyes of uncertainty.

"You're looking at the proud owner of Leigh Hall," he blurted.

She gaped. Too stunned to speak?

"I purchased it not to trap you or guilt you into not crying off. I purchased it because I've found a place where I belong. It's here that I've found love. I'm in love with… Sidvale… and… the villagers… and everything here, really. I want to make a home here, not in London. I… We don't have time to talk now, but I have more to say. Please, give me a chance to say it all. If you choose to cry off now, I'll understand, but I only ask for a chance."

Lord Dunley, devil take the man, returned to the drawing room, interrupting before she could reply. "Is aught wrong? Does Miss Amy require a maid?"

Percival gave Abbie a pleading look before he escorted her into the dining room.

How curious to be seated with Mrs. Sullivan to one side and Mrs. Rockford on the other rather than his betrothed. Lord Dunley, he noticed, sat next to Miss Clint on one side and his mother the other. Impertinent man. Abigail sat on the opposite end of the table from Percival between her brothers-in-law. Assigned seating at a betrothal dinner was a ridiculous notion, but every host had their preference, and so it would appear Lord Dunley had his. Not that the man should care where Percival or Abbie sat when he had no real interest in either of them. A glance to Lady Dunley revealed no malice either, as she was deep in conversation with the Clint family, her face animated and enraptured by whatever Mr. Clint posited.

To keep sane and stop himself from watching Abigail's every move, Percy made conversation with his dinner companions, asking after their children, their lives, the weather, their bonnets, anything, everything, whatever would keep them talking and prevent his head from swiveling to the woman who was about to cry off the engagement he wanted to keep.

A clink of glass. A clearing of a throat. A scrape of a chair.

Percival's eyes widened. His teeth gnashed. His gaze moved from one guest to the next to halt the passage of time before his eyes came to rest on the person standing to make an announcement.

Lord Dunley.

Percy closed his eyes and exhaled. Thank heavens it was not Abbie.

"I propose a toast to all of the guests here today to celebrate two auspicious betrothals. May every gentleman in such a position be as happy as I am." His tone as bored as ever, Lord Dunley raised his glass. "Allow me to say a few words and invite Mr. Randall to do the same. It is not every man who can boast a friendship between his betrothed and his mother, for is it not true that many men of our time marry women their mothers detest?"

The table remained silent. Percy tried not to smirk, for that had been Dunley's attempt to make a joke.

The speech continued, overlong and overdull, until at last everyone raised their glass.

Dunley cleared his throat again. "You have a few words to share, yes, Mr. Randall?"

Dratted man.

Pushing his chair back and tossing his napkin in the seat, Percy stood, his eyes meeting no one's but Abbie's. Her expression mirrored his inner turmoil.

"If I may ask Miss Walsley to stand with me, in the event she too would like to say a few words?" He nodded to her, offering her the opportunity to crumble his world.

She stood, cheeks pinkening.

Eyes unwavering, locked with hers, he said the truest words he knew that would enable her to decide their fate and come out the victor no matter the outcome. "I want everyone here to know that from the moment I met Miss Walsley, I knew she was too good for me. With each passing day of her acquaintance, my esteem for her rises by leaps and bounds. I'm certain now she's the noblest woman I've ever met. I wish her the greatest happiness. For those who know me well, you can attest that I don't often make good choices. Lord Monkworth can speak for the time I thought it would be fun to outrun a bull. Lady Camforth can tell of the time I swapped the hair powder from her dressing room with the pearl ash from Cook's pantry. The stories are numerous, and my reputation sorrier for it."

He paused for the chuckles and chortles to die down.

"I made myself a promise recently to bring only pride to my family from this point forward. Should Miss Walsley come to her senses and realize she can have far better than the likes of me, I will forever be grateful she gave me this opportunity to know her. And should she choose to do so, who could blame her for sending me back to London?" He raised his glass to his betrothed. "Abbie?"

Her bottom lip was tucked between her teeth in that way that made his heart flip-flop. He hoped his words gave her an out, an option, but also enough hope to give him a chance, at least to explain himself and his feelings.

"It's, um, funny you, uh, should mention returning to London," she stuttered in response, sending his world reeling, "because we always said that, um, well, if there were a reason for me to send you back to London, it would be because of our different opinions on the, um, curtains. You see…" She trailed off, her face reddening. "Would you like to make the announcement, or shall I?"

All blood drained from his face. He stood still, unresponsive.

"I suppose I shall," she continued. "Percival has purchased Leigh Hall."

The dinner guests applauded; a few gasped; a few offered congratulations. Percival remained still, watching Abbie's expressions, waiting for the hammer to fall. Or was that it?

"I'm as shocked as you all must be," she said. "And I'm as proud of him as his family must be. Thank you all for a lovely dinner." With a hasty nod, she sat down.

Percival heaved a sigh of relief. When he returned to his chair, he shivered from the beads of sweat that trickled down his back. Of all the high-tension moments he had experienced in his life, that was the tensest. He had no illusions about the state of their engagement or that she would not cry off, but he had been given a reprieve, a second chance, an opportunity to explain himself. So help him, he would make the most of it. His glance to Abbie was rewarded with a heart-pounding hint of a shy smile.

The day after the dinner, the church was full to bursting with both Abbie's family and Percival's. The villagers were in awe of their grand guests. *An earl*, they kept whispering behind their hands. Despite the devotion he showed to his wife, there were more than a few young girls in near swoons over the Earl of Camforth—wealth, title, chivalry, *and* good looks. Only the greying at his temples gave away his age. That and the presence of his adult children. The girls ogled him all the same. A few tried to eye the heir, Baron Monkworth, but one look from his wife sent them cowering into a corner of their pew, not bound to make the same mistake twice.

Abbie had eyes only for the middle son, Percival. He glanced at her frequently. She knew because she watched him throughout the sermon.

Yesterday was to be the cry off. They were to have done it together, a united front, two incompatible people. At first, she had planned to make the announcement in the drawing room before last night's dinner, but she decided against that when she realized how awkward dinner would be afterwards. No, that was actually not true at all. She had procrastinated the announcement because she was enjoying the company of his family too much to break the spell. Falling in love with his family was as natural as falling in love with him.

More to the point, the hope burning steadily in her heart held her tongue.

His pleas for a chance, his announcement about the hall, it all sent her head spinning. Was he serious? Did he feel the same way about her? It seemed so impossible. And yet the letter…

She had had another opportunity to cry off after dinner when they had returned to the drawing room for tea. Every look towards Percival had stopped her. Being there with him, his eyes trained on her, his open admiration worn in his expression, it all felt *right*. The impossible seemed possible.

The congregation gathered outside the church after service, parishioners vying for an introduction to the Randall family or desirous to reminisce with the vicar's daughters. Abbie stood to one side of her father, searching the crowd for Percival. He had been standing right *there*. And then poof!

"Now's our chance," a voice whispered from behind her.

She felt his palm cupping her elbow before she saw his profile as he stepped up next to her. The touch, even through the sleeve of her dress, sent a thrill through her body.

"Allow me to walk you home while everyone's distracted?" he asked, his tone full of meaning and insinuation that went beyond a simple walk home.

This was the chance he wanted, the opportunity to speak with her. It was not a chance to escape an engagement. It was not *his* chance, rather *our* chance, he had said. Their chance to…to what? Be together? Her breath quickened.

She knew her own feelings for him and what she wanted. She also held tight to that hope his affections were sincere. How could they not be sincere? The letter from Mr. Stitch, the flowers, the gift, the note, all things only she saw, no notch to his reputation or saving grace to his predicament. The speech at the dinner had been public but she had recognized her liberty to make the final decision. And there was the purchase of Leigh Hall, an action he took after being granted an escape from the shackle. He gained nothing from deceiving her and less than nothing from continuing the engagement. How could she not believe him sincere?

The familiar walk to the vicarage with Percival at her side invited her to tuck her hand in the crook of his arm, her shoulder bumping against him every few steps. They strode in silence, the sounds of laughter and happiness behind them.

Not until they settled in the parlor did either speak, the first words via speaking glances as she blushed to see him take in the array of flowers perched around the room.

"Tell me about the hall," she prompted when he began pacing.

"Yes, that's a good place to start. I prepared a speech last night, but my nerves are too frayed to recall it. Yes, let's start with the hall."

A speech? Her brows rose in surprise.

"No, let me say this part first, at least. If you feel nothing for me, I'll understand. I'll back away, leave you in peace, and move into my new residence to begin a fresh life. But if you feel something, anything, reconsider. I don't wish to break off our engagement, Abbie. It may have started as a misunderstanding, then moved into a business partnership, but it has since become something real to me. I want it to be real."

He kneeled before her, clasping her trembling hand in his warm, strong palms.

"I come to you not as a man needing to fulfill an ultimatum. I'm not a dependent of my father, needing a bride. I come to you as an independent man wanting *you* as my wife. I've purchased a home I adore and have set a meeting for next week with the mill owner to discuss an investment. I can offer you security and happiness. I'm not the rogue you think me to be, and I vow there will never be anyone but you, only and forever you. Before this moment, I've never proposed to anyone, not because I have an aversion to marriage but because I've never met someone I wished to marry. I don't make my offer lightly. I place my heart in your hands. My devotion is true and runs deep. If you'll have me, I'll love you not until death does us part but well beyond that, beyond the grave, and beyond the gates of Heaven."

Her hand still held captive, Abbie tugged at the handkerchief in her dress pocket, desperate to wipe the tears before she made a blubbering fool of herself in the middle of his pretty prose.

"I want to know when your novel is published," he continued. "I want to know the progress of your next novel. I want to be with you to celebrate the moment you become the premier novelist of the age. I want to be there with you and for you when these dreams come true."

Her handkerchief dabbing at her nose, she made to speak, but he put a finger to her lips.

"Not yet. There's more," he said.

He tugged at his pocket, trying to pull out what looked like a bit of folded paper. Abbie took the opportunity to wipe her face of tears. As dreadful and blotchy as she must look, she did not care. She wanted to hear more. In fact, she never wanted him to stop.

Smoothing out the paper, still kneeling before her, he read, "'Dear Lucy. It is I, Mr. Stitch, your trusted advisor. I have a confession. We never met at a dinner party as I once claimed. I do not have a wife you know, also as I once claimed. You'll be shocked to learn that I am the very Mr. R. you have reservations about. This means all my advice has been full of motive and bias, except the last letter wherein I instructed you to spot the differences between a sincere gentleman and rake. Well, that letter, too, was full of motive and bias, but not the kind you think, for it was my ardent hope you would read those words and realize me the very best of men and see my love as truth. I know not what your aunt Mrs. Button will say to this revelation, but I have only to say that I love you with all my heart and soul.'"

Abbie's tears were interrupted by her laughter, causing an embarrassing mixture of hiccupped stutters and shudders. Percival did not seem to mind. He handed her a fresh handkerchief and clasped her free hand once more, the paper tossed to the floor.

"I'm not Sir Bartholomew. I've not lived a chaste life. I don't even slay dragons. And if Granny M ever loses her sheep, I won't promise to help find them. To be honest, I would probably invite the dragon in for tea rather than slay it, and I would buy Granny M new sheep. I am nothing more than a humble second son, no accolades to my name, but I will love you more deeply and for much longer than Sir Bartholomew ever could, for unlike that chivalrous knight who wanders the country in search of fulfillment, I already know my place. My estate is in need of repairs and my name is soon to be sullied by the word industry, but will you consider, just consider, if you feel anything at all, if my words have not fallen flat, will you consent to be my wife? Will you, Miss Abigail Walsley, marry me?"

After the longest, most disjointed speech Abbie had heard in her life, she launched herself into his arms, peppering his face with wet and snotty kisses. The two, kneeling together on the floor, wrapped arms about each other, their lips meeting in a feverish and unchaste kiss.

When their lips parted for the slightest of moments, she took the opportunity to say, "Yes, I'll marry you. I've loved you for too long not to."

"Have you really?" He leaned back to study her face.

She nodded, tugging him back to her lips.

Their embrace continued, lips slanting, tongues probing, hands exploring, until the parlor door opened.

Both her family and his spilled into the room, all laughter and conversation. Then they spotted Abigail and Percival, kneeling, locked in a lascivious embrace. Silence shook the couple from their private moment.

Clamoring to their feet, not the least embarrassed, they clasped hands and faced their families.

Percival said, "You may all wish us happy."

"Yes," Abbie continued for him, "for Percival has proposed, and I've accepted."

Each family member looked from one to the other in complete perplexity.

Except the vicar.

Leland smiled, looking from Abbie to Percival. "Splendid. I can finally read the banns."

Epilogue

1801

The feather of her quill brushed against her chin as she re-read the lines.

Lady Araminta peered out her tower. A queue of knights crossed the drawbridge.

Hmm. Should her ladyship see the queue first, the knight of her choice first, or remark on her own independence first? For the third novel, her publisher had welcomed an independent heroine as the main character, but just how independent she could get away with, she was unsure. Abigail tapped the empty quill against the paper, lost in thought. Flipping to the page before it, she studied the last lines of the previous chapter rather than watch where she was walking.

When her shin met the arm of an unsuspecting chair, nearly sending her flying over it, she looked up for the first time in her walk down the hallway to the drawing room. Half the furniture had been overturned, the other half covered in the old curtains. Covered was putting it mildly. The curtains draped over several pieces of furniture, forming odd sorts of tents and tunnels. What in the name of sanity was going on in here?

A growl. A screech. Curtains shuddered and hovered. Another almighty growl sent a knight brandishing a wooden sword shrieking his way out from under one of the tents. Abbie's five-year-old son Edmund was soon followed by his three-year-old sister Emma, who was armored in a tiara and veil and squealing with piercing conviction to *ruuuun*. The pair raced behind Abbie and hid.

The curtain bumped and humped and shifted until it flew into the air, revealing a fierce dragon on the rampage. Percival charged, wearing—good heavens! Was that her old basil-green open robe with train? Yes, she believed it was.

"Rawr!" Percival exclaimed. "I'm a hungry dragon! I eat all who enter my lair!"

The children clutched Abbie's legs. "Save us, Mummy! Save us! Papa's going to eat us!"

Undaunted, Percival stalked her, his hands turned to talons.

Abbie patted their heads, her manuscript clutched in her other hand. In a demonstration of bravery, she walked right up to the fearsome dragon and kissed his cheek. "Don't you know the best way to defeat a dragon is to invite it for tea?"

He grinned just long enough to throw her off her guard. Then with a duck and scoop, he swooped her into his arms, her shrieks joining those of the children's, her manuscript pages flying into the air and onto the dreadful curtains they had both hated. The princess and knight circled back to save mummy as the dragon roared and carried her to his lair.

Flash Fiction

Arrival

C risp air slashed his face. Nicholas bent lower, hugging the stallion's neck.

The ill-timed missive had threatened the most important business opportunity of his life. He didn't care.

He rode hell for leather against the sharp winter wind. She needed him. He shouldn't have left her. *A month to go*, he'd thought the morning he left for London. One month to close the deal, securing their future as coal mine owners.

Only a week had passed.

The house loomed ahead, silent and foreboding. Naked tree branches reached for souls to snatch.

Leaping from the horse, he raced past a groom and a footman, the front door slamming into the wall in his wake.

The foyer stood empty, only the neighing of his horse behind him and the voices of the staff ahead. Shouts sounded from the first-floor sitting room, voices raised in fear.

Need drove him forward. He had to see her. She had to know he'd come.

Racing through the gallery and down the hall with the squeaking floorboards, he saw her father, grim and imposing. The man stood guard, a face of stone, a will of iron.

Undaunted, Nicholas barreled into the brick chest, pushing it aside. Or trying to. The wall of a man didn't budge.

"You're not going in there," thundered the voice.

"Like hell, I'm not. She needs me," he insisted, desperate to get by.

"You're too late."

The words stopped him cold. Limply he stood, his body slack, his soul dissolving. He hadn't ridden fast enough. He'd come too late.

Life flashed before his eyes. Her life. Their life. A young girl he'd loved at first sight, a heart he'd worked long years to win. Vibrant blue eyes, golden hair, a laugh that chimed. She'd tamed his recklessness, brought sense to his world, given meaning to his life.

Three difficult pregnancies later, they remained childless, heartbroken. Each lost babe claimed a piece of her vivaciousness, a corner of her smile. And now, the fourth had taken her life.

"The physician's with her now," said her father. "He'll call you in when he's finished."

"To hell with the physician. I need to see her." He pushed against the man with renewed strength.

A punch to the gut bent his father-in-law's will, and Nicholas shoved past, bracing himself for what waited behind the door.

"You're too late," said his mother-in-law, a handkerchief catching her sobs.

He pulled her into an embrace, forcing his eyes to the sitting room's chaise longue, afraid to see the ashen face, or worse, the faceless sheet.

"You're too late," repeated the voice of an angel. "Your son refused to wait."

The vision of perfection blurred from the tears he wiped on his mother-in-law's shoulder. The sobbing woman muttered about miracles as the physician swaddled a newborn. His wife gazed lovingly at the wriggling baby.

His wife. Alive.

He came to her side, the physician and attendant howling with rage that the new mother wasn't prepared to receive, and other useless yammering that barely registered in the flood of his relief. Smiling, his wife held out her arms. He dove into them.

"I thought I'd lost you," he muttered against her neck, inhaling the sweet smell of jasmine and sweat. "My brave, brave, Fiona."

Placing a hand to his heart, she said, "We both must be brave now. We've a babe to raise."

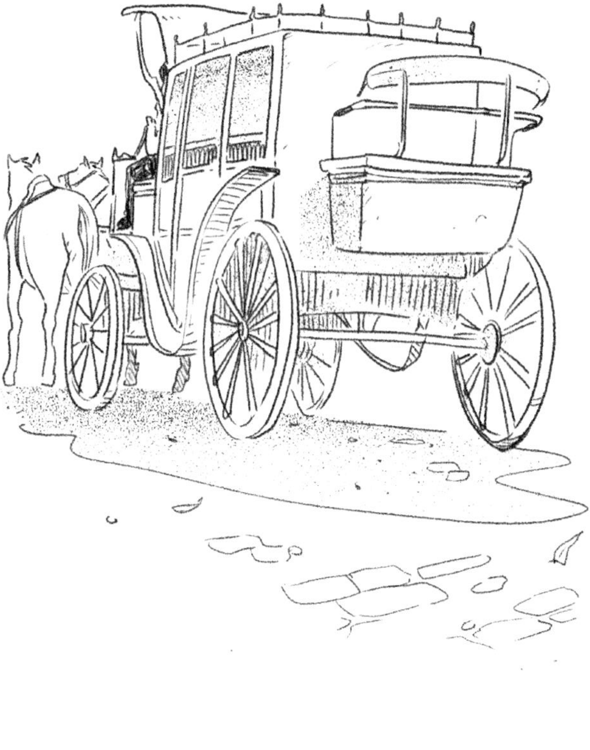

Beguiled

The anonymous letters first appeared in the newspaper on February 1st and caused such a stir, she hid at home for a week. No one doubted they were written for her. How many Lady Ts of Shropshire were there, after all?

The latest letter, featured in the Valentine's edition, was the most scandalous:

To the bewitching Lady T. of Shropshire:
Thine eyes be green and thine hair red.
Please, accept me so we may wed.
I loved you at first sight
And hope you don't take fright
When you lay your precious eyes on me.
Tonight, at last light, together we'll be.

The ball began at dusk.

Her dance card filled before she'd reached the receiving line to greet her hostess. The eager faces of bachelors all claimed with their waggling eyebrows to be her secret admirer. Would he make himself known tonight? *Would* she run in fright?

Though no one spoke to her, all eyes found her from behind fans and hands.

Between the twirls and promenades of each dance, she scanned the crowd for clues. Whispers followed her, taunting her with tales of a clandestine romance.

And then she saw him.

A shadowed figure watched her from behind a potted plant. Her pulse raced, a roar in her ears masking the voices around her.

Their eyes met, and her world tilted. Hazel eyes peered at her from beneath heavy lids framed with dark eyelashes. Those eyes seemed to read her soul. Never had she believed in love at first sight. Until now.

He took a step towards her.

She stepped towards him.

A din of voices resounded around her, crescendoing when he took another step.

And then a clink of glass, drawing the attention of all in the room.

"But a moment, please, but a moment. I have an announcement," voiced the hostess. "It is a propitious Valentine's ball, indeed, for I have the pleasure of announcing the betrothal of my eldest daughter to Lord Keyes."

Her eyes never left his, though he took five more steps forward. She counted. How many more until he reached her?

He stopped. Her breath caught. He wasn't walking towards her, but rather to the center of the ballroom. A young miss affecting well-practiced ennui took his arm.

How could this be? *He* was the betrothed Lord Keyes?

No! She'd only just discovered him. She'd only just found love.

Oblivious to the girl on his arm, he continued to stare at her, his eyes ablaze.

Before she made a cake of herself, she tore her gaze from his and escaped by way of the terrace doors. Grasping the railing outside, she filled her lungs with air, staring at the sun setting behind a copse of trees.

Footsteps sounded behind her. A gossiping matron or a vapid girl to tease her?

A rumble intoned, "Elope with me."

She whipped around to come face-to-face with Lord Keyes. They stood but an arm's reach from each other.

"I don't know you," she whispered.

"Yes, you do. You knew me at first sight, just as I knew you." His cologne enveloped her, enticing her to move closer. "Come away with me."

"But what of your betrothed?"

"Inconsequential. I want you, only you. Come with me. Gretna Green awaits." He held out his hand. "Will you be me Valentine bride?"

Her family's disapproving faces flashed before her eyes.

"Yes." She slipped her hand into his.

They fled the terrace, darting hand in hand across the park to the circle drive.

Swift words to a curious coachman and a bump and jostle later, they were on the road, bound for Scotland. Her stranger pulled her against his chest, his arms wrapping around her shoulders to shield her from doubt. He kissed her deeply, soulfully, conveying to her all the words they'd not yet said, affirming his heart mirrored what hers did for him.

At length, she leaned away, smiling, memorizing his face, reaching a hand to trace the scar that ran from his left ear to his chin.

"I've loved you since the second letter," she confessed.

A crease deepened between his brows. "Letter? What letter?"

She laughed at his coyness and kissed him brazenly.

Until it dawned—he hadn't returned the laugh.

The carriage continued to Scotland, his question echoing in her mind.

Highwayman

My dearest Estella,

Mourning ended yesterday. No longer must I feign sorrow. Do not think your dearest friend wicked or unchristian. For too long I sought the good in my husband. For too long I hid the pain he caused me. His death was a welcomed release, embraced with tears of relief. Today, I shed the cloak of gloom. My cousin arrives on the morrow to fetch me, for it would seem a widow should not live alone. Hoping to see you during the Season.

Your Faithful Friend, Laura

Estella,

I write to you from an inn between my old home and my new one. Cousin arrived punctually. The journey is tedious in his company. He is a kind, staid gentleman. For all that, you will be surprised when I say he proposed within the first hour. Yes, dearest Estella, the dullest gentleman of my acquaintance has proposed. My heart did flutter, but only from the resulting indigestion.

As politely as I might, kerchief in hand, did I dab at my eyes sorrowfully and say, "But my dear Lord Bluton has too soon passed from my heart. Give me time, Cousin." To which, he replied, "Lord Bluton would desire your security. Do reconsider my offer."

Only just have I been freed from my bonds, and now another wishes to capture me! I will not give in.

Your Determined Friend, Laura

My dearest friend,

Oh, Estella! Such monstrous adventure! I write to you from the safety of an inn near my family home. It shan't be long before I am safe in the bosom of my parents. But that is the last place I wish to be. What has happened to prompt this letter, you ask? A highwayman, Estella!

He came upon us after nightfall. A man in black. He seized the carriage, wrested the door from my cousin's grip, and with one hand pulled my cousin free of his seat. Grunts, shuffling feet, and hushed tones ensued. I knew not what

I heard. Quiet followed, a strangled quiet that had me biting my knuckle. I was afeared, Estella! Oh, how my heart did pound. What happened next, you ask? You shall think me mad or else a fibber.

A masked face thrust into the carriage. He must have been startled to see me, for he paused to take my measure. In that moment, I knew not fear — only yearning. It was his eyes, Estella. Eyes not of danger but of adventure and daring. Though I could not see his face to know if he were hideous or handsome, I fell for his eyes. I said to him with my own, "Take me with you!" Perchance he does not read eyes, for his response was a gentlemanly bow before departing.

Fear not for my staid cousin, for the dullard returned to the carriage before long, scuffed but unharmed. He mumbled about spies then told me not to worry my fair head when I queried his meaning.

I wonder if I shall see those eyes again. Oh, how I long for an adventure! Do you think me mad, Estella? I do not believe him a highwayman. Fanciful tales I have weaved since I saw him, but I do believe he is a spy for Crown and country! Though what he should want with my cousin, I know not.

Your Lovestruck Friend, Laura

Estella,

I am bored silly. The country assemblies are nothing more than rooms of dolts and boobies. I wish not for their company. Cousin has applied for my hand twice more. I want to escape. I want to live. I want to be free of these fools.

When Lord Bluton passed, I knew my chance had arrived. And yet, here I sit at the escritoire, wasting away of boredom. Return soon to regale me with tales from the continent. Certainly, you are having more fun than I. If I stole a horse and paced the King's road, do you suppose a highwayman with daring eyes would rescue me?

Your Bored Friend, Laura

My darling Estella,

This shall be my last letter for I know not how long. Do not fret for my safety — I am launching myself into an adventure*!*

Last night's assembly was another dull affair. The same dances, the same partners, the same jests. But then, a late arrival was announced, a Lord Rohr. At first, I did not turn, for what is one more dullard? Words flitted around me — rogue, beast, spy. It was the one word I longed to hear.

I turned, and what do you think I saw? The eyes. *Eyes of daring cut across the room to settle on me. Around the perimeter, he prowled, resolute. I knew, then, my adventure was about to begin. With steady, determined steps, he came upon me. With a bow and mocking smile, he said, "Come."*

And I did.

Shipwreck

C olin braced for impact.
Shoulder met wood.
The floor became the wall.

A symphony of groaning and creaking lumber accompanied his curse. The room rocked, sending a crate toppling across the cabin, narrowly missing his head. Outside, the storm raged. Waves beat against the window, a startling white-capped sight when lightning lit the sky.

He had to get out. He had to help the crew. He had to do *something*. He had to get out.

The room tilted, wall becoming floor once more as the ship pitched. Lurching to his feet, the pain in his shoulder simultaneously throbbing and piercing daggers down his arm, he wrenched open the cabin door.

Water slammed against his chest, grabbed his shirt points, and pulled him under.

His eyes fluttered open. He shivered from the cold, the icy hand of Death cradling his body. Next to him perched an angel. An angel in the body of his ladylove, encircled by a halo of vibrant light. He reached for the ethereal hand. All went dark.

Gasping for breath, he came to. Instead of the inside of a murky coffin, he found himself staring at a wooden canopy. Gulping air, he clawed about him, fighting to orient himself in time and space, life and death. His fists curled around damp bedsheets—wet with his sweat? With seawater? Steadying his breathing, Colin crooked his elbows to hoist himself up. A lancing pain sliced at his leg. His arms slid back to his sides. His body responded in kind, pulsing with torment. Limp. Helpless. Unconscious.

He awoke fuzzy, groggy, the foul taste of parched sleep in his mouth. With a tentative twitch of his arm, he tested his body and sensed his surroundings. Definitely a bed. Dry sheets. Pain now a dull throb. Manageable. Opening his eyes against the crust of sleep, he saw the same wooden canopy. How long since the storm? A day? A month?

Inch by inch, Colin turned his protesting body onto its side, propping himself on his elbow. A room. Moderate size. Modest wealth. Brocade curtains framed a sun-drenched window, illuminating the mahogany-red furnishings and Rococo art. A chair sat next to his bedside, hosting an empty vigil. The bedside table held a stubbed candle, a bowl of water, and cloths.

A door at the far end of the room opened. Colin tensed. Against the pain, he readied for fight or flight.

Carrying a bundle of linens, paying no mind to the man on the bed, was a slender maiden with flaxen hair. *Julia.* His stomach clenched, and his heart seized. Only when he exhaled noisily, a breath turned cough, did she look at him, her eyes wide, cheeks flushed, eyebrows raised.

"Mr. Trowbridge, you're awake."

"Am I dead?" he rasped, his throat scratching words.

Shaking her head, she brought the bundle to his bedside. "You'll be fit as a fiddle soon and able to return to work."

"The crew. Where are they? Where's the ship?" Colin tried to push the bedsheets aside, but a hand blocked his progress.

"Please, lie back. I need to change your bandage." With a familiarity they had not shared in years, she pressed a hand to his chest to ease him back.

His head nestled into the pillow. "What bandage? Where are my men?"

"The bandage on your leg. The physician was able to remove all the wooden splinters, but you need time to heal."

Panic clutched his throat. His leg? A physician had hacked at his leg? Bolting upright through a blinding pain, he tore away the sheets. His eyes feasted on the sight of his legs, both legs, still intact and looking normal aside from bruising. A bandage wrapped about one thigh.

Only after he had settled against the pillow again did he realize he wore nothing but a nightshirt, and not even his own nightshirt, as his ladylove from years past tended to him. Good Lord!

He squeezed shut his eyes, clenching his jaw against the ache as her hands unwound the old bandage.

"A bit of wood impaled your leg. Nothing too deep, the physician assured, but the muscle needs time to heal."

"And my men?" he grunted.

"They're being tended. You must rest and not worry. All are well and in rooms of their own. You're in my home, you see. There was nowhere else large enough to take them." Her hands worked deftly to secure a new bandage. "The ship, I'm afraid, didn't fare as well."

Braving a peek, he admired her head bent over his leg, her bottom lip captured between her teeth in concentration. Colin's heart swelled to see her again. The years had been too long. Years and a continent apart…

Then it struck him. *Her home*. Had she married? Had she not waited for his return? All his work for naught.

Years, a continent, and now a shipwreck. He dared not wait for death to tear their love asunder.

"Julia. I may not look like much at present, but I've returned to you. Tell me you've not given up hope. Tell me you'll marry me."

Her eyes glistened with unshed tears. Shaking her head, she blinked them away, covered his leg with the bed cover, and gathered the linens to leave.

"I can't."

The pain in his heart ripped his chest in two. She had married someone else. He could not face another day.

"I waited," she said. "I hoped. I planned. Then you washed into the cove, you and your men, and father knew you'd come back for me. He was furious. He said I could never marry a deckhand."

Eyes wide, Colin turned to face her. Her cheeks were pale, lined with rivers.

"I'm no longer a deckhand, Julia. That was my ship. Your father said I must prove myself worthy, and I did. I worked from nothing. Now I *own* the shipping company, Julia. My solicitor has purchased the old Gaines manor and is refurbishing it. Oh, tell me you aren't married. Tell me your father will grant me an audience. I did it all for you."

Color flooded her cheeks, and her lips curved into a wide smile. Throwing herself against his chest, she hugged his neck, her face burrowing into the pillow with muffled shrieks of laughter.

She mumbled into the linen, "Yes. Oh, yes! I'll fetch him now, this very minute." She rose above him, her face inches from his. "Should he ask, the maid saw to your bandage. And…" She blushed. "I only peeked once."

Colin laughed despite the fire in his lungs, a happy man indeed. After all his hard work, his dreams were at last coming true.

Entangled

Velvet greenery caressed Emmaline's fingertips. Yew hedges, soft to her trailing hands, towered on either side.

At the sound of heels against stone, she quickened her pace.

A chase was afoot.

Turning a corner, she dashed down a darkened path. A quick glance back. No one. But he was in pursuit. One path behind her? Two?

She took another corner, frantic, her feet tingling.

Jerked to a stop. Collapsed into the hedge.

A tug at her dress. Her heart galloped.

A branch. It was a branch! She laughed. It had snagged the silk of her dress, caught on the petticoat beneath. Wrenching free, she grasped at the yew to propel herself forward.

Another turn. And another.

Dead end.

Spinning, she backtracked, desperate. A third turn revealed a long dark path.

Around her echoed the titters of women and guffaws of men as they chased each other through the hedge maze, the highlight of Lady Levinford's annual May Day fête. In the center: a maypole.

Emmaline stumbled forward, turning another corner, nearly toppling two partygoers. Without sparing them a glance, she raced down another path. He would find her. The rogue would win.

Lanterns swayed, shifting their haloes at unreliable intervals, the world dark at the dead edges.

Another turn. A dead end.

She had to pause to catch her breath. Bracing herself against the hedge, she sucked in quick breaths. One hand held her steady, the other clutched her side, a sharp pain twinging from the exertion.

A crack penetrated the air, startling her. Color lit the sky. Someone had found the center. The maypole dance would begin.

She was alone, then. Alone in a dark dead end, awaiting her fate.

It was the shadow she saw first. A crackle of color illuminated the man, his silhouette cast on the stone ground. His outline loomed, prowling towards her, stalking with silent grace.

"You've found me, Lord Levinford. Now, what will you do?" she asked, only the tremor on his name belying her anticipation.

A low laugh slipped from his lips. In swift strides, he was to her, pinning her into the hedge.

"I'll have my wicked way with you," he promised.

Emmaline gasped. His hand grasped her thigh, sliding upwards, lifting her dress and petticoat, hoisting her leg around his *derrière*. The heat of his body scalded her. His tongue invaded her mouth.

Her petticoat about her waist and her heart in her throat, she clutched a fistful of his hair. He captured her mouth with his and kissed her near to madness.

In the distance, shrieks and applause accompanied the anticipated maypole dance.

"Next year, I'll catch *you*," she vowed.

A chuckle tickled her ear. "As you wish, Lady Levinford."

Midsummer

It began with a kiss.

An eager thirteen-year-old lad and his bashful ten-year-old neighbor. Beneath the cypress, beside the lake. The sun at its highest point on the longest day of the year.

With that kiss, Rothchild knew himself wed.

But life had other plans.

Every year, they met at the lake on the summer solstice. Every year, a kiss renewed their childhood vows. Every year, until he purchased a commission.

He had written. She had replied. Six years of promises. Travel was frequent, battles more so. Last year, he stopped writing. She would understand.

Bloodshed, mayhem, chaos. A bayonet to the face. He returned home a baronet, scared, scarred, and broken. He did not write. She would understand.

Two reclusive years lost in the shadows of pain and regret. She would understand.

At last, he faced the man in the mirror. Worn. Wounded. Dignified. An elder in a body of no more than five and twenty years. The day had arrived.

In the library of Mr. Kempwood, father of his ladylove, the longcase clock ticked the passage of time, ominous. Fifteen minutes and counting.

Tugging at his waistcoat, he waited.

Running a hand through his hair, he waited.

Smoothing a gloved hand over riding breeches, he waited.

The study door opened with a swish and closed with a click.

Ferocious as ever with bushy brows speaking their own dialect above narrowed eyes, Mr. Kempwood grunted in greeting, strode behind his desk, and harrumphed into his chair, the inquisitor at the ready.

Rothchild swallowed, the sound echoing in the silence.

"Well?" barked Mr. Kempwood.

A bead of sweat etched a path down Rothchild's temple. Facing the enemy's cavalry could not be more tense.

"I've come to ask for your daughter's hand in marriage. As a baronet with a new estate, both granted by the King for services to the Crown, I have much to offer."

"You're too late. I've already accepted Lord Hammerly's suit. If that will be all?" Mr. Kempwood did not await an answer before striding from the room.

A bayonet to the face could not compare to a dagger to the heart. She had not understood. She had not waited.

A painful heat behind his eyes, he left the study for the front door.

"Rothchild?" came a soft voice.

One hand on the banister, one foot on the first step, she stood at the top of the stairwell, a traitor in the guise of his love. Eyes wide, cheeks flushed, a hesitation about her stance as though she might take flight. She had not changed. And yet she had.

He turned away and left for home.

The silk-spun memory of her had given him reason to hope, reason to return, reason to recover. She had not understood. She had not waited.

To smother his heartache, he attended a house party. What more did a man need than a house full of women lusting after eligible men?

Except love had lost its allure. As he could not have Cecily, there would be no one for him. Evening after tedious evening, he sat in the same leather chair, observing the tittering women swooning over false men.

With a change in the air, Lord Hammerly arrived, all shoulders and smugness. Apprehension beat in Rothchild's chest.

Lord Hammerly winked, sparkled, and dazzled. From behind palms, Rothchild stalked him. From behind garden walls, Rothchild haunted him. From behind columns, Rothchild spied him. How could Cecily throw over her true love for a preening peacock?

The night of the dance, Lord Hammerly vanished. Rothchild paced, fretted, and searched. But what was he to do, challenge the man? No offense had been made other than stealing his love.

Giggles and groans from behind a parlor door halted his steps. He should ignore them. This was not his business. Was it *her* behind the door? With her betrothed?

Eyes narrowed, jaw clenched, hands fisted, he threw open the door. The Devil! Piled on a settee were Lord Hammerly, Lord Bumbarden, and Mrs. Snow. Unclothed.

"Deuces and devils!" Rothchild said louder than he'd expected.

"Close the blasted door!" shouted Lord Bumbarden.

A crowd formed, curious about the entangled limbs on the settee.

Rothchild should have celebrated. Exposed, Lord Hammerly would be ruined. And yet, she had not understood. She had not waited.

Midsummer, he sat at the lake, skipping stones across the blue, nostalgic.

"Rothchild?" came the voice he knew so well.

The hair on the back of his neck stood at attention.

"Oh, Rothchild! It is you!" A rustle of fabric and she stood next to him, blocking the sun, casting him in shadow. "Your scar… You're so dashing now."

His heart caught in his throat. The memories of being here with her flooded back.

"I waited for you, my love," Cecily said. "Please understand. Lord Hammerly lost a gamble and saw my fortune as his savior. He tricked my father into believing I'd been compromised. Papa didn't believe my protests. But now, I'm free. Papa insisted the betrothal be broken after Hammerly's disgrace. I'm free. And I'm yours."

He tilted his head to meet her gaze.

Her eyes revealed the truth. "Will you have me?" The depths of love shone in her tears.

She had waited! She had understood.

And so beneath the cypress, beside the lake, with the sun at its highest point on the longest day of the year, they compromised each other.

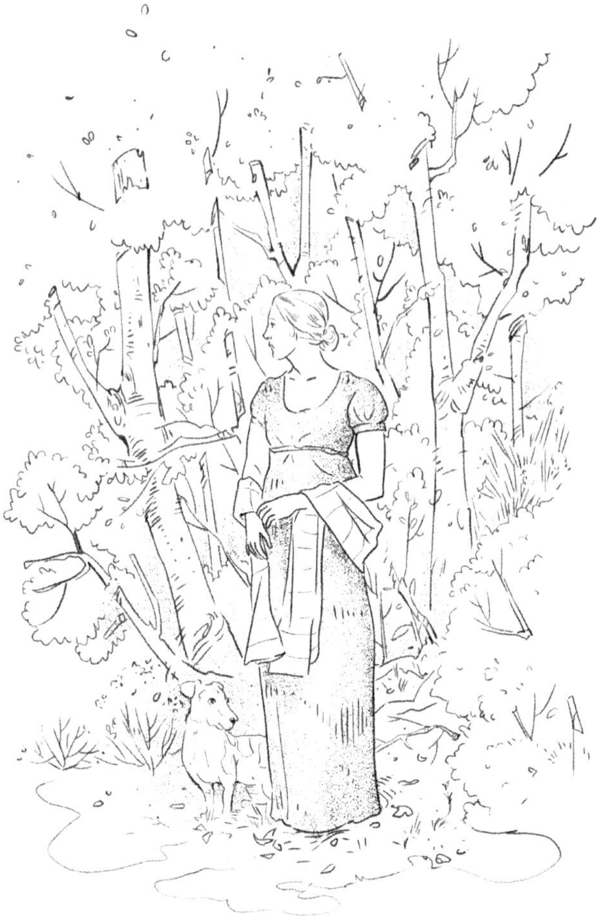

Candor

Lord Eagleton died on a Wednesday. The townspeople rejoiced.

Friday, they gathered at the inn over ale and pasties, plotting.

"We won't suffer another tyrant's rule!" shouted one man.

A din of voices rose in assent.

"How do we know the cousin will be different? Same blood runs through his veins!"

The people jeered.

As meetings go, many voiced an opinion, most agreed, and nothing was accomplished.

When Cami left for home, it was not yet dusk. She chose the woods that separated Eagleton Park from the village. She knew the route well, and her terrier, Ferguson, made an efficient enough protector from the highwaymen the deceased Lord Eagleton had employed to line his pockets. His bandits plundered the fanciest of conveyances while terrorizing the villagers. As Lord Eagleton had taken a hefty portion of the profits, the highwaymen knew immunity for their crimes. All crimes.

But Cami could hold her own. As a vicar's daughter, she was acquainted with sin and villainy.

Beneath the canopy of the forest, the world darkened. Her feet trod on his land, trespassing. She smirked and trod farther. Slats of light shone where the setting sun parted leaves. She inhaled the woody scents, Ferguson trotting at her heels, ears erect and nose sniffing, on the watch for trouble.

It found her in a succession of flashes.

Ferguson barking ferocious yips. The responding neigh of a horse. Black horse flesh rising before her eyes. The world tilting as she fell.

A blade to her throat.

She dared not move. Ferguson continued to bark, the sound muffled and distant. The horse pawed at the ground, unnerved by the terrier. Her eyes focused, time slowed to a normal pulse. Sabre in hand, a masked rider loomed over her.

A highwayman! Fear made flesh in the shape of a man.

Her breath suspended. Oh no, no, *no*. Erratic, her heart pounded.

"When did highwaymen trade pistols for witchery?" the man demanded.

Eyes wide, Cami mouthed her confusion.

Brown eyes studied her. "You must've bewitched the woods to take me by surprise. Nary a sound I heard from you or the pup. Is witchery your only weapon, or shall you also employ your beauty to wrest my gold?"

Ferguson moved between them and growled, prepared to defend his lady.

Finding her voice at the end of the sabre, she asked, "Are *you* not a highwayman?"

Gruff, he barked, "Do I *look* like a highwayman?"

A pointed glance found the blade. "You'll pardon me for saying, but at the present, you do."

With swift movement, the stranger sheathed the sword then removed his riding mask. He reached a hand to help her rise.

His face was too angular, his nose too hawkish, his eyes too dark to be handsome. Still Cami found herself breathless. Licking lips that had gone dry, she grimaced.

"My apologies," he said. "Are you injured? You've surprised me out of my manners, my lady."

"Mrs. Black, actually, and I'm uninjured." She made a show of shaking the dirt from her dress.

"Is Eagleton Park far, do you know?" As if to prove his good intentions, he kneeled before Ferguson and reached out a hand. The traitor of a terrier abandoned his bark, wagged a tail, and licked the palm.

"You're on the property now. The house is a mile west."

"You shouldn't walk the woods alone, Mrs. Black."

"Yes, well, it's not your concern. My home isn't far." She made to leave.

"You are my concern, Mrs. Black. Allow me to introduce myself." He sketched a bow. "Lord Eagleton. Newly inherited. I clean up well, I assure you. I shall see you safely home."

His smile twisted her stomach into knots. It remained so for their entire walk to her cottage.

He had such ideas! A new canal to prevent flooding. A raise in wages. Investment opportunities for the tenant farmers. Building improvements. He spoke sincerely, with an air of excitement. Was it all to be believed? His eyes spoke truth.

But the people had suffered too long under the former Lord Eagleton. They would never trust this new one.

Something bubbled in Cami's chest. A bold and daring idea.

"You need an ally," she said. "Someone of the people, someone they trust."

"Do I?" he asked, brows raised.

She ignored his skepticism. "Allow me to be that person."

"Why you?" His eyes searched her face.

"I've lived here all my life. I believe what you say, but for the others to believe, you'll need an ally. I'm the vicar's daughter and the rector's wife. You need me by your side."

"I hadn't realized I was in search of an advisor."

"Not an advisor, my lord. A wife." Her knees trembled beneath her petticoat, her words far bolder than she felt. "Wed me, and the people will trust you."

"And what do you suppose the rector will say?" he asked, kneeling again to rub Ferguson's belly.

"I'm widowed, my lord. He was my father's best friend. It was a convenient match…" *if a miserable one*. She chastised herself for the thought. He'd not been unkind.

"I see. And ours would be a match of love, or of convenience?"

She flushed, questioning now the wisdom of her impetuous proposal.

Rising smoothly, he said, "I'll give you my answer before week's end. For now, know me to be bewitched." With a touch to his hat, he leapt on his horse and cantered away.

Cami slept not a wink for a week. How could she have been so bold? She had proposed to a stranger! The new Lord Eagleton, no less. But how could she not? She was a good judge of character, and she knew he was a good man. She dared not deny the flutter in her heart.

The end of the week arrived with a town meeting, the new Lord Eagleton presiding.

"Put action to words! Words are empty!" they shouted at his ideas. "How can we trust you? You'll cheat us!"

When the meeting reached its unruliest, his lordship stood, holding up staying hands. "I promise to show you. I will not be a tyrant lording over you. I will work alongside you. Consider me one of you."

When he held a hand to her, their eyes meeting, Cami dreaded she may swoon.

"Allow me to introduce my betrothed."

Chin high, she stood and walked to the front of the room. Placing a gloved hand in his, she turned to the townspeople and smiled through her shock and disbelief.

Gasps mingled with sighs and applause. "He is to be one of us," whispered the room.

Love or convenience? she asked herself daily, weekly, monthly.

The first time he hosted a town meeting to encourage farmers to invest in a canal, she hoped it to be love. The first time she witnessed him stripped to his buckskins, bare-chested and sweaty, shoveling the new canal alongside the laborers, she wanted it to be love. The first time he gazed adoringly into the eyes of their first born, she knew it to be love. A love that grew from a moment of whimsy into a lifetime of respect and trust.

As Lord and Lady Eagleton danced under the stars at the sixth annual fête, the villagers looked on and knew themselves most fortunate for never could there be a more loving lord and lady, with children who played with those in the village, the lines of greatness blurred.

Most importantly, she knew herself to be loved when he touched the back of his fingers to her cheek and whispered his affection. "I was right to first mistake you for a highwayman, Lady Eagleton. You've stolen my heart."

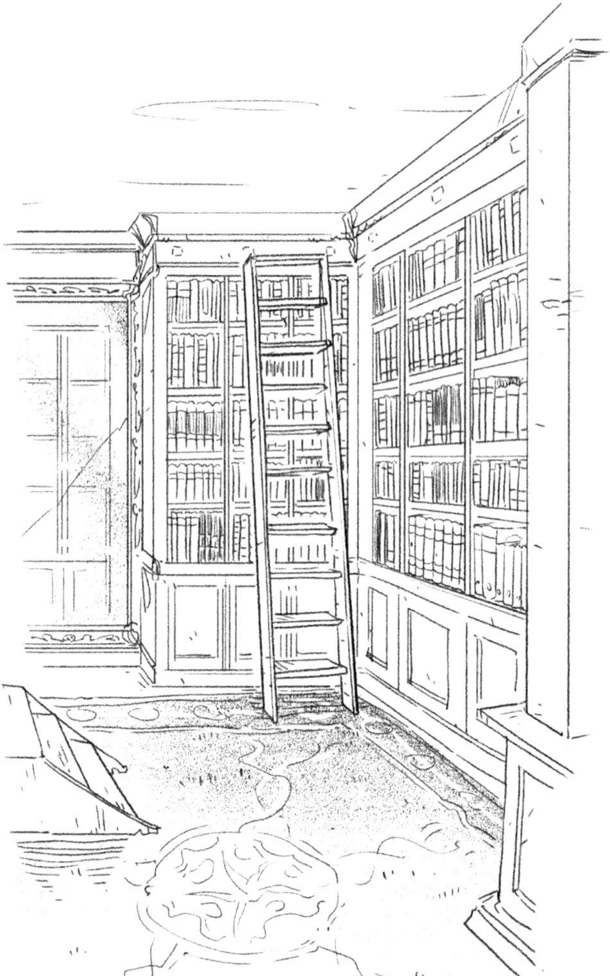

Requited

Polished wood slick against her gloveless palm, Penelope took the stairs to the library.

The familiarity of the gallery leading to the forbidding oak door awakened so many memories, few good. Two naughty siblings oft reprimanded, suitors who courted her father's title, mandates for her come out, the visit from the solicitor after Father's death, her acceptance of a position as lady's companion…

So many memories, few good. At least her brother had not inherited their father's iron will along with the estate and title. The house was now steadily filling with the sounds of children's laughter rather than tears. She smiled—a tight smile, but a smile.

Penelope palmed the library door's handle just as it opened from the other side, pulling her forward into the arms of an unsuspecting man.

Nose met hard chin. Bodies collided. Shoe met toes.

Holding the throbbing bridge of her nose, Penelope said, "I'm terribly sorry. I should have—"

Voices overlapped as the gentleman said, "My apologies, I never thought—"

And then their eyes met.

Had her gasp been audible? Was the thudding of her heart visible?

"Liam!"

His eyes widened in recognition. He took a step back and studied her, searching for something. But what was there to find?

When he recovered his shock, his posture stiffening, he gave a brisk bow. "Penelope."

"What are you doing here?"

"I'm your nephew's tutor. It's good you know that I come on Thursdays so our paths don't cross again. Had I known you would be here, I…I…" He took a breath. "Excuse me."

With a curt nod, he was gone in a whiff of aromatic shaving soap.

Pressing a hand to her bosom, Penelope stepped into the library and closed the door behind her. *Oh, Liam*. She would not cry for the past, for what could have been. He was the one who'd left all those years ago.

Visits to the lake, glances exchanged behind turned backs, secrets shared, hands held in the meadow. Their first kiss had sealed her love. Nothing more than a stolen moment behind the stables before her brother arrived to claim his friend, and yet it had changed her life. He was the only boy she'd ever loved.

And then came the day that ended it all. Penelope blinked away tears she had not shed for ten years.

Had she known he would be at the house, she — she what? Would not have come home? Penelope had had no choice but to return to her brother's care, at least until she could secure another position.

Her week passed filled with indecisiveness. Should she confront him? Did the reason matter after all this time?

Outside the closed library door she stood, waiting for her nephew to leave. As dull as the Latin lesson sounded, she pressed her ear to the wood, living a lifetime in the deep tones of Liam's voice.

Rustling. Movement. A chair toppled with a thud. Feet padded in quick succession.

Penelope stood back as her nephew wrenched open the door and ran down the hallway, screeching with delight that lessons were at an end. Turning, she faced her past.

Lips scowled at her below furrowed brows.

"My brother never mentioned you worked for him," she said.

"Why should he? We are nothing to each other."

The words slashed at her, sharp and vicious. At one time, they had been everything to one another.

Stepping over the threshold, she steeled herself to ask, "Why did you leave? I deserve to know."

Planting clenched fists to the tabletop, he pushed himself to his feet. The turn of his lips, the determination in his eyes, the scent of his starched linen, all so familiar. "You know why I left."

She wrapped her arms about her waist, protecting her core from more heartache. "My brother said you joined the army."

"I did."

"But why? I waited for you until dawn. You never came. Why?"

Liam cocked his head to one side, staring quizzically. "You rejected me, Penelope. Has time erased your words?"

It was her turn to eye him in question. "I did no such thing. We arranged to meet at midnight. I was there. My bag was packed. You never showed. Two weeks later, Nathan announced you had joined the army. How could you leave me?"

Liam covered his face with large hands. In silence they stood.

To her shock, soft laughter sounded behind those hands she knew so well, hands that had caressed her after their coupling beneath the willow, that had stroked her cheek, their touch accompanied by promises of love.

She'd had the misfortune to fall in love with her brother's best friend, the youngest son of a baronet. He had pretended to love her. With words of ever after, he had taken her virtue then left, never to look back. She had alternately hated and yearned for him through the years.

"I need not ask why you never replied to my letters," he said, his laughter dying. His hands fell to his sides, limp.

"Letters? You never wrote to me."

"Penelope," he whispered, her name haunted on his lips. "I hated you for years for trampling on my heart."

He stepped forward as though to approach her, but then sighed and halted. "I went to your father that morning and asked for your hand so you wouldn't be estranged after an elopement. He knew everything. That we had been meeting. That we had been intimate. How else could he have known except from you?"

When she shook her head to deny the accusation, he held up a staying hand.

"Your father said you regretted your actions, withdrew your promises, and came to him for forgiveness, frightened you would be saddled with a nobody. I wrote to you, demanding the truth. Finally, he took pity and purchased a commission on my behalf."

The truth hit her with a gut punch. She struggled to breathe, her heart racing at the realization of the life stolen from them.

In a blink, Liam's arms were around her, strong and warm.

His lips pressed to her scalp, his next words murmured against her hair. "You never spoke to him, did you? He never told you I came. You never knew. Oh, I am a fool. Young and gullible, I thought… Oh, never mind what I thought. Is it too late? Penelope, are we too late?"

She burrowed against his chest and wrapped her arms about his waist, not wanting to lose another minute with the man she loved. "It's never too late to reclaim our lives."

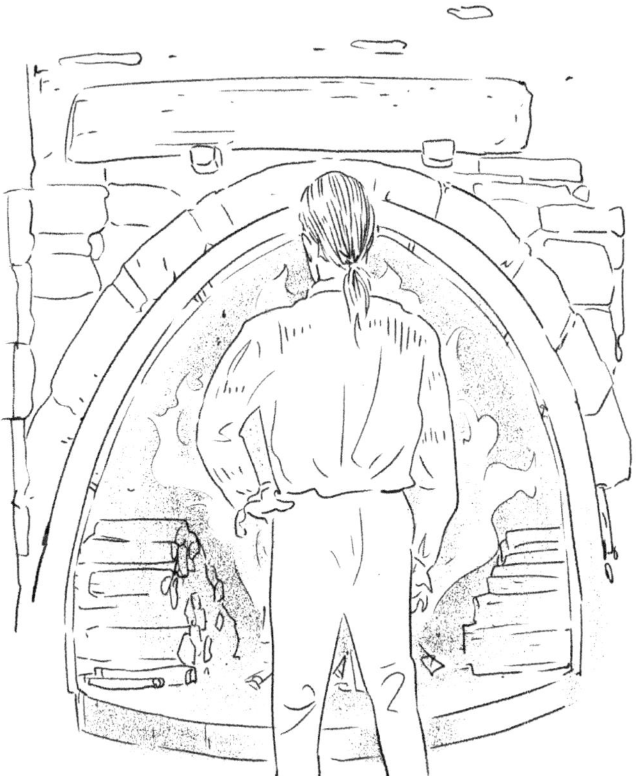

Persephone

The lattice of the casement window segmented the amber world outside into the yellows and reds of autumn.

"It's done." Her father's voice, firm and controlled, threatened to discompose her. "The contract is signed.

Chin quivering, Sofie pursed her lips to save her dignity. She would not give him the satisfaction of seeing her cry.

"I should thank you," she whispered, commanding her voice not to shake. "Never again can you lord over me."

Tearing her gaze from the window, she met his hard eyes, curtsied, and left.

The haven of her room had been divested of her belongings. They had packed away her life. A final, lingering look was all she gave.

In the foyer waited her mother, the one person Sofie had hoped would fight on her behalf against an arranged marriage to a stranger.

"This is for the best, dear," Mother said instead in her sweet soprano. "Sir Nathaniel is to be elected Lord Mayor of London. It's a good match."

Sofie bowed her head and stared at her hands, willing them, too, not to shake. "Yes, I can see how beneficial it would be for Father."

She was nothing more than a bartering chip in the politics of men.

An hour later, she was tucked in a hired carriage with her maid. They headed south to meet her betrothed at an inn halfway to London. Once officially acquainted, she and the baronet would proceed together for the wedding and his election.

The carriage bumped along, lulling her maid into a deep slumber but jarring Sofie out of her protective shell. The heel of her palm wiped tears from her cold cheeks.

Three tiring days later, the carriage was within an afternoon's distance of *the* inn. The one where she would meet her prescribed life's mate. If only she could meet another man, her perfect man, and elope out from under the villain who had arranged a wife of good family for political gain.

A light drizzle pattered against the carriage window, blurring the scenery. Sofie had never traveled farther south than Durham. Would London be so very different? Was it truly the mouth of hell? She shuddered. Sinking into the collar of her pelisse and wrapping her arms about her, she leaned her forehead against the window and closed her eyes.

A jolt woke her. Darkness shrouded the carriage. Rain pounded.

Were they far from their destination? Her maid's face pressed against the window in search of salvation.

In a fractured moment, the carriage swayed, tossing Sofie on her side. The world slid, shook, tilted. A scream pierced the storm, ending with a thud as her maid was flung against the carriage wall. The vehicle toppled to the ground and slid across mud. Sofie clung to the leather strap, her body prone on the side of the coach, her face staring up at the door.

All around her, men shouted, and horses whinnied. Her maid lay unconscious. Sofie had to get them out. She reached up for the door and shook the handle. Struggle as she might, the door would not budge. She pushed; she pulled; she prayed.

The door flung outwards, wrenched out of her hands. Rain splashed in her face.

"Are you injured?" a baritone rumbled.

Wiping her eyes of droplets, she peered up into a shadowed face framed by soaked hair.

"Give me your hands," the darkness commanded.

"My maid. She's injured. Please, take her first," Sofie shouted above the din of the storm.

"I can more easily get to her if you're out of the way. Take my hand."

A powerful forearm hauled her to safety. Once he saw her to firm ground, he climbed back on the carriage to retrieve her maid.

Several men dashed about in the rain, working to free the horses from the overturned carriage. Far from the ditch, another carriage stood, unharmed, beckoning with dry security.

"Follow me," said their savior, striding ahead of her, the maid cradled in his arms.

He nestled her companion on the opposite bench and turned to Sofie. "My man will see you to the inn."

He looked at her for no longer than a moment, but eternity stretched under his gaze. Sofie shivered in her drenched pelisse. The blackness of night hid his face, but she felt his compassion. Would he be scandalized if she threw her arms around his neck and kissed him?

Only when the carriage lurched forward did she realize she had not uttered a word of thanks.

The inn was nicer than expected, a large and clean establishment. The innkeeper's wife saw Sofie to her room, had a temporary maid sent up, and promised to tend to her companion, who had thankfully come to with a single sniff of smelling salts. Their luggage waited, not lost in the mud.

Had Sir Nathaniel arrived yet? Would he send for her to dine with him or wait until tomorrow? Her maid had chosen a lovely dress for their first meeting, but Sofie could hardly think of that now. She was tired and chilled. A cup of tea was what she needed most.

In dry clothes but with damp hair, she found her way downstairs. The public room was crowded with travelers seeking shelter from the storm. She searched impatient faces for the innkeeper or his wife or — no, she would not admit that she came in hopes of seeing her evening's hero.

But who was she to deny fate?

A flash of movement stole her attention. Broad shoulders bearing a drenched, multi-caped greatcoat strode into the inn, soaked black hair fanning about a chiseled face.

He made for the private parlor. The door closed behind him, leaving her hesitant. But she only wanted to thank him. What harm could come from a quick word of gratitude? This would be her only opportunity.

One step. Then another. Her hand perched on the handle. *Breathe*.

She saw herself into the private room.

"Excuse me. I don't mean to intrude, but—" Sofie choked on her remaining words.

The parlor was empty except for the man beside the fire. The greatcoat had been tossed across a chair. The cravat, coat, and waistcoat had followed. Before her stood a man in nothing but boots, buckskins, and a nearly transparent shirt that clung to his torso in sinful ways.

His hands swept his hair away from his face as he turned to her, his expression one of shock mixed with anger.

"This parlor is reserved," he barked.

She hardly heard. Angled features, square jaw, cleft chin… Her breath hitched at the sight of the bare chest framed by the shirt's open vee, the tapered waist, and the muscled thighs.

"Oh, it's you," he said, interrupting her admiration. "My apologies. I had thought to have the parlor to myself until dinner." With a lunge, he snatched up the soaked waistcoat.

"No, I'm the one who owes you an apology. I shouldn't have barged in. I only wanted to thank you for helping us."

"Damsels in distress are my speciality," he said with a wink. "I had planned to invite you to dinner after your respite. Seeing that you're already here, would you care to join me?"

The side door to the parlor opened.

The innkeeper stepped in, his eyes on the tray he carried. "Coffee, sir. And I've sent our boy to your suite until your valet arri—" He halted, the tray meeting the table with a *thunk*.

His mouth gaped as he looked from Sofie to the half-dressed man and back again. Taking a step back, he bowed and mumbled his apologies.

"Thank you, Mr. Fremont. I trust you've taken good care of my wife's quarters?"

"Yes, yes, the very best, as you requested." The innkeeper exited as quickly as he entered, leaving them alone once more.

Her first horror was at being caught in a room alone with a half-dressed man. Her second was learning he already had a wife, here at the inn, no less.

Amidst her shock, the man laughed. "Was it arrogant of me to announce you as my wife?"

"Your wife? You mean, Mr. Fremont thought you meant *me*?"

"But of course." He crossed the room in quick strides, grabbed her by the shoulders, and kissed her. A dizzying, spine-tingling kiss, his warm, moist mouth pressed to hers.

When he released her, she grabbed at his chest to hold steady. *This*. This was what she wanted. Not an arranged marriage, but *this*.

He raised a hand to her cheek, caressing her with the backs of his fingers. "Now it's your turn to rescue me, my lady."

"I'm afraid I can't. I…you see…I'm already betrothed."

"Yes, you are. *To me*. Sir Nathaniel Gilbert." He leaned in, teasing lips brushing hers once more. "At your service."

Haunted

They said he bore the mark of the devil.

Poppycock, Rosalind thought.

Fools nattered in her ear — a castle shrouded in darkness, ghouls lurking, a master who ate the hearts of babes. *Utter rubbish*. Granted, the circumstances were unusual, but there was undoubtedly a rational explanation for the earl's behavior.

Every year, the flame of fear was fanned by the Earl of Tepes' exclusive house party on All Hallows' Eve. The earl himself invited — nay, challenged — thirteen unmarried ladies and their chaperones to dine at the castle. The lady who lasted an entire night would meet the earl as a potential bride. As of yet, no one had stayed until morning.

No one had seen the earl, either. Plenty claimed to have, each with horrific tales as unlikely as the next.

Never in Rosalind's dreams would she have considered accepting an invitation to such a silly contest, but life found her in desperate straits. Her uncle, despite his wealth, considered her a burden. Unmarriageable, long in the tooth, and headstrong, she would find herself with packed bags in hand before next month ended. In comparison, marriage to the "monstrous" Lord Tepes sounded divine.

Surveying her companions, Rosalind felt notably out of place. Each had a proper chaperone, whether their mother, elder sister, or aunt. She, however, had a disgruntled maid. Not that it mattered. The ladies sharing this carriage, and likely the others following, would not last long, all afraid of their own shadow. Not Rosalind. There were no such things as ghosts or spooks that went bump in the night.

A glance out the window did little to bolster her confidence, however. The castle rose above a low-lying fog, an overgrown garden stretching the length of the drive.

Carriages queued before a portcullis with latticed iron spikes. *Cheery*.

Departing safety one trembling foot at a time, the ladies and their chaperones watched agape as a one-armed footman turned the lever to raise the gate. The butler, stooped by a shoulder hump, shuffled towards them.

"Good evening," he said, one lazy eye roaming. "If you'll follow me, please."

The other ladies exchanged wary glances. Rosalind rolled her eyes and took the lead behind the perfectly amiable butler.

Twenty pairs of eyes watched them from mounted portraits, each with a gaze that followed the group from foyer to drawing room. One young lady whimpered. *Linear perspective*, Rosalind scoffed.

Garnet damask curtains shielded the windows. Candles illuminated the room. Shadows danced across brocade wallpaper—crimson with gilded acanthus leaves. A chill tremored skin despite the fire and warming wine. With no sign of host or ghost, the guests speculated what horrors awaited them this night.

An hour they waited until the hunched butler shambled them into the dining room, which glittered and glowed from candles extraordinaire. Decadent plates appeared with a *saut de basque* dance of footmen. Rosalind hid a smile. She could accustom herself to such a life.

A scream ripped through the room.

All heads turned to the youngest lady, a hand to her mouth, her gaze riveted on a blushing footman. Ah, *not* blushing. A pink face puckered with burn scars looked back at the young lady with such sorrow, Rosalind's heart bled for him. Ducking his head, the footman left the room, as did the girl and her mother shortly thereafter.

And then there were twelve.

Two courses served, the entourage relaxed to discuss the latest fashions in bonnets. Through such barren conversation, Rosalind eyed the room and footmen, the former opulent, the latter damaged. *Curious*.

Entertainment accompanied the third course.

It began with a *thump* and *scrape* above them. *Thump, scrape. Thump, scrape*. The sounds traveled across the ceiling. All eyes turned upwards. Downward it followed the wall, then scratched the length of the room, sending a girl into a swoon. No sooner did her aunt grab the smelling salts than a banshee screech shattered the air.

Four pairs of guests fled the castle with the devil on their heels, their dinners unfinished.

"Oh, for heaven's sake," Rosalind said to her remaining companions. "It was only a fox."

From side to side the guests eyed each other, wary. Only one of the sounds had been explained.

Eight contestants and their protectors finished dinner and returned to the drawing room for the delights of two brave girls' musical talents. One sang. One played. Unfortunately, the soprano resembled the strings of a violin in the hands of a novice. The neighboring werewolf felt as deafened as Rosalind, for not ten bars into the song, a spine-chilling howl bayed into the night.

The accompanist pounded discordant keys and shrieked herself off the piano bench. The howl ushered three more guests and their mothers out of the castle.

"This is ridiculous. There are no wolves in England," Rosalind rationalized to her four rivals and their guardians.

"Then how do you explain the night-howler?" questioned a matron whose eyes were as beady as her ward's.

"Well…perhaps…" She tapped her index finger to her mouth. "One of the footmen stubbed his toe on a table. Wouldn't you howl at such pain?"

The matron's expression soured.

A haughty girl, sitting unnecessarily far from the group, lowered her nose long enough to say, "Don't think he'll marry you even if you win the contest. No one wants a spinster for their countess."

So, the talons were unleashed at last. And they called the earl a monster?

Rosalind smiled. "I take it you're already planning your nuptials with our vampiric host."

"You can't frighten me," said the harpy. "I don't believe a word of such rumors. He, like so many men, wishes to avoid marriage. This is all a lark."

Brows arched, Rosalind stood. "Then I'm no competition for you. If you'll all excuse me, I wish to retire early. Good night."

Ignoring the harrumphs, she headed for the door. Two of the pairings joined her for an early rest. No sooner did the group reach the foot of the stairs than behind them erupted screams and footfalls. Lady Haughty and another contestant raced through the foyer to the front door, leaving cries of singing ghosts in their wake.

And then there were three.

For how long Rosalind lay in bed staring at the muralled ceiling, she could not say. She counted by sounds rather than by time. Another fox. Another howl. A curious dragging sound punctuated by thumps. If they had not arrived at the castle determined to last an evening without losing their soul to the beasts lurking in the shadows, no one would have been bothered by the peculiar combination of noises.

The staff were a curiosity, certainly. Victims of a monster? Unlikely. The host merely had a penchant for hiring the unwanted. That fact made him admirable.

Ah, a new sound. A giggle in the wall behind her bed, as though from a child hiding. Straining, she listened. The giggling moved along the wall. Was this the drawing room ghost?

A bang shook the paintings. Rosalind leapt out of bed, clutching her dressing gown. Ghoulish moaning ensued. The wall shuddered, the moans intensifying.

After lighting her bedside candle, a fumbling challenge in the dark, she donned a robe and made for the door.

Peering into the hallway, she saw only emptiness. Until the two doors down from hers opened to the flying nightgowns of the last guests and their relations, leaving Rosalind alone in the house except, of course, for her maid, though she had not seen the girl since undressing for bed.

Ears perked, she listened for the ghostly sounds. Silence.

With a shrug, Rosalind bowed her head back into her room, but not before catching a flash of color. Peeking once more around the door, she grinned. An earthly maid and footman crept out of a closet together, the footman adjusting his fall flap. Haunted castle, indeed.

Thump, rattle. Thump, rattle.

Eyes wide, Rosalind looked the opposite direction down the hall. Empty.

Thump, rattle.

Courage in her throat, she followed the sound. *Thump, rattle.* It came from behind the wall. Fingers strangling her chamberstick, she pressed an ear to the wood. *Thump, rattle, scrape. Thump, rattle, scrape.*

She rapped smartly on the wall. The sound paused before continuing around the corner into the gallery. She followed. Abruptly, it stopped again, pivoted, and went the opposite direction.

Had she not first heard a door open, she would not have been swift enough to douse her candle and duck behind a decorative bust. As it happened, she did hear a door. The peculiar part was there were no doors in the hall. Eyes straining in the darkness, she watched.

As though walking through the wall, a frail man appeared in the gallery, tray in hand. He took five steps to the opposite wall and disappeared again. Even that was not as notable as the clubbed foot he dragged and the rattling cutlery on his tray. Rosalind barely suppressed her mirth. Ghosts in the wall, indeed.

The footman thumped his way inside the opposite wall, leaving an empty hall behind him. Retracing his steps, she studied his exit point. It seemed ordinary enough. She pushed against the wood, feeling the grain for a seam or lever or something.

Click.

The wall angled and slid, a handy pocket door. A quick glance beyond revealed a well-lit servant's hallway. Sconces decorated the walls every few feet. To the right, the hall continued, and to the left it ended at a set of spiral steps. To the left she went. On second thought… She dashed back to set the candlestick by the door to mark the exit.

While uneven and narrow, the stairs climbed only one story before ending at an arched wooden door. Lifting the iron ring, she pushed open the door and stepped inside.

Before her was an inviting tower library. A fire roared in the hearth. The smell of leather-bound books enticed her. Though not a large space, it was warm and cozy. Lounging in front of the fireplace was the night-howler—a sizable bloodhound, its head on its paws. Facing the fire, its back to the door, was a winged chair.

Thunk, click.

The door shut behind her.

The bloodhound moved first, lifting its head to investigate. He thumped his tail and climbed to his feet to lumber to her. Rosalind calmed her beating heart by petting the bloodhound, whose baying bark had become a familiar sound that evening.

"About time you arrived," the voice from the chair growled. "I'm ravenous."

"Good heavens, do you mean to eat me?"

The beast was on his feet in a flash, hand braced against the mantel, teeth bared.

With his back to the firelight, his face hid in shadow. From all else she could see, he appeared a normal man. No, normal would be a disservice. He was a physically thrilling man with long black hair worn loose around broad shoulders, a hard chest visible in the vee of a starched shirt, and muscular thighs framed with buckskin breeches.

Her eyes roamed over his deliciously attractive physique in its state of half-dress. *This* was the monster? Had her stomach not fluttered so fiercely nor her cheeks warmed so feverishly, she would have laughed.

"I hadn't realized my butler would bring dessert before dinner," he said at last, recovering from the unexpected intrusion.

Her body flamed from his implication. Under normal circumstances, she would have thought of a witty retort. Alas, all she could do now was pet the dog.

"Haven't you heard, my lady? I eat virgins." He growled again, the effect lost when the bloodhound thumped his tail and trotted over to his master to nuzzle a pale hand.

Sucking in her breath, hand on her stomach, she said, "Well, I suppose that gives us both something to look forward to. I do believe that's a benefit of marriage, yes?"

Lord Tepes barked a laugh. For a moment, all tension was eased. But his laugh ended sharply.

"What are you doing in my study?"

She took a brave step forward. "Looking for a husband."

In the silence that stretched, she could feel the earl's gaze sweep over her. The sensation quickened her pulse.

Pushing himself away from the mantel, her host strode across the room, stopping mere feet away, and turned to catch the firelight on his features.

"Be careful what you wish for on All Hallows' Eve."

Tentative, nervous, excited, she approached to better look at him, a smile on her lips.

One blue eye and one brown watched her with intensity. A long streak of white laced the raven hair from temple to tip. Starting at the temple and stretching down to a clenched jaw was colorless linen-white skin.

And so, this was the devil's mark. Her smile broadened. He looked to her to be kissed by an angel.

He crossed his arms over his chest. "Now that you've seen behind the curtain, shall I arrange for a carriage?"

She reached a hand to touch his forearm, the skin hot through his shirtsleeve.

When he flinched at the touch, she said, "On the contrary. I'll sleep soundly this evening, if not smugly. You see, Lord Tepes, I don't believe in ghosts. I do, however, believe you owe me breakfast."

His expression relaxed into the semblance of a grin. "If I don't frighten you, then what of my staff?"

"People who have met with unfortunate circumstances. Certainly not goblins or ghouls." Taking a step closer, she reached a hand to the discolored cheek. "What I don't understand is the contest."

He stood still, allowing her to touch his face and hair, seemingly unaware of how erotic she found the fingertip exploration.

"I protect the unwanted and deformed as I protect myself. The contest perpetuates rumors and discourages callers. However much I might have hoped someone like you would last the night, I never expected it. For too long, I've been ridiculed and afraid, just as my staff. Now, we can do the laughing and cause the fear."

"You could make friends, you know, rather than hiding."

"You who are so perfect know nothing of society's cruelty. I've tried making *friends*. At one time, I thought my inheritance would be freeing. I was ready to start a new life as a peer, not an oddity. They took one look at me and turned away in horror. Perhaps with a countess—"

Standing on her tiptoes, Rosalind kissed the pale skin, her lips brushing his hot flesh.

In a breathless movement, she was pinned against the door, his lips pressed to hers, a kiss more passionate than she dreamt possible. Her arms wrapped around his neck, his hands exploring her waist through the dressing robe.

Lost in the kiss, she nearly missed the whimpering of the bloodhound. Reluctantly, their lips parted. Turning in unison, they spotted the pup staring at a far wall.

"One of your footmen must be carrying biscuits," she said with a laugh.

Brows furrowed, he said, "There's not a servant's hall behind that wall."

The dog ran in a circle and howled as an apparition floated through the wall, across the room, and into the adjacent wall, humming to herself.

Lord Tepes tightened his hold on Rosalind, as though expecting her to flee after all.

"I'm sure there's a logical explanation," she said, tilting her face in invitation.

He chuckled, his lips returning to their rightful place against hers.

Masquerade

Mist enshrouded the castle, a sea fret of cold gloom. Lady Evelyn tugged at the edges of her threadbare traveling cloak, chilled by more than the November air.

She had come to win the heart of the reclusive Viscount Marr. Her competition lined the drive. Ladies of various ages and statuses stepped out of carriages and entered the mouth of stone and iron.

Shivering, she accepted the footman's hand and exited her own carriage, her aunt in tow. It was her aunt's influence that had gifted Evelyn this chance. While no one wanted a destitute bride, Aunt Augusta held enough persuasion to ensure her niece at least received an invitation.

Together they followed the other guests to the drawing room.

Not long after, a tall gentleman in a nondescript graphite ensemble, spectacles perched on his nose and raven hair closely clipped, stepped into the room, signaling for silence.

"Welcome, venerable guests," he said, his voice a velvet tenor. "I am your host, Mr. Brice, solicitor. Your safe arrival on this auspicious evening bodes well for our plans to find Viscount Marr a bride."

Murmurs hummed.

"No need to swoon, ladies, for there is no secret as to why you've been invited. His lordship will choose his bride from among you. On the eve of the masquerade, seven days hence, she shall be named. A plethora of entertainment awaits your pleasure, beginning with a musicale this evening, a picnic on the morrow, fireworks at dusk, and more. Please, drink."

The partygoers tittered as footmen circled with trays of claret.

Women in jewels and revealing bodices decorated the room, their chaperones hovering. Each measured the other, sizing up their opponents. An equal number of gentlemen attended, their eyes feasting on the available flesh.

Staring into her untasted wine, Evelyn frowned. Even with the persistent presses of Aunt Augusta, she could not entice herself to court a stranger, and certainly not one she had yet to meet. Viscount Marr had not left his castle for two decades. He was rumored to be near death and in desperate need of an heir. His wealth knew no bounds.

She looked back to the solicitor, in a corner away from the guests. His long fingers tapped his wine glass, his gaze studying each person, astute.

He cut a fine figure, though it was the intelligence behind the spectacles she found enchanting. If her aunt were not present, Evelyn would have sought his company. Ah, but he would not welcome hers. A man of no name or fortune would have little to gain from a woman who had name but no fortune.

Mr. Brice turned, his eyes meeting hers. Breath hitched, she smiled. He tilted his head, as though confused by her attention. Only when he returned her smile did she exhale.

The day after, a chill Wednesday with a leaden sky, the guests gathered on the lawn for bowls and gossip. Evelyn slipped away. The evening before had been tedious enough, wasted in the company of panting gentlemen and women whose words dripped with venom in their pursuit to poison the opposition. All for naught since the viscount was not among their numbers. In fact, no one had seen him.

A folly overlooked the lawn, a temple of ruined stone and climbing vines. It afforded Evelyn the perfect view to watch the play of avarice. Folding her hands in her lap, she enjoyed from afar the theatrics of fluttering fans. If only she had brought paints and canvas.

"Striking vista, no?"

Mr. Brice leaned against the stone.

She stood, acknowledging his reverent bow.

With an adjustment to his spectacles, he approached. "The entertainment isn't to your liking?"

"The company, more like. Oh, how discourteous of me to say." She stuttered a laugh. The way he looked at her made her stomach flutter and her skin flush in sinful ways. "I've no wish to gossip or flirt. I'd much rather paint, actually. And you? As master of ceremonies, should you not be mingling, taking notes for the viscount?"

Mr. Brice's lips curved at the corners.

With a low chuckle that tingled her toes, he asked rhetorically, "You think me a spy for his lordship?" He winked, bringing her attention to eyes of golden hazel. "I've taken enough notes for one morning. Besides, no one wants the company of a humble solicitor."

She waved her hand to the bench. "Join me?"

His expression curious, he sat. She settled beside him, increasingly aware of his proximity, his leg inches from her own, his body warming hers without touching.

Time warped, in one moment concave, in the next convex. For how long they spoke, Evelyn could not say, but she knew she wanted to see Mr. Brice again. How inconvenient to fall for a solicitor of little means. Despite the age and mystery of the viscount, Lord Marr was the better catch to ensure her family did not face ruin and starvation.

When a rainy day later in the week trapped the guests indoors, the two met again. As the others speculated about the viscount's condition, some believing him infirm, others deformed, Evelyn slipped into the library with Mr. Brice.

After an exchange on the inspiring views of the north tower, Evelyn asked, "Have you been Lord Marr's solicitor for long?"

His smile slipped. "Since June."

"Do you enjoy the work?"

"It's… different. I've been a solicitor for ten years and love what I do, but it will take time to accustom myself to these surroundings." Crossing one lithe leg over the other, he steepled his fingers. "The presence of a Lady Marr will help."

Evelyn tucked a curl behind her ear, both thrilled and anxious at being alone with him.

"Why is he choosing a stranger as a bride? Does he not care whom he marries?" If only she could ask instead if Mr. Brice was looking for a bride and how he might feel about a dowry-less woman.

"Don't believe the rumors of him being a hermitic goblin. He's merely a busy man with few social interests. I'm conducting the initial reconnaissance, for he does not want a shallow or greedy wife. And yet, how does one disguise boundless wealth?"

"Yes, I see your point. It's a pity he doesn't join the party, though. The few older gentlemen in attendance are receiving all the attention." She laughed when he stared blankly back at her. "You see, the ladies believe any of the elderly men could be the viscount in disguise."

Mr. Brice's shoulders shook with laughter. "As if he were a grand prize. Age? Pox scars? Hunched back? Nothing dissuades a woman from a wealthy match. And yet, here you sit in the library with a solicitor. You're a curiosity, Lady Evelyn."

Blushing, she stared down at her folded hands. "My family put me up to accepting the invitation. They're desperate for me to make a good match, a wealthy match, as you aptly said. We've no money, you see. At least not much, not enough to sustain us for another year. And so, here I am. But I've not the heart for it, not when my interest is otherwise engaged."

With a long look to Mr. Brice, she gifted a tentative smile.

He returned it.

Two more days of secret meetings passed. Evelyn avoided the crowd following an aged guest, a man who hobbled on a cane and scowled, insisting he was not a viscount. The ladies were undeterred.

The day before the masquerade, she met her suitor in the north tower. Though he brought a canvas and paints, not a single stroke met the untouched surface.

Instead, Evelyn found herself backed against the stone wall, her fingers grasping Mr. Brice's hair as he molded his form to hers and sought her lips. His mouth slanted over hers in a warm embrace, his tongue teasing her lips open.

However difficult it would be to face her family, she could not marry for wealth. This was what she wanted. This feeling. This man.

The morning of the masquerade, he caught her before descending the stairs and pulled her into an empty parlor. Hugging her to him, his lips pressed to her temple, he asked what she would do if Viscount Marr chose her as his bride.

"Don't be silly, Stephen. He has no reason to choose me. I've avoided everyone and all entertainments."

"All the more reason to choose you. You're not swayed by greed or society. What will you do if he names you?" he persisted.

She pulled off his spectacles and looked into the depths of his eyes. "He won't choose me." As he made to speak again, she said, "If he does, I'll simply say no."

"In front of all invited, in front of your aunt, to the despair of your family, you would turn down a fortune and a title?" His brows furrowed, his tone incredulous. "For…for me? A no-name solicitor?"

"You're not a no-name solicitor. You're Stephen Brice, and I love you."

The evening of the masquerade brought all manner of fancy dress. Fey, vegetables, literary characters, and jesters mingled. Evelyn searched for the only person she wished to see. Her eyes fell on a figure in a domino, stooped, cane in hand. Stephen's worried questions echoed as the cloaked figure in black watched her, stalking her through the ballroom, never letting her out of his sight, his mask concealing his identity.

Anxiety churned her stomach. What if Stephen already knew what was to happen? What if the viscount chose her? It was one thing to tell herself she would refuse him, but it was quite another to do it.

Had she the courage to say no to a viscount? Much less in front of all these people. Her aunt's face could be her undoing, for in that face would be both disappointment and fear. Evelyn's entire family depended on her making the right choice.

Guests swirled on the dance floor, bold in their movements with their faces disguised. Not once did she see Stephen. The viscount, however, hovered on the fringes, watching. Whispers rose in crescendo as all realized he was in attendance.

Evelyn's pulse raced as the longcase clock struck midnight. The orchestra stilled. The tapping of a cane echoed. All eyes turned to watch the domino ascend the steps at the end of the ballroom.

In a creaking voice, the figure said, "It is time to choose my bride. May you all rejoice with me."

She was bumped and jostled as the crowd gathered before him. Aunt Augusta pushed to reach her niece, grabbing Evelyn's arm and patting her hand. In this moment, all their financial problems could be resolved.

This was the moment, her aunt repeated. This was the moment.

Evelyn's eyes fixed on the viscount. Her heart pounded. Her palms perspired in her worn gloves.

"Allow me to introduce the bride of my choice," his lordship said, deep voice crackling. "Would Lady Evelyn Woodward join me?"

Evelyn remained rooted. Gasps and mutterings enveloped her. Aunt Augusta squeezed her hand and pushed her forward, tears at the corners of her eyes. Before Evelyn knew what was happening, she was being propelled towards the viscount. A wave undulated through the crowd, thrusting her onward.

No, no, no. Why were her feet still moving? Why was she approaching him? No!

Her heart and her mind battled as her legs betrayed her. A glance behind her caught Aunt Augusta's hopeful expression. Her family depended on her. This was their chance.

She looked up at the cloaked man. A gloved hand reached out. Pausing before the steps, Evelyn stared at the hand, her own trembling and hesitant. What of Stephen? What of love?

But what of her family?

Her betrayal lanced through her.

Squeezing her eyes shut, she slipped her hand into the viscount's.

The grip was firmer than she expected as it tugged her up the stairs. She looked to the mask staring sightlessly at her.

"No," she whispered.

His head tilted to one side. "No?"

Afraid of her own words and the fate she was forging, she said with a tremor, "I will not marry you, your lordship."

"Is it my age?" he asked.

As silence stretched, she prayed Stephen's affection was sincere. "I'm in love with your solicitor."

While the crowd strained to hear the exchange, the viscount chuckled.

Straightening, he rose before her into a towering man. Releasing her hand, he removed his tricorn and mask and tossed them aside.

She gasped, the sound rippling through the crowd. Stephen stood before her, smiling, a cane in one hand, his other outstretched to take hers once more.

He bowed over her knuckles and said loud enough for all to hear, "Allow me to introduce myself. Stephen Brice, Viscount Marr."

"But…but…" Evelyn stuttered.

The room was abuzz.

"I apologize for my betrayal. I had to be sure you wanted me. I *am* a solicitor, you should know. I inherited this summer upon the death of my great uncle." Stephen winked. "Will you still marry me?"

With a jubilant cry, she threw her arms around his neck. For all the guests to see, Lady Evelyn kissed her true love.

Homecoming

They had met on a day such as this.

Frost whitened the ground. The leaden sky promised snow. Mistletoe hung from doorways. The family gathered around the hearth, singing merriment, until their noses teased them into the dining room with the scents of pudding, goose, and wassail.

Ten years ago, their eyes met across the dining table. They knew with the first heart flutter it was meant to be.

She sat today at the same dining table, heart fluttering again, but at the sight of the empty chair, the backs of her eyes and throat burning.

Look to the man on your left, her mother had advised before dinner. *A wealthy man, recently widowed, looking for a new bride.*

She looked nowhere except the empty seat. Memories flooded her mind, drowning her eyes. Their first kiss, under the mistletoe, with slightly parted lips. Their first night of passion after the wedding one month later. Their first child, a wrinkly boy who smelled of promise and had his father's jewel-green eyes. Their last night before the war, cradled naked in tight arms.

The letter. Eyelids squeezed against the final memory. She would not think of it.

How could she look to another when her heart remained lost on the battlefield? His headstone marked an empty grave.

"Pardon me," said the man to her left. "I believe we met in London many years ago. You were friends with my wife."

Blinking grief aside, she looked. Eyes of sapphire looked back, astute, intelligent.

"Yes," she responded. "She was the most compassionate woman of my acquaintance."

"Then we have something in common. Would you sit with me in the drawing room after dinner?"

No.

"Yes," she said. "That would be lovely."

Her eyes resumed their study of the empty chair.

Boisterous children filled the drawing room after dinner, running to and fro. Her three played among them, all with eyes of green. Beside her sat the wealthy man, recently widowed, seeking a new bride for his had passed too soon. He aimed to fill the void of quiet nights, of empty chairs. Perhaps she, too, should try.

"Would you allow me to call on you?" he asked from his side of the settee.

No.

"Yes," she said. "That would be lovely."

Thunder echoed in her ears, along with hooves and drums, the sounds of war keeping time with her heart. The sound of their first Christmas apart was too loud to bear.

With the *tap*, *tap*, *tapping* of a door knocker, the room hushed, silent except the cacophony in her head.

"Madeleine," whispered the memory of his voice.

Her heart fluttering, she looked.

A ghost stood in the doorway, its face gaunt, marred by war. Eyes of jeweled green met hers. *Tap, tap, tap*, he moved into the room, leaning on a cane.

Her legs shook. Her hands trembled. Her vision blurred.

"Papa!" screamed three children at once, their thundering feet galloping across the floor.

Void overflowing, she rushed to join their embrace. Cradled in tight arms, she wept on a starched cravat.

"Only with you am I alive," his lips mouthed against her temple. "Merry Christmas, my love."

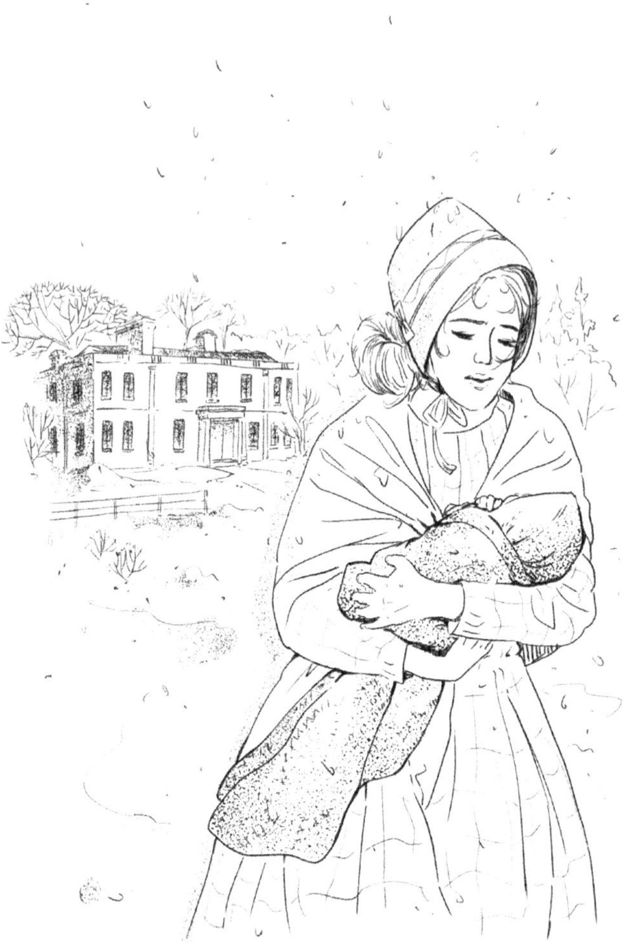

Beneficence

The snow-blanketed night wrapped her in a silence that chilled and blinded, its crisp white reflecting the moonlight. Snow trickled into her slippers, biting numb toes, slowing her gait.

Not long now until she spied the gabled roof. Had life continued without her, or had the world stopped, breath bated?

Two years had passed, harsh words forever haunting. She was not to return, never to darken the doorstep with her scarlet shame.

Her burden weighed heavily on her hip, swaddled in layers.

Between the nude branches of the sycamores rose the spires of the hall. *Home.*

The silent silver night transformed with an increasing clatter. The cacophony of the Christmas Ball shattered the peace with voices, heels, and hooves. Hundreds of candles blinked their yellow cat eyes, stalking her approach.

Go back! warned the flickering lights.

Resolved, she defied them. The servants' entrance snaked around the corner, but her soleless shoes pivoted too late. A couple in glittering finery spied her huddled form.

"A beggar!" The woman snarled. "Fie on you!"

Another couple stepped out to attend the banshee. Then another. Deafening shrieks, shouts, and chides shrouded her.

Then—silence.

A man approached, faltering.

"Bethany? Is it you?"

Her voice trembled. "Aye, Papa. 'Tis me."

Her bundle stirred, wriggling in her arms.

Crying into the night, a woman rushed past Papa, enveloping Bethany in warm arms scented of lavender.

Pinched and kissed and coddled, she was escorted past startled sycophants.

At the door waited all her happy memories embodied in one man, the one not chosen. She tucked her head against her babe's curls, hiding her face, her shame. Hands pushed her forward, past Robert's wrinkled brow.

The scents of sandalwood fans, sweaty warmth, and Mama filled her nostrils. *Home.*

Guests lumbered, lurched, minced, and shambled to the door, to escape the returning transgressor or to circle the reuniting family, hungry with curiosity.

The wet cheeks of her parents pressed against her face as they begged forgiveness despite *her* sin.

Words of contrition accompanied loving hands reaching for her babe. They cooed and caressed the golden ringlets and pink cheeks.

Weightless, she wandered, searching the faces until their eyes met. He smiled. She frowned. The sea between them parted. She staggered, eyes fixed to floor until shoe tips edged into view.

"You should have told me," he said in greeting.

"I couldn't bear your judgment."

"You never noticed it was I who loved you. If you had told me…" Pained words trailed off, his emerald eyes a tempest of emotion.

"Oh, Robert. It was I who loved *you*. I feared you wouldn't want me, not after—" Her words splintered. "Oh, Robert. If I had known…"

The family circled.

Robert took the babe in his arms, eyes wide with wonder.

"Mistletoe!" a voice exclaimed.

Green mischief appeared above their heads.

Robert leaned. "My kiss is conditional." Eyes atwinkle with promise, he asked, "Marry me?"

And with a single Christmas kiss, her babe nestled between them, Bethany's every wish came true.

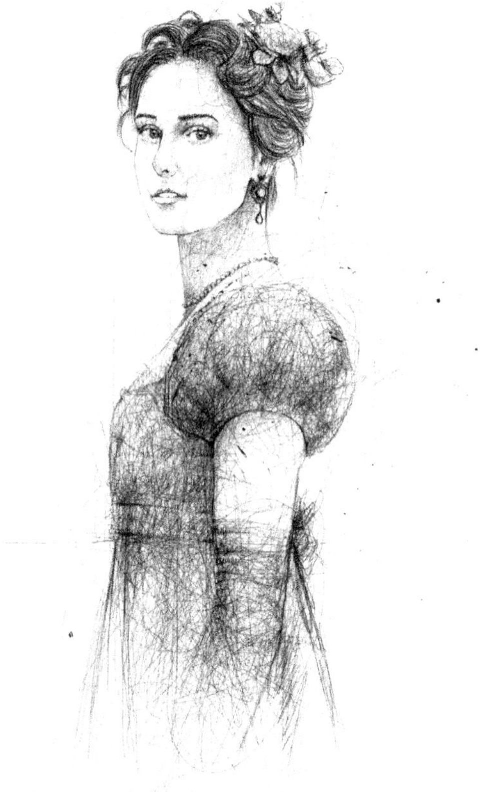

Gorgeous

The flicker of flames danced over the ballroom, casting a spell on those entwined in the cotillion, a spell that stopped at Marianne's slippers.

Darkness enshrouded her. No one saw her lilac muslin, raven braids, or glistening tears.

They celebrated the soldiers' homecoming, victorious. Voices hummed, bees seeking honey.

The sea of red undulated.

She searched the faces, hardened yet happy, faces of friends and family, none belonging to him.

Five years had passed since their rendezvous at the lake. Five years remembering his shadow blotting out the sun as he leaned over her. Five years remembering the feel of his cheek chafing hers accompanied by a rhythmic pant. Five years spent yearning.

Every week, the butler had brought letters signed *Yours Always*.

Now her heart broke anew every morning when the butler gave her a sorrowful expression in place of a letter. Two months without word.

No one spoke of him, the silence deafening to ears that longed for a single word.

Spoken from behind a tree, startling a fifteen-year-old from meditation, his first word to her: "Gorgeous."

Not for another five years had she learned he hadn't meant the view.

Ten years as a neighbor, as a friend, as a lover. And now her cheek would never again feel his rough stubble, her lips never again taste his.

Figures pranced and swirled on the parquet floor, oblivious to her pain.

She sank further into shadow. The drone of bees increased, deafening. She closed her eyes to drown them out.

Something brushed against her. She angled away, blinking an ocean from her eyes.

Syllables brushed her again. A word whispered for her ears only.

"Gorgeous."

Eyes opened wide. The world glowed. Luminous. He stood before her wearing regimentals, clean cheeks, a disarming smile, and a newly minted scar slashed across his devil-may-care face.

She leapt from the shadows into his arms, enfolded by their strength, engulfed by the light.

"I'm home," Simon whispered.

And so, at last, was she.

A Note from the Author

Dear Reader,

Thank you for purchasing and reading this book. Supporting indie writers who brave self-publishing is important and appreciated. I hope you'll continue reading my novels, as I have many more titles to come.

I humbly request you review this book on Amazon with an honest opinion. Reviewing elsewhere is additionally much appreciated.

One way to support writers you've enjoyed reading, indie or otherwise, is to share their work with friends, family, book clubs, etc. Lend books, share books, exchange books, recommend books, and gift books. If you especially enjoyed a writer's book, lend it to someone to read in case they might find a new favorite author in the book you've shared.

Connect with me online at www.paullettgolden.com, www.facebook.com/paullettgolden, www.twitter.com/paullettgolden, and www.instagram.com/paullettgolden, as well as Amazon's Author Central, Goodreads, BookBub, and LibraryThing.

All the best,
Paullett Golden

About the Author

Celebrated for her complex characters, realistic conflicts, and sensual love scenes, Paullett Golden has put a spin on historical romance. Her novels, set primarily in Georgian and Regency England with some dabbling in Ireland, Scotland, and France, challenge the norm by involving characters who are loved for their flaws, imperfections, and idiosyncrasies. Her stories show love overcoming adversity. Whatever our self-doubts, *love will out*.

Connect online
paullettgolden.com
facebook.com/paullettgolden
twitter.com/paullettgolden
instagram.com/paullettgolden

Printed in Great Britain
by Amazon